Between Cups of Coffee

Between Cups of Coffee

Tajalli Keshavarz

Matador
5 Weir Road
Kibworth Beauchamp
Leicester LE8 0LQ, UK
Tel: (+44) 116 279 2299
Fax: (+44) 116 279 2277
Email: books@troubador.co.uk
Web: www.troubador.co.uk/matador

ISBN 978 1848765 009

British Library Cataloguing in Publication Data.
A catalogue record for this book is available from the British Library.

Typeset in 11pt Aldine Roman by Troubador Publishing Ltd, Leicester, UK
Printed in the UK by TJ International, Padstow, Cornwall

Matador is an imprint of Troubador Publishing Ltd

To Jila

'Meanwhile I talk to myself, as one who has plenty of time. No one tells me anything new; so I tell myself to myself.'

Nietzsche

1

It had rained heavily; I had time to think while walking slowly down the shiny alleyways with tall buildings on both sides. It was a short walk but when I got back to my flat I knew things were going to be different.

I had bought milk, bread and paper. I was putting them on the kitchen table when there was a knock at the door. Carol came in with the usual expression on her face; stress. She had a light fabric skirt on with small pinkish flower patterns. She threw her bag on a chair and dropped into the chair next to her bag. It was a hot day.

'I am going, have decided, going tomorrow. Have the ticket.'

Had she bought the ticket weeks ago; now telling me about it? Perhaps she thought, in the little quiet times that she had, that I would be devastated, that I would pick up a big fight. I was thinking of the bulk of marking to do and how to organise my time to read the book I had wanted to finish for a long time.

I said, 'but why?' I thought her bra was too tight, that the skin around the edge would be red. I thought of the feeling of liberation that releasing the bra will bring her.

So she had planned her going away well in advance, perhaps months ago; all those times we were together she was thinking about leaving.

I do have an admiration for women. I generalise but maybe I am entitled to. Women do things; men make a mess of things. Women make decisions and act on them, maybe slowly but they do. Their action is based on a conviction; they are – at least most of the time – convinced. Those women who have passed a couple of 'interpersonal transactions' are decisive, determined and nothing can stop them! Oh! I love this: '*interpersonal transactions*'! But men, they get into an animated state of affair, they have to prove things, to themselves more than anyone else, but all the same they have to prove.

I look at Carol sitting in front of me with her hair sticky, with some drying sweat around her hairline. I imagine her walking in the heat, I am thinking about her and she is leaving me!

I repeated:

'But why? Why such a sudden urge?'

'You knew it. Didn't you? You should have at least guessed something was not right? Don't tell me you knew nothing. I cannot believe such a blunt denial, not from you.'

So, she was experienced! As if I did not know it. Could anything move her? She was always in a state of drama. No, not in the way you might think. I am not imposing a general view on her responses here. But she was always in trouble with something. This had a degree of attraction for me in the beginning. I guess this was the way I got attracted to her. When I think about it, I get absorbed in momentary cases. Momentary pictures, changing of the light, movement of a face, a profile, a short journey of hand to face, to hair, to a glass of wine; and then what? How would that glass be moved to the lips? How would it stay in one hand or be embraced in two hands, getting warmer and warmer while words pass by? Words that escape from the door of a small crowded café, words that remain inside, get repeated, rehearsed silence get heavier and then precipitate with a sudden impulse on the table between two faces.

I remained silent. This was a question I did not want to answer; did not want to ask myself. I wasn't sure if deep inside I did not wish her out; out of my life in spite of all those times we had spent together, apart from, I suppose, the good times talking: words to fill in gaps between events of the skin. As if it was a moral duty, not only for me – for both of us – to explain intimacy. But for me when her hand approached her shirt, the buttons opened one by one with a certainty that defied romantic scenarios, it was intimate. For me, it is a meaningful dialogue when a skirt loosens and falls, when a clip opens. It is a personal statement. But if I wanted her out, it was perhaps because her statements were just words put together to form idle, meaningless paragraphs. I could imagine her as a studious pupil in her childhood when her teacher would tell her to write a page a week because it would improve her composition.

I said, 'you haven't left enough time for us, to spend at least a few days together.'

'Did you want to?'

'Of course.'

She remained silent.

'What time tomorrow?' I asked.

'The flight is at 2 p.m.'

'So we have today and tomorrow…some of it at least…I hope.' I said.

'If you like. I have some chores to do though.'

I had meetings the next morning. Well, they had to wait. Any hint about the meetings would create uproar:

'You see, you pretend to miss me. You pretend to be shocked and upset about me leaving. All you think about is yourself!'

I could not guess what there was behind her words; she was looking into her bag for something. I thought she was leaving and at least for the last hours I should be able to keep things calm, maybe more loving, at least for the last hours. I said:

'Would you like me to book *Jasmine Leaf*?' it was the one that we used to go to when we felt upbeat.

'OK'. She was standing next to the window. Perhaps she expected something else, an eruption, anger, sadness, perhaps even pleading. Then, she was gone. I thought last minute shopping!

The restaurant was unusually quiet when I arrived. A couple of businessmen were sitting at a table in the corner. Nobody was at the bar. Three stems of small carnations in a small vase were sitting on a white tablecloth on each table. They had changed the decoration. On the wall, there were old drawings of game birds. The waiters were standing idle between the bar-stand and the door. I imagined that one of those loyal customers, a regular businessman, had bought the place to change the whole thing to his liking. Like those who marry a woman of certain type to make a better person of her. And look what happens: there are no customers; the place is like a funeral parlour. There was no similarity to the restaurant we used to go to.

Then, she came in. I saw her as she came in through the door. She had a long scarf around her head with frills falling down over her right shoulder. As she saw me she touched the scarf. She did not seem to have noticed the changes, the drastic alteration of the décor, and the change of the background colour from that deep beige into very bright pink.

'What would you like?' I asked. She was looking at the empty tables around us.

'I don't know.'

Now she was removing her scarf.

'What about the usual? Or you want to try something else?'

Her hair was now hitting her shoulders, just, and only part of it. It was shorter in the front. A younger look? She did not need it. I thought now that she was leaving me she needed the confidence of being young. And who was it? Or maybe there was no one else? Why should there always be another person for an affair to end? The air is full of sentences:

'*Listen, we had a good time together, but…*,' '*I have seen someone.*'

I thought that perhaps I like to convince myself that there is another person because if she left me for no-one else, then it would mean that she was bored with me;

that I was no good at all, that she was so desperate she wanted to go at any cost.

I looked at her as she was sitting there looking around. I was not sure if she had had her hair cut. When I first saw her, she had it curled and a pair of sun glasses was resting over her head. What did we talk about? I could not remember, nothing to remember. And now, what would I remember of this '*year-long*' affair? I wasn't sure what would excite her, what would move something in her. For me in this relationship, it was just fine to be together, even if it was for part of the time.

The waiter was bringing the food and the restaurant wasn't any busier. Only a couple of businessmen had come in. Where had all those people gone? I wished we were in a crowded place. We could sit together in peace without the lapses of silence which I could not fill in. There would be no questions, no excitement or anger, only eating! But why was I so defensive? These occasions have always been very embarrassing for me when people sit together face to face without a word. I would feel awkward even if there were five people sitting around silently saying nothing, expecting someone to break the silence.

She was sitting there as though nothing had happened. It was she who came to me saying she was leaving. It was she who should have had something to say. But nothing was uttered now, no explanations, no excuses. 'Good suggestion to come here,' she said.

How could it be good if she didn't even detect the obvious changes to the restaurant? Whatever she said, it made her more distant from our past times together.

I could picture her sitting on the bed with her bathrobe on, having one knee bent to be able to reach her toenail. Did I like bright red or dark, nearly black? I was standing by the window and the sun was shining into the room canvassing her fingers. 'Red', I said, 'definitely red.' Her eyes turned towards me.

The businessmen in the corner were having a heated debate now. I could hear odd words. Tomorrow there was going to be an important meeting in their department. They disagreed about something. What was my programme? I was supposed to have a couple of meetings; one with a colleague and one with a student who wanted to change his course. Well, I was going to miss the meetings, something I had never done before. I also needed to put the final touches to a report I had been working on over the past year. Actually, I had started it the day after I met her and now I would finish it just after she left.

'Don't you want to drink that coffee? I didn't know you liked it cold,' she said.

Now she was angry. Was she trying to say that she hadn't been part of my life anyway? As if I cared!

I say, 'I don't, I didn't notice it coming.' Now it was her turn to postulate. *'Is he so much affected by my going that he missed the coffee coming?'* She smiles.

'So when is your flight?' I ask.

'I told you. Tomorrow 2 p.m.'

2

The first time we flew together was two months after we met. She had her hair pulled back tightly, had a red top on and a pair of jeans. I was surprised to see her so agile, prepared and jolly. That was a trip full of agreement. Each word was absorbed, received with delightful acceptance on both sides. Then we returned and we started to treat each other with a sense of caution. I could understand why I felt that way, but I could not understand it from her side. Was I to be bothered? After all, when I should have bothered, I didn't. I didn't care at all. And that was in a totally different case. I say 'case'. Sometimes I wonder about myself and my choice of words. As if they have come out of a redundant dictionary. Yes it had nothing to do with Carol. It was Kate our silent librarian with long rather dull hair.

Kate had been with us for five years already and I had seen her on and off in the library, always in a rush returning a book or borrowing a journal. But it was that evening when I stayed longer to look up some references and needed her help. And I think that was the way it started. It all started slowly. I don't think that either of us had any intentions of having a relationship. But it happened. I suppose we were a good match. A man in a hurry, always, and a calm and composed woman; one who had time to look at things, to read books, to see people, to walk to the sandwich shop slowly, and had decided what she wanted to have during her morning coffee. I always had to pause a second or two in the shop to decide on a sandwich, always momentary feeling or no feeling at all, very animated, just a chicken sandwich, that will do. A packet of crisps would change the taste if necessary. So it was interesting for us to go out to have dinner together to exchange ideas on topics.

Carol is playing with her dessert. Piercing the chocolate with the tip of the spoon, spreading the cake on the plate making shapes. I wonder what Kate's last meal had been, lying on the bed waiting. Assuming she *had* eaten the last several days before the final moment. It didn't take long for her. Not at all. It was a case of going in and dying. Not exactly like that but pretty much so. It took just a week or two. I thought how very untypical of her. She was so thorough, patient, systematic. I thought she would fight it and come out calmly with her modest smile. But no! Perhaps she wanted to die systematically. And what did I do those two weeks and before that? Nothing. I did not see her in the hospital, I didn't see her before that either; practically since she stopped coming to work. I assume she wore a tight scarf around her head, she didn't like a wig. Perhaps she didn't get to that stage. I could not imagine her with a wig. Had I gone and seen her, what could I have said? But then, I didn't go. And that was that.

Carol was in when the phone rang. I took the phone.
'Kate is dead.'

It was Elizabeth, the deputy head librarian.

'I thought I should tell you. You might want to do something. They phoned me a minute ago from the hospital. They had tried to contact you as well but couldn't find you. Apparently, they had found your name in Kate's papers next to her bed.'

Short and simple!

'Are you a coffee or tea drinker?' I asked.
Kate had a light white shirt on and had cut her hair short.
She laughed:
'I do not discriminate.'
She was jolly that day. We walked by the bank of the river and spent some time looking through the books at the outdoor stands with second-hand books.

Lying on the bed I was looking through the book she had bought for me. When I looked up, I saw her shirt on the chair next to the bed. She was standing next to it. She leaned towards the shelf, took the candle holder with a long stem and blew off the small flame. As I was lying on the bed, I was looking at her body under the light of the two remaining candles next to each other. It was the first time I was seeing her skin in full. She moved towards me. It was a calm night. We were both silent throughout.

Putting the phone down I kept my composure. Carol had a thin peach- coloured summer skirt, moving around bare feet in the kitchen, having an ice-cream, her fingers sticky. She was a sloppy eater. For me there was an erotic element in all that. I went to her and caressed her hair. She had that determined, yet attractive, look in her eyes. I continued my caress.

I would never know what was behind that look. Was it saying: 'well, this is yet another chore to get over and done with' or, 'he thinks that he is in charge, but this is my call.' Now that I think about it, I question the element of attraction in all that; I don't go as far as to say 'love' was behind that attraction. Was it a power game? I do not see myself as a man who seeks power against women. But maybe I am wrong to think this. After all, what about my mother? After all those years of submission as a child, as a young boy, don't I want secretly to prove myself to a woman? A woman who is cunningly inviting me to submit to her? Albeit in a predictable manner? But all the designs are essentially the same throughout the years; all different shapes of the sticky fingers and the bare feet. How many of them are working on the same principle at this moment around the world?… And the obvious thing is that by their nature, they are designed to look innocent, innocent secrets! Keep them if you wish, avoid being obvious. Exactly contrary to men who are so obvious in their physiological responses that I doubt if a single man could do anything in his life that could go unnoticed by a woman who chooses not to ignore it.

I was caressing Carol's hair as we were going to the other room. As if I was driving a car and I was getting close to a roundabout. Then, she turned around and asked me: 'What was in that phone call? You are not yourself.'

Of course she knew about Kate. Not that she knew her in any particular context. I suppose she was just a name to her. A name that was associated with me. But in any case, it was not relevant to her and I did not want to tell her about Kate, about what had happened. I felt strangely private about it. As if I was protecting Kate's dignity. Did I consider disease as something to be ashamed of? I hadn't told her about the cancer because this was not part of our mutual life. But now, having her in my arms, and her asking me about the telephone call, I was pushed into a corner. I had to defend Kate's 'dignity'. Her death was a secret between me and her. Funny thinking that, after all, I did not even go to the hospital to see her, even for a short visit. But it wasn't about the period of the visit; it wasn't something to do, to tick off. Now I was defending the relationship. I told her: 'one of those things. It is boring. Do you want to know now?' I looked at her while she was busy with her red shirt. It was the time for ignoring, for silence and forgetting.

But silence is for the outside. Inside, are all the noises, the events happening and demanding explanation, justification, defence! I remembered, and I don't know why, that Kate was setting up the table for dinner. She loved candles and I didn't. I don't think that she ever knew how much I disliked the flickering of the light as we sat for dinner. I thought it was a betrayal of the relationship with Kate, remembering my dislikes. Carol's body started moving next to me and while I moved to adjust my movements with hers, I thought that it was a betrayal of this relationship too, remembering the dislikes while pretending I was interested in the movements.

And perhaps it was a betrayal of myself as well thinking about both situations while I wasn't interested in either of them.

I suppose this is an accurate description of myself as an addicted man. I am addicted to guilt. To follow my desires has been a huge betrayal of people closest to me: my mother, my lovers, and who else? I cannot think, Oh yes, my colleagues. Here, I do not include my father. I always kept out of his way but had a sense of respect for him. This sense grew as I grew older so I became more and more distant from his views, his outlook to life which I found too rigid. He followed all the rules and regulations to the letter. For a large chunk of my life, he was my ideal hero. And then, it just sank into the sea. I cannot say why. There was no sudden discovery, no breakage of image. If anything, as time went by I found him to be more a man of principles and morals. The point is that I found that I had a different outlook to life. I noticed that we were two different persons, very different. And what about friends? Do I feel guilty towards them? I cannot answer. I have come across people, have had good times with them, but could never define or understand the word 'friend'. They set premises and make conditions: 'If you are a friend then you do not....' or 'friends never....' I just don't look that way at a relationship. So do I believe in such a thing called friend? Do I have friends? Have I ever considered friendship?

Kate turns towards me as she is lying on the bed. Her

long nightgown loose, part of her small breast with her nipples exposed. She says: 'what time is it?'

'9:30' I say.

'Oh.'

I know she thinks she has overslept but she doesn't say anything. She does not move. It is a Sunday. There is no need for awareness of time. But her time is trapped into boxes of responsibilities. This, I suppose, is the more serious one: a mother in hospital, alone. But we haven't talked about it in any details. She mentioned it to me in passing. Not that she wants to keep a distance, but this is one of those boxes she does not see relevant to our relationship. And I am, of course, happy about it. I have always preferred, even tried, to keep myself in at a distance with regards to others' personal circumstances.

She is now showered, dressed, her long hair wrapped back. She stands by the door and next, she has gone. I stay in bed; I have the rest of the Sunday. I look out of the window. I can see the sky, a grey day. It is the start of autumn. My mind is empty, I can't even think of the chores but I desire something, I don't know what. I will go out for a coffee and a cake in the small bistro I like. It is full of people like me on Sundays. Hopefully, I will find a seat in the corner. I will flick through the newspapers. I will look at occasional couples, sleepy; some with a satisfied look, some anxious, some silent, pausing, preoccupied. Next, I shall dissolve in the streets to be found later in a pub for lunch. I hope it would be sunny by then.

When I think about it, all my relationships have been

snapshots with no coherence. Have I lost something? Have I been lucky? Passing by the events, the tragedies, the catastrophes, trying to maximise momentary pleasures? But this bothers me: a man sitting in the bistro waiting for his coffee reading a newspaper with nothing in his mind, nothing to worry about, nothing to look forward to.

'Your hands are cold', I said.

She was silent. This wasn't something new. She would go into these bouts of silence. I never asked what she was thinking about, where her mind was. She might have known about her cancer from the early days. Perhaps she was thinking about its effect on our relationship. We were sitting in this café where we used to go near the university; tables with flowery plastic covers, the waiter wiping them with wet towel, always coming close to you. Wiping the table next to you, as if he craved to hear a tantalizing dialogue, finding a secret! He would bring the coffee with an egg sandwich on brown. Now that I think about it, it is so stereotypical: a vegetarian librarian with a lecturer talking about Virginia Woolf to avoid becoming too personal. But I suppose it was personal for her. As for me, I wasn't bothered I avoided things becoming personal; I think I have been successful in that. The waiter comes with the plate of sandwiches, a couple of pieces of drooping lettuce next to the brown bread.

I take a bite; it is dry in my mouth. I think what was her last meal? Did she know that what she was eating was going to be her last? The taste of bread, water, a sweet piece, salt....as the piece melted in her mouth, thinking this was the last experience, time to say goodbye to it. What is there in the last glance? Is it the colour of the ceiling? An unceremonious end to a watchful eye! A librarian watching all those people every day with their questions, with their books hugged tightly next to their chests, taking books from the shelves, returning back to the shelves. People coming into the library in winter with their wet coats, umbrellas, shawls, scarves; paging through the books and then looking outside the window watching the snow eventually coming down after so many days of wet weather ….Now the last glance. Maybe it was a look at the pale skin of the nurse?

3

Coffee was sitting on the table. It was cold. Carol had finished hers.

'So it is 10:30.'

'Yes.' I said

She didn't say more. I was thinking of how to get out of there. Imagined I was in my flat watering the couple of pots I had. I am a lousy gardener. I say gardener as if I have a couple of acres under my harrow! It is a joke. I walk by the fields in the countryside feeling as if I am walking through my own land, as if I have just come down from the combine harvester to rest my muscles. I am a joke, a bad one at that. The image that I have of myself! I am more and more alien from this character, David, sitting alone reminiscing events, stories that carry no weight and yet remain active, alive.

Now I was picturing the small pots in my mind. I sat there facing Carol and thinking about the smell of the pot plants. I wanted to be alone, having nothing to do with the things around me, the people, the events surrounding me. How could I carry on the conversation with Carol until the waiter brings the bill? I thought she was a hard case. What did she want after all?

The waiter smiles and leaves the bill on the table. It is inside a wooden box. What an absolute joke. This is supposed to be chic, respectful, stylish. For me it was pretentious fit for those nouveau-rich city guys with their pin-striped smelly jackets. Carol is looking at the box. I say, 'are you really sure you want to leave?' She says, 'what do you think?'

OK, she wants to play it hard. There will be only a few words between us until I drop her at her flat. I think about tomorrow and the scene she would make in the airport. She, with her suitcases, fidgeting, talking about her life with the girl at the counter while people get restless behind her. Perhaps the best is to drop her quickly with no words to be said again.

I had already started to imagine myself in the car returning from the airport. I was comfortable. I said 'what time do you want me tomorrow?' I thought she might say, 'don't you want to come in?' She said, 'I will need to be there two hours earlier, so elevenish?' 'Fine,' I said, and I was happy to see myself alone in the street with the sound of my footsteps.

This is a contradiction. I often thought there should always be someone next to me talking. A woman with intriguing dialogue more sophisticated than one with simple flirtatious sentences, clichés; someone that would challenge my ideas. But now, I was enjoying myself being alone.

I go to the small coffee maker again. It is starting to rain outside. The mug warms my hands as I wrap them around it. On its side there is a colourful picture of a sailing boat; an activity totally foreign to me. I can't even remember how it has come to the flat. I don't like it but I clean it every time soon after I drink coffee. It seems that there is a resistance movement among the coffee particles. *'You drink our people and we, the resistance will stay! We will stick to the walls of your beloved mug!'* My room smells of coffee, newly brewed hot coffee. Carol can drink it cold. She pours the coffee then leaves it there; you think she has forgotten all about it. Sometimes she even goes away to the corner shop and returns half an hour later and drinks it with pleasure as if it was poured a minute ago! I cannot understand this. Cold coffee? The whole idea is to extract the essence under hot water. Drink it hot and absorb the aroma. I think she likes to ignore the cup. She enjoys the feeling that something is waiting for her, and she loves it when she ignores it. But how can she enjoy it when it has lost its heat? She can go, do the shopping, come back, have a sip and still leave the rest of the coffee for later.

4

Carol was all ready to go with her big red suitcases, smaller yellow rolling suitcase, and the two handbags. Checking-in took a long time. I wondered how come so many children travel even during the term time. She seemed happy. She was engaged with a small boy in front of her talking about the book in the boy's hand. Apparently she had read it! I thought I had never understood her. I could never imagine her sitting still reading a book, let alone a children's book; magazines? Yes. Reading magazines was a ritual for her. She knew the day each one of the three magazines came out. I thought I was like her when I was a boy but I had only one magazine and was loyal to it even when other boys talked about the story in the rival magazine. I used to go out first thing in the morning to get it. I kept them neatly one over the other even though once I had read them I would hardly go back to them.

The queue was moving slowly. She was still talking with the boy. I waited for her to go through the passport control. As she went through, she stopped briefly to look back with a smile. And then she was gone. I walked out. There was a breeze; I liked the freshness of the air.

I had come down with a cold. I think it had all happened during the night while I was asleep but it had started to show itself now. It kept itself hidden for Carol to leave! I was tired with a blocked nose and heavy eyes before going to the airport. And now I was sitting in my office, straight from the airport and having missed two appointments.

The phone rang. It was Elizabeth with her stern voice as usual. I imagined she had pink lipstick on her thin lips.

'Hello David, I have been phoning you. Can I see you briefly?'

'Sure, I suppose it is to do with next year's reading-list?'

'Not really, but it wouldn't take much of your time.'

'No problem, can you come over to my office?'

'That's excellent. See you a bit later?'

'Yes. What about 4:30?'

'Excellent!'

I wondered what she wanted. I used to see her from time to time in meetings. Sharp at 4:30 there was a knock at the door. She came in.

'I won't take too much of your time. I know you are busy.' She seemed rather embarrassed. She was talking in short sentences. 'I know Kate was a friend. She was like a daughter to me… since she joined us two years ago; so dedicated, so responsible.' She paused. 'Of course I took care of her, I mean went to see her every day, when she got admitted. It was a shock for me, you know, I thought we were close, I mean, I thought we were close enough for me to know something about it. It came like a shock to me. She rarely talked; and her only relative, her brother, being miles away busy with his job…'

'I didn't know she had a brother.'

'Oh, yes. She was fond of him too but you know she rarely talked about people or herself really. She was so involved with books and students. She did tell me though that you were a friend, she had great respect for you. I think she admired you for what you did in your work.'

'Yes.' I paused. 'She loved books.'

'And to see all that go so quickly…I was so shattered to see her declining. I did take some books for her but all I saw were several travel magazines…all opened but clearly unread. I wonder where her mind was. Of course she was very poorly…'

Elizabeth didn't ask me any questions. I was waiting for the inevitable one about how much I knew her. But no! She paused again and took out an envelope from her briefcase.

'She asked me to give you this after…'

She gave me the envelope. It was a white office envelope closed with my name in the centre, simply saying David.

Elizabeth stood up.

'It is funny how one misses people. We take things too much for granted. My office is so lonely these days.'

'I am sorry, I know what you mean.'

As she stood up, she looked around my office without concentrating.

'I wish I were as tidy as you are.'

I stayed silent. She paused and then quickly said goodbye and left the room.

I worked well after she left. There was no interruption. I had the envelope on the desk in front of me but I didn't want to open it. It was as if I was forced to concentrate to avoid opening it.

The office was cold. It wasn't a simple case of marking papers. I was looking at a student's report. It was so badly handwritten I couldn't decipher it. My throat was sore. I had a headache and I wanted to gather my energy to take myself to the flat. I thought of Kate lying on the hospital bed. Did she have too much pain? With her long hair unwashed for days, sweating, drying, dried sweat over cold skin, and an ache throughout her body, her bones. And losing weight, whatever weight that was left of her. And then I remembered her in a light summer dress, with big white circles on a red background. I had never seen her like that. So unusual for her to have her hair done, her neck and part of her shoulders showing, even a red lipstick. And the way she smiled, even laughed then. Later she told me that it was her mother's dress. She rarely talked about her but then in a sudden burst of talking she told me her mother was too loud, wore bright colours and didn't care if what she wore suited her age or not.

Apart from those moments when we were engaged in our debates over coffee, she was normally silent and this is how I always remember her. But then it was so unusual of her wanting to go around the world. She had put on some weight. Her slim face had grown a bit puffy. I thought it was a whim. She was so serious about her job. She loved to help all those students going to her asking about the most obscure topics, patents, books, electronic articles. Now getting ready to go out to dinner she was telling me she wanted to take a year off to travel; if the personnel didn't accept it, then she would resign. She was so solemnly serious about it. She was telling me this as if she was sharing a secret with me. And I was thinking that we were getting late for the restaurant, that she was too melodramatic; it didn't occur to me that it was her last wish. She was now sitting at the kitchen table. I touched her face with the back of my fingers and we went out.

She did not go on that world trip after all. Soon after that conversation she was admitted. But throughout our dinner that night she talked about her dreams for the trip. She had read about all sorts of things, about details of travelling in obscure countries with detailed itineraries. I listened to her as if she was talking about a third person. Someone she admired but I didn't know. She did use, by the by, and only once, the word "we"; that we could get a flight to an obscure place, I can't remember where, to start our journey. I didn't think much of it at the time. I don't even think I registered what she meant. I was thinking of having an early night, spend some time together and start an early day to finish the backlog.

'Do you like travelling?' she asked.

Do I like travelling? I ask myself. Maybe life is too short to think about travelling. Students travel after their degree. But for me? Now? What is the attraction? People bring so many reasons for it. Some people start to travel the world when they find out that their time is soon to come. I am totally opposed to this. If you are to die, then you might as well concentrate on things close to you, not waste your precious little time on a train from one miserable town to another. You might go to your local café, sit inside if it is cold, see people passing by and remember your days had passed, live with your memories in your last days.

I said: 'what a question, of course, everyone likes travelling.'

I was thinking of holidays. Perhaps she had already planned her travel. Maybe she had collected several travel plans from different travel agents; the magazines sitting tidily on her bedroom table; now an uninhabited room waiting to be altered by whoever settles in it, the new tenant.

But was she seriously thinking of travelling alone while she knew she was ill?

5

I looked at the envelope on my desk. I put it in my pocket. Just then there was a knock at my door. This student, Richard, came in. He wanted to know about the exam dates. The timetable was already published on the usual board. It was also announced electronically and each student should have received from the admin a personal e-mail giving them their timetable. I explained the whole thing to him. I was tired and wanted to go home. He wasn't convinced by my explanation, stood there looking at me working and then reluctantly left the room.

A few minutes later, the phone rang, it was Carol. I thought she must have been airborne by then.

'OK,' she said, 'if you don't want me to leave, then you will be happy to know I changed my mind. I decided to stay; after all this is just a ticket.'

I wanted to say, 'no! It is not only a ticket, It is much more than that, and what about your mother who is probably having coffee in the airport smoking away waiting for your arrival?' But I didn't say anything. I had already prepared my mind about her leaving, not being in my flat with the smell of her perfume everywhere. But I didn't utter a word. Of course now she needed to stay somewhere; my flat would be a reasonable choice until she found a place again. I coughed. She said:

'Do you have a cold? Did you hear what I just said?'

'Yes! This is all your decision. You decided to go and you are welcome to stay.'

I said it in an indifferent and somewhat annoyed voice. But she took the 'welcome' and considered my annoyance as a sign of me being hurt that she had decided to leave without telling me properly in advance.

She said, 'I knew you were not like that, like any other man.'

I coughed again. She was in the mood for talking:

'We will have a hot soup and you will sleep better.'

'I have an urgent document to finish. I wouldn't be early.'

'Don't worry I will be waiting for you.' Obviously she hadn't thrown away the key to the flat.

I put the phone down. There was another knock at the door. Richard came in again.

'Sorry but I do not know why you ignore my request. You are my personal tutor. I want to know about my exam dates.

'I told you what to do.'

'All I am saying is that you don't pay attention to my case.'

'I explained everything in detail. You are not a first year student. You should be able to deal with the timetable.'

'But I cannot find the information.'

'Your other colleagues can.'

'I don't know about them.'

'Don't you see each other in classes if not outside?' I was trying to tidy up.

'I cannot see why I should not ask my personal tutor about my timetable.'

'In that case you will need to come back some other time. I have other priorities at the moment.'

'It is always difficult to find you.'

'That is my business. If you want to contact me you can e-mail me for an appointment or you can phone my office.'

'OK, can you give me an appointment?'

'What is it about?'

'My exam timetable.'

'Sorry. For that you should see the announcement board or check electronically.'

He said something with closed mouth.

'Did you say something?'

'I want to ask you for a favour.'

'What do you want?'

He was very polite. His stance had changed.

'Yes?'

'Could I borrow your calculator? I have a test and my calculator is broken.'

I opened my drawer and gave him the calculator.

'I will bring it back to you after the test.'

'Don't worry, just put it in my pigeon-hole.'

'Would it be OK?'

'Yes!' I was sharp.

He left the room.

I don't know why I got into that conversation with the boy. I was tired, my throat was hurting and the prospect of going home was not appealing. I still had quite a bit of work to finish and without a tidy desk I couldn't concentrate. The course leader's report to show destination statistics of students who had finished last year, the number and performance of current students compared to last year and the reasons for any variations, a critical self-assessment! What B.S. I add a 'c' after it and the degree is given! And it is the degree they are good at! After three years of B.S. They get a B.Sc. what a load of garbage I thought. This is the time I should spend on research. By the time I finish the report and go home, Carol would be back at the flat; probably with her suitcases semi-open in the middle of the room. She would be drying her hair or applying nail varnish.

I was coughing and started counting the number of students on the computer list.

The telephone rang again. It was the Chair of the Department.

'Hello Michael. What can I do for you'? I said.

He was formal: 'What is the situation about this student.'

'Which student?'

'Richard Farmbaker.'

'Nothing much, bit of a bore really. He is hustling me for the exams timetable.'

'He says you won't give him his timetable.'

'What do you mean?'

'Why won't you give him his timetable?'

I said: 'Because I am not going to spend my time on something obvious. I am here to help students with real academic problems, not to act as an information board. The timetable is announced for all, they should have received an electronic alert as well, and they can also check their bloody timetable on the Intranet too, we are talking about information overload here. This is a university not a kindergarten, at least that's what I think!'

'Come on now. Don't you think you are over-reacting? We need to keep them happy.'

'Look, he is not a new student. He is supposed to have finished his studies by now. This is his bloody last semester and if he cannot find the timetable he doesn't deserve to get a degree.'

'Wait a minute now. You are going too far. He is your tutee and we cannot afford to be complacent. What harm does it do you to give him the dates?'

'Look, I have loads of work to do. This mundane thing has taken too much of my time and yours it seems.'

'I have to go now; I'll miss my 6:35 train. I will send him to you. OK?' Michael said.

'Not OK! I have already made myself clear on this.'

I see that I am shaking. I haven't been angry for some time. And now, this nincompoop is affecting my circulation. I remember myself as a student. I cannot remember a single case of talking to my tutor on any issue with mundane demands. He would ask me in the corridor, 'all OK David?' and my answer was always positive. Not that I didn't have problems. They were either too personal as I considered them at the time or they were not important enough to be mentioned.

I asked myself, 'am I feeling sorry for myself yet again?' Why am I doing this? So what if a student has silly demands? Michael is right. Give the brute the blooming timetable and get rid of him. What is this sense of righteousness? I am here to lecture on science not on codes of behaviour, not on how mature one should be! After all look at Carol's behaviour. She is sitting in my bedroom, where I always avoid inviting permanent residence, and is having her nails varnished after a protest departure! And what was my role in all this? Now I have to live with the saga of a messy relationship.

There is a knock at the door. It is Richard with a triumphant look in his eyes: 'Dr. Michael told me to come and see you. He said it will be OK.'

Only a minute ago, I had convinced myself to give the brute the timetable. But now I just couldn't. As if my whole being was invaded. I looked at him with complete ignorance.

'What about?'

'Oh! I thought you knew. It is about the exam timetable.'

'I think I made it quite clear for you. I have other priorities. If you cannot get yourself organised for your exams, and this is your final semester, then you have a problem. Now I have other things to do, OK?'

'But...'

'No buts, all the information you need is provided for you in different ways, you just waste your time and mine here.'

It was evening when he left the room. I could hear

the door to other rooms closing as others left their offices along the long corridor.

I worked for another hour. I printed the module report and left it in Michael's pigeon-hole. I also e-mailed him a copy. Then I left my office.

Should I buy some stuff from the supermarket? My plan was to go to the small bistro on the corner near my flat. They make delicious soups. This was something I had missed since I started going out with Carol. We went there once together and she hated the place. Anita, the Polish waitress there, didn't like her either. I thought they had a mutual agreement not to like each other. This, however, created a problem for me. Now, I was looking forward to going to the place in the corner for their soup. But it wasn't to be. I was going to meet the big red suitcases in the middle of my bedroom. And as for the soup, Carol had other ideas.

6

Outside, the air was fresh; a sharp breeze was blowing with intermittent drizzle. As I passed the corner near my flat, I saw Anita serving the only occupied table in the bistro. There were three men at the table. The light in the café was pale white as usual. I moved fast to get to the flat, I was feeling cold and the drizzle was changing to a persistent but light rain.

Getting to the flat I could hear loud music from outside. I opened the door. Carol shouted from the bedroom: 'I am in here!'

'So how are you?' I turned the volume down.

'More to the point, are you feeling better?'

'Not really. My throat is not doing well and I have a headache.'

'It's the shock of me leaving, come here, you will feel much better.'

She was lying on the bed wearing my bathrobe.

'I need to have a soup or something, had a long day.' I stood by the bed.

'You are underestimating yourself, come over.'

'Really, I am not in the right mood.'

'What's happened? Is this the way to show your

excitement for my return? Show some appreciation!'

'Listen, now is not the time for it. Can we get something to eat?'

'I will be ready in a second.'

She dropped the robe.

'We can go to the *'Matches'*. We should celebrate my coming back, don't you think?'

This was an expensive restaurant the other side of town. I did not say anything.

'Don't say you are tired! Don't be a bore.'

'Have you told your mother you are not on the plane?'

'Oh yes, what do you think? You want her to give me a roasting from there? As soon as I came in I phoned. You don't mind do you? I phoned her on her getting ready to go to the airport. She was so disappointed. Thank God I have someone who cares for me.'

'Did she ask you why you are not going?'

'No! She is so wise. She understands me. She knows I am not a bore. After all, she knows that if I do something, there is a reason for it.'

'And what might that be?'

'If you can't say, I am not going to tell you.' She was still naked, throwing dresses out of her suitcase.'

'No, I cannot say. Actually I am baffled.'

'I take it as a compliment. You find me an enigma!'

'It wasn't meant to be a compliment.'

'For me it was! You are such a negative man. I do not know why I returned. I am trying my best here and look how you respond. I might as well pack up and go.'

I smiled. She was wearing a thin yellow and green dress now.

'Listen, it was your decision to leave and it was you who decided to return. I had nothing to do with it. Now, if you want to go, again, it is your decision.'

'Come on darling! Do not be so confrontational towards a good guest. I promise not to stay in your flat a minute longer than necessary. I start looking for a place as from tomorrow.'

'The flat you left might be still available!'

'Oh! Don't pretend you want me to stay! Who wants to go to that dump of a place? I might as well leave town!'

I had taken two days off to find that flat for her.

'Let's go. It is getting late and I have another long day tomorrow,' I said.

'I am all yours.' She smelled nice, I could sense it despite my cold. She came close.

'You'll catch my cold.'

'Do you think that can stop me? I have cancelled my departure to be with you!'

My hand was in my pocket. I felt Kate's letter.

'Of course.'

'You don't believe me? I will prove it to you!'

'All I need now is to eat.'

We went out. The rain had stopped. The roads were shining cold under the lights. We were in the restaurant in half an hour, I was happy with the taxi driver going fast.

We spoke little during the dinner. I think she gave up on me conversing with her. The soup was lukewarm; something I don't like even in my best mood. Now my neck was stiff too and I was angry with myself, repeating the question in my mind: 'why did you come out? You could be in bed sleeping.' But I knew the answer. Coming out with her was the only way to avoid her. She was quite happy with her dinner which she finished with appetite. She had a good chat with the young waiter who was more than happy to please.

'Madam, you might care to taste our warm Crème Brulée with raspberries.'

I wondered where they had got fresh raspberries from and I thought of how to take myself out of bed to work tomorrow. I started thinking about the items that I had to deal with and this didn't help my headache. 'Where are you?' she asked. 'Don't be such a wimp. After all it is just a cold. You've always been a hypochondriac.' I was just going to say, 'how well you have got to know me in such a short time,' but I successfully shut myself up. As we started to leave the waiter rushed to us and accompanied us to the door. He opened the door with a smile:

'Hope to see you soon,' he said looking at me.

'He is too busy,' Carole said, 'but of course I will do my best to convince him.' She smiled at him.

In the taxi I was grateful to the driver for talking to her about his flat in the south of Spain somewhere, I was half asleep all the way. I wondered what energy taxi drivers have. To drive all day or night in all sorts of weather dealing with all sorts of customers and still have time to talk with them from the other side of the separating glass. They usually assume a certain posture to talk and see the passenger at the same time. But then, there are only special types of customers they talk to. I am sure he wouldn't even think of talking to me. I had dozed off with the background voice of the driver when we came to a halt.

'Have a good night Madame.'

I opened my eyes and rushed some money into his hands. I thought I would go out like a light as soon as I got to the bed. But in the bed I just couldn't go to sleep. It wasn't that her soft skin was touching me, it was as if I was lonely in a far away island. I knew I had a fever but it didn't bother me. I was thinking of tomorrow and the load of things that needed to be done. Then I remembered the envelope in my pocket. I felt as if I had forgotten an important appointment. I wanted to be left alone. That way I wouldn't feel lonely. But now, there was no such chance. I coughed.

'Don't touch the railings. How many times must I tell you not to touch the railings? Can't you see all these patients with all sorts of diseases touching them?'

My mother was all over me whenever I had a cold. And my cold always lingered, would grow into bronchitis. Then of course it had to be the danger of tuberculosis in her mind.

'Doctor, please tell me the truth. Is this child going to survive? Maybe he has tuberculosis, that is why he is coughing all the time. Why don't doctors tell us the truth? I can handle it. I can live with it. Just tell me what is wrong with this child.'

Then she would start crying.

'This is the story of my life. Look at me. I have spent all my youth on this child; ill all the time. What sin have

I committed to deserve this? Do you want some juice? I can make it with grated apple for you. Have it. It is good for you.'

Carol's skin is soft and smells nice. She always sleeps naked. I can hear her deep breathing. I ask myself why I don't desire her. I answer back, 'don't be silly; in this state?' But I am not convinced with my answer.

It was an interrupted sleep. I woke up several times and each time I felt something was wrong with me: my throat, my head, my whole body. But when I eventually tried to get up there was a ray of sunshine coming in. It was 11 a.m. I still had a splitting headache and could not breathe well. Carol had gone with all her stuff spread around the flat. I had to make a phone call to the department. Michael was on answer machine. So I contacted the secretary and told her I had flu and couldn't go to the office, had no lectures so no urgent arrangements were needed. She said Michael was looking for me earlier. I told her with the state that I was in I wasn't sure when I would be in next.

The CD player was left on from yesterday. I put on a calm CD and sat on the chair. I had a picture on the wall in front of me: a child walking on a narrow dry country road with his head turned looking back. I hadn't looked at the picture since I had hung it. Kate and I had brought it together on one of the rare occasions when we spent the whole day together having an early lunch, going from bookshop to bookshop, talking over afternoon coffee and watching a movie that we both liked.

The chair in the kitchen felt uncomfortable. I didn't have the energy to take a shower. I went to my jacket, took the envelope from the pocket and went back to the kitchen, heated up some milk and sat on the sofa in the sitting room. I kept the envelope in my hand for some seconds. Then I tore it from the side. I took the letter out slowly and started reading it. It was written on a simple white paper. I could see she had taken time writing it slowly:

'*Dear David,*

You are reading this letter so I am gone. Strange. All my life I was thinking what is the use... so what if I am here going to the bookshelves everyday, picking books, reading some and going home reading some more. I used to watch the students as they came into the library chatting away loudly, carrying with them their secret love affairs, laughing carelessly hiding their cheating and bitchiness towards each other. I always asked myself what is the use... I didn't have the resolve to continue to search for the answer. Now that I am writing this letter to you, I have such a desire to remain; to see you again; to just have a conversation. And of course this is not to be. So my diminishing hope is that you never read this letter. Perhaps I keep it deep in my box to refer to it by chance every now and then. Perhaps I will tear it into pieces so that I myself cannot decipher the words that I have written. But it all happened so sudden... and the time is short now. No need to contact you...no need to be in touch. There is this curtain between my space and the next. I hear noises deep at night and I forget them in the morning. It is good that I don't get a proper sleep, that's when dreams come in... something I do not have time for any longer. I doze off and see us walking by the river, stopping at the booksellers' and raising those philosophical questions...I still have no answer for them, by the way! I know it's silly to assume an answer but the point is that I am so ashamed of myself. I have always led a puny life; a meagre life. Only those times when we were together, those times give me hope that perhaps I could make a difference. But there you are. You are reading this so I am gone. I have left my meagre life.

It remains for me to thank you. I wanted to start my letter with thanking you for those moments of excitement; the moments you enabled me to show my excitement despite my aloofness. I think we've had good times together; short times, but good times. People call it quality time. I hate that phrase. I think our life is getting too much defined by buzz words. What I want to say is that I hope you have the same feeling; that I have been useful in my life and have been able to give joy as much as I have received. There is no more to say but of course the eternal question: you want to ask me, now that I am in this situation, is there something more to look for? To be quite frank, and perhaps bitter (what is new you might say!), I don't care and if there is, I think it is something of a mess just like the one everyone lives in everyday. The scope and opportunities might be more, but all the same, the same mess.

I think it is always better to stop unexpectedly, so: Bye.
Kate.'

I stayed with the letter in my hand for some time. I didn't want to break the moment but then I took my eyes away from the letter and started looking at the objects in the room. Through the open door I could see the bed, the bed cover half hanging onto the floor, the red open suitcases at the bottom of the bed, the small table by the bed, the lamp, next to it the book I have been trying to finish over the last six months. I had bought this book with Kate as well, the beige carpet, the picture, the peach coloured walls. I thought how good it felt that there was no wallpaper, a symbol of misery! And I looked at the ceiling, a lamp, no lampshade. I should buy one!

7

I was ill for four days. I stayed put apart from short walks to the corner shop to buy basic food. I saw Carol on and off everyday but she came over every night to stay. She was sorry that I was 'under the weather.' I did manage to do some work at home on the fourth day and decided to go to work the next day however I felt. As it happened I was feeling much better. The weather had changed to milder with a hazy sunshine. When I left to work, Carol was asleep. I left a note for her, 'if you are in tonight we shall properly celebrate!' I couldn't imagine why I wrote that note but I felt a degree of satisfaction by writing it, I suppose it was because I was feeling better.

Coming out of the flat I was happy to have the faint sun against my face. In the corner I saw Anita in the bistro. A single man was sitting at the corner table having a coffee and reading newspaper. She was cleaning another table. She had her long blonde hair wrapped back and I could only see her from behind. She had a grey-blue dress on with a narrow waist.

My office was cold. I listened to the messages left for me. There were two calls from Michael and several external calls. I had a couple of hundred e-mails and had lectures to give all afternoon. I made myself coffee and sat at the computer. I started to answer an urgent e-mail on a research project. The phone rang. It was Michael.

'Are you feeling better?'

'Yes, you had left me two messages to contact you. I've just arrived.'

'Yes. We have a bit of a problem here.'

'How can I help?'

'Heh, by not making them!'

'What do you mean? What has happened?'

'I did ask you to give that chap the timetable…'

'Not the timetable again!'

'Oh yes. You should respect people more, David.'

'Wait a minute now. Who has been disrespectful? I pay people so much respect I lose any patience I have left!'

'The chap has written to the provost. The provost called me as an urgent matter telling me he did not want any discontent. He asked me what the matter with my department was! "Can't you answer a simple question from a student?" he said. So I started to explain. Do you know what he said? He said, so what? Is it too difficult to give the timetable to a dyslexic student? Then he asked me if I knew the student was dyslexic. Of course I didn't and this didn't help either.'

'Wait a minute. I think this has gone too far. We have all the mechanisms in place for the students. We are bending backwards to help them. How much spoon feeding can one do? These kids need to be prepared to face society!'

'Yeah yeah yeah! We all know that but you really must have got it by now that we are providing a service and the customer is always right.'

'Sorry Michael but I am not working in a shoe shop. This is a place to exercise and promote intellect and for it a minimum requirement is demanded from those you call customers!'

'Well you say that. In any case I do not have much time. The boy is coming to see you! Give him the wretched timetable! You are his personal tutor.' He put the phone down. I thought I was red in the face. My coffee was cold now. I took my jacket and left my office heading to the coffee shop across the road.

It was unusually quiet. The young Chinese boy by the counter said 'cappuccino, very hot?' I smiled and said yes and sat at the small and uncomfortable table. It was particularly bad when it was crowded and people wanted to pass by you. The boy brought the coffee in a large cup. I remembered Kate. It was here I saw her last. She looked pale. We drank cappuccino and shared a Danish pastry. She said she was going to be away for a month to see her family up north, she said she needed it...she hadn't seen them for a long time and she was obliged to see them. This was the first time she talked about her family. I just ignored it as mundane talk. She looked at me with curiosity as if she wanted to know something. I had a lecture and had to leave the coffee unfinished. 'See you soon then, the whole month, isn't it too long?'

'Not really, I haven't seen them for a long time and if I wait for them to come down, it would never happen.'

'Try to have a rest while there...home-made food can do miracles!' I smiled, rushing.

'I shall. It will be a very long rest.'

She smiled. Her hair was hanging on her shoulders. She leaned her head forward and having the cup in her both hands she started looking at it. I thought she was warming up her fingers.

The boy said, 'a Danish perhaps?' I said 'no, not today.' I looked out. The sky was grey again. The cappuccino had gone cold. The froth was still on it. I came out; I had to go back to the office; had to finish the chores. As I got to my office, I saw that Richard was waiting by the door. I ignored him, went in, closed my door and started to deal with the paperwork. There was a knock at my door. 'Yes.' I said.

Richard came in.

'Yes?'

He talked as if we hadn't had a discussion before: 'Can I get the timetable now please?'

'So you were unable to get it from the sources I told you last time.'

'Yes.'

'And other students have.'

'I don't know about others.'

I took the phone and phoned the admin.

'Hello Bob, listen I have a student of mine who cannot access the information on his exam timetable. Could you help him?'

'But everything has been announced.'

'Yes I know, I know, but apparently for some reason

beyond me, he cannot get it. Would you please help?'

'One of those then.'

'Exactly.'

'OK send him to Gail at the desk. She will help him.'

'Great. Thanks Bob. I really appreciate it. I know it is an unnecessary bother.'

Richard was looking into my library books. 'Can I borrow this one.'

'No! Can't you get it from the library?'

'All copies are out.'

'I am sorry, I cannot help you. I need the book. For your timetable, go to Gail at the desk and ask her.'

'So you cannot give me it?'

'Go to Gail, the central office downstairs at the desk and ask her.'

He reluctantly left the room.

I looked out of the window. It was raining. I looked at the computer keyboard. It was dirty with rings of dark dust stuck around the keys. I started cleaning each key with a damp tissue. I felt as if I could do that all day, sleep on the keyboard, wake up, have a coffee and continue like that. I had to go to a conference abroad, only for three days. I didn't have the energy to organise the tickets. Go to the Net, do the bookings, get a cheap flight, book the hotel that I have been to several times where I always end up having the room against the lift.

I looked out again. It was raining harder. I took the phone and dialled this colleague at the other university; we had written a joint paper to present in the conference.

'Hello Fiona, I was lucky to catch you.'

'Luck is all mine David, all ready to go?'

'I'm afraid not, have had a couple of set-backs...'

'You're not chickening out are you?'

'I know it's un-typical of me but I have to stay put this time. I really did look forward to a few days of respite.'

'I'm sorry too...well...I suppose I need to do the presentation?'

'If you don't mind, the slides are all ready if you are happy to do it my way...anyway, I'll e-mail them to you...do change them as you wish.'

'Wouldn't make much difference, the essentials are the same...Oh...I was looking forward...'

'I would have come if I could change things...anyway we shall be in touch.'

'Absolutely.'

I put the phone down. It was still raining when I left the office later.

8

A week later Elizabeth contacted me again. This time she was more businesslike: 'There is a matter I assume we should deal with together, it concerns Kate.'

'Yes?'

'Of course you can say no at the outset.'

I thought 'obviously!' She was stating a fact but clearly she wanted me to say yes. I was happy for her to behave business like, the way she approached the topic, as it conveyed the message that she was closer to Kate than I was.

'So what is it I wonder?' I said.

'Her belongings.'

'What about them?'

'They need to be dealt with. The flat's owner wants to let it again and the flat needs to be vacated.'

'And how could I be of help? What about her family?'

'I'm not aware of any but her brother, she only had one brother up north and it is so difficult to find him. He is often off-shore. I managed to pin him down eventually but he told me he was happy for me to deal with it. He has already talked it over with the flat owner. He wants me to do whatever I like with her belongings.'

'So things seem to be sorted already,' I said.

She paused. 'As I said you are by no means obliged to do anything. It is just that I thought you might want to be part of this. After all you were close to her.' She paused again. 'Of course this will help me a lot, I feel a bit awkward going to her flat alone.'

'I understand. I do not suppose there is much to do.'

'No. It is not laborious. Just an evening or an afternoon should suffice. Would you be able to spare an afternoon? It will be better for me.'

'Yes, fine.'

'I am free Tuesday and Thursday afternoons.'

'So, what about next Thursday?'

'That is very good, thanks David. Shall we leave after lunch?'

'We can have a sandwich lunch together and go.'

'Good idea, see you Thursday 12:30.'

I tried to picture Kate's flat. Of course I had been there several times but now it was difficult to put things together and picture them in my mind, the patterns on the curtains, the colour of the kitchen walls... But I remembered the thickness of the carpet and her bathroom slippers as they were tidied away by the bath next to the pink fluffy mat.

I could picture her when she told me she was going away for a month... the way she talked softly. She did everything so smoothly, silently with no effort. I could have easily believed that she was back; phoning me: 'I am back, fancy a cup together?'

And I waited for her to come back and I left it at that for a month to pass...and for another... going out to dinner with Carol, having late nights. I thought about the unfinished book that I bought together with Kate and had a sudden urge to read it there and then. The book was sitting somewhere in my flat, perhaps under pieces of Carol's garments.

I was feeling uneasy. There were the voices of students talking in the corridor and I wished I were somewhere else. I took the phone and dialled Fiona. She wasn't in her office. I left a message: 'Hi, it's David! I assume you are back from the conference by now, wondered how your speech went, I'm sure excellently. Give me a call if you get the time.' I knew there was no need for the call and she would've phoned me at some point but I felt like talking to someone. At the end, it was worse, I couldn't talk with her and I had left a banal message. Then there was a ring. It was one of those aggressive rings telling you that you have messages... it was a call from the registrar's office saying it was urgent and important. There was a new form to be distributed next semester to all students. This would happen through different channels so that all students would receive it. The form will be sent to all staff later but this was a prior notice for us to be well aware in advance. The form would clearly and in an itemised fashion lay down the procedure to complain against lecturers and other staff within the university. I thought, why don't we spread the leaflets by a chopper? Like those emergency air drops bringing food and medicine to the needy, to the storm-stricken, to the earthquake victims. Why don't we provide them with specific complaint examples? A "Good Complaint Practice Guide, GCPG form"? It was as if we were inviting the students to complain even if they did not have any grievances. Were we directing students' minds to the right things? Oh! After all, what is right and what is wrong? Now I knew I was talking about something that I liked, the discussion over a coffee bringing all those arguments from Descartes and Nietzsche and moving from Kierkegaard to the Bible and back; a science lecturer in discourse with a young librarian. Perhaps I'd better print the form as soon as I receive it and keep it handy for that useless Richard. I suppose his room is full of this sort of junk.

I was still disturbed. The registrar's message had not helped of course. I sat there looking at the wall opposite my desk. I had a set of pictures pinned onto the cork board, pictures of my students in the lab... smiling, group pictures of departmental parties, pictures of participants in a meeting all standing on the stairs in eight rows, a postcard that I bought from a museum showing the statue of a god. I wanted to talk to someone, about anything; I even thought it would be good if Richard came in! I was ready for a good argument! But there was no noise from the corridor any more. I thought that I must change the water filter, buy some filter paper for the percolator and clean the small coffee table in my office. I thought I would be much more efficient then. I could always buy a doughnut and bring in biscuits. I wouldn't need to go to the coffee shop any more, there would be no use going there sitting alone anyway. I should start thinking seriously. Enough of dilly-dallies. And my research? 'What about it?' I could go faster perhaps getting more serious with my team. Do they think I am soft? Too easy on them? Do they like me for my science? For myself... being what I am? And should it matter? Where are they going in their life? Do they have any aims? A bit of research here and there! Now I was getting bitter. Why was I undermining them? And what about the degree students? 'Don't joke with me it is not the time!' I told myself. "Get real", Michael told me! And I always thought I was a realist. Now Michael was bringing me up to speed with the policies: 'Bums on seats mate! The customer is never wrong. Do give him the timetable!' I might as well open a coffee shop!

The wind outside was sharp. I walked to the nearest pub. I usually avoided it but this time, it was a necessity. Inside it was warm and smoky. I bought a beer and sat in a corner. I was in the mood for discussion and I could easily spend an hour having a dialogue with myself. And my colleagues? I suddenly felt the heavy air. I wanted to have a discussion on so many topics, none of which I could start meaningfully with my colleagues. It wasn't a case of them having no opinion, on the contrary. But they weren't interested. Any interest was only geared towards proving their superiority, asserting themselves, Asserting! Yes! I remembered the case of teaching tasks; what was called 'transferable skills'. Who were we kidding? We had to provide sessions for students to learn how to be assertive! How to be a leader! Did I believe in any of such activities? Clearly not! So why did I practise them? If I was so critical of the students and the lecturers then why did I stay in my job? I was one of those lucky ones not to be too dependent on the cash coming from their job! So what was it? Was it possible to love my job and yet dislike so many aspects of it?

The pub was getting crowded. I started looking at the black and white pictures of the 1930s to 1960s actors on the wall. Then I saw Ian, an older colleague of mine, coming in. He came straight over:

'Do you mind?' He took a stool and sat in front of me without waiting for my answer. 'Chilly outside,' he touched his nose, 'what's yours?'

'Thanks I am OK.'

'You can have another one, I'll get you a large one.' He went to the bar.

He came over with a pint of lager and a glass of white wine for himself. He put the lager next to the one I was drinking.

'Thanks,' I said.

'My pleasure.'

'Always wanted a calm life.' He paused. 'My in-laws are with me now. They are staying for a month; have come all the way from the back of beyond.'

He had a sip of his wine. I thought for a man of his age, to have in-laws was strange. But he had a young wife. He said, 'I nearly lost my collection last week; you know; the storm.'

'What collection?' I asked.

'My stamps. I had to keep them in the attic. I had to move them to the attic as the in-laws were coming, small flat you know! And what happens? Of course it had to rain the same night they came. You should have seen me, should have seen us! Thankfully the rain didn't get to the albums. Only some corners got wet. I had to move the stamps though. It was an all-night job. But some of those in the cardboard box did get wet. I am not sure how damaged they are. And what does she say? She is not supportive you know, has never been. And of course I am rude. An old rude dreamy man! The rude romantic! Hah hah! And I get all these lectures from my wife. Thirty years younger than me! Mind you, the parents were understanding. When she told them, they were embarrassed somehow and they had jet-lag! Couldn't sleep. I preferred to be alone rearranging all those stamps but I was worried about them in the other room where they were sleeping. And of course she would tell me that I was very rude not to let her parents have a good rest on their first night after arrival. You fidget too much, she said!'

'I had told her I was a man of principles. I told her at the first opportunity I had, that is, when we were alone. And that was that. I told her from the outset.' I made it clear from the start what I expected from us being together, that is if she was happy with it.'

He had a round-neck maroon jumper on and was fidgeting awkwardly on the stool, sitting in front of me.

He went silent. I was surprised. I didn't know him that well for him to talk to me about his personal, family life; and it was very sudden. I had thought there would be no-one to talk to until getting back to the flat where Carol would be on the phone. I started thinking, did I like a calm and quiet life? How would it feel if I remained alone with minimal relation with people around me?

9

As I had imagined, Carol was on the phone. She continued for a while. As she put the phone down, she said, 'are you back darling?' I said, 'Darling is back and darling is very hungry.'

'We have to do something about it then. Where are we going tonight?'

'Nowhere, we have something in the fridge.'

'I thought you'd love to go out.'

'Not really.'

We ate at home. It was a cold supper but I preferred the cold food to going out in that cold weather. She said, 'I saw Fabrizio today, he has put on so much weight I nearly didn't recognise him.'

'How is he?'

'Fit as a fiddle, apart from the weight.'

'And Gail?'

'She was on good form too, in control. He does adore her. He told me quietly he was going to buy her something nice.'

'Oh! And what would that be? What is the occasion?'

'For him, there is no need for an occasion. He is so

thoughtful. But didn't want to divulge! He is such a lovely man, such a lovable man.'

'And did you have time to check the estate agents?' It was a full month now that she had been staying with me.

'You don't want me to make a wrong choice do you? You don't want me to feel miserable. It is hardly a month since I came here. Don't worry, before you know it I'll be gone. You can have the whole mansion to yourself! Do you know? I don't know what I have done to you to deserve this.'

She started to prepare herself to cry. Had I ever believed a woman crying? I am sure I did. I must have, the glance, the movements, the silent moments between the tears. But, then, when did I start to doubt it? She had the paper napkin in her hand tearing it only with one hand into small pieces. Then took what was left to her nose. Her red nail varnish was intact.

'You never loved me,' she said.

I thought, we never had any conversations like this before. Where did that come from? We were never on those terms. Now she was bringing in a new element. I felt tired and wanted to go to bed. She continued:

'You know, I thought I had a friend in you. How wrong could I be? They are together from yonks ago and Fabrizio still is prepared to leave his office to go and buy a present for her, he thinks about her for no particular reason. And us? How long have we been together? Can you say? I bet you don't know, it is hardly a year. And all you think about is to throw me out in the street, and that, when I have changed all my plans and come back to you, cancelled my flight just for you.'

She paused and I thought it was the right time for a full throttle crying, a loud cry. But no! She came over to me, went behind me and leaned towards me from behind my head. She brought her mouth to my ear and said, very calmly, 'but I don't care. You are like that and I like you the way you are.'

Then she went back to her seat, poured herself some wine and started looking at me with a loving expression.

Next day, I woke up early. Persistent rain was hitting the window. It was windy. Carol was asleep next to me with her mouth semi-open. Her skin was warm. Her shoulder looked fresh out of the duvet. It was cold. I made myself a strong coffee and left the flat. It was Thursday and I wanted to do as much as I could before lunch time. At the corner of the street I saw the Polish woman in the bistro. She was looking out. Saw me walking fast under the rain and waved. I waved back at her and went faster; I jumped on the bus that took me straight to the university. I was determined to clear my desk. The corridor was dark. I was the first one to arrive. Decided not to look at e-mails and by 11 a.m. I had managed to send off two reports and see two of my researchers. I had discussed and sympathised with them on their equipment failure and family issues. I made another coffee in the office and started reading my e-mails. There was an e-mail from Michael: 'Richard was here and made sure I missed my train. I had to get the timetable for him. He said you ignore him all the time. I thought I should draw a line under this ridiculous situation. He still might file a complaint against us. I tried to be accommodating. Anyway, as I have missed my train and there is no other for another hour, I thought I would share the intrigue with you.'

I started to compose a reply. Then I deleted it and phoned Elizabeth. 'I know it is a bit too early but if you like we can go earlier.'

'Not really. I am struggling to finish my errands here before 12:30. Is it OK?'

'Oh yes. I just wondered.'

'So see you at half twelve then.' She put the phone down.

We had a hasty sandwich lunch and did not talk much. Elizabeth's mind seemed to be somewhere else. I wasn't particularly interested to have lunch with her like that. I hoped to take the opportunity to discuss the new library facilities with her but this wasn't going to happen. As she continued with her sandwich I started looking at the students coming in to buy sandwiches; in groups, alone, most of them with their mobiles. I still had a residual cold and this was a good time to feel it again. One of the students came towards me:

'I haven't seen you for some time,' he said.

He had a baseball cap on, reversed, with a tiny earring pierced into his left ear.

'So I have been unlucky!' I said.

He laughed.

'Perhaps it's because you haven't been around,' I said.

'Yes, my mum got a divorce. I helped her move out.'

'Oh, I am sorry.'

'Not necessary. I will have a larger room in the new flat.' He was chewing and laughing.

'So you have a better place to study.'

'Whatever!'

'Good luck.'

'Yeah, I need it.' He left.

Elizabeth had finished her sandwich and we were ready to go too. Outside, I called a cab.

10

Elizabeth brought a key-ring out of her large black plastic handbag. On it, there were perhaps eight keys. She paused and carefully chose one and put it in the chipped blue door. The door opened easily. We walked up two floors I had gone through with Kate a couple of times and passed the narrow staircase with the old red flower-patterned carpet. Then there was the new pine-look door. Elizabeth paused again and chose another key from the key- ring which she had kept in her hand. Her fingers looked older than her face, with cracks on the skin around the nails. The door opened with a push and we entered. There was the short entrance opening into a sitting-room with the raised step leading onto the open kitchen.

The curtains were open in the small sitting-room and there was a faint light coming in from a hazy sun. A beige dress was lying tidily on the back of a chair. On one side of the sitting-room there were four rows of simple shelves, all filled up with books. I remembered the shelves faintly. A couple of magazines were placed on the coffee table. Under the window pane in the small kitchen there was a pot of herbs, dried up. An ironing table was leaning against the wall in a corner of the kitchen.

Elizabeth was standing between the corridor and the sitting room: 'I suggest we start here. There is only one other room and it shouldn't take long, really.' 'Yes,' I said.

She walked to the other side of the room, pensive.

'The sofa and the chair and the knickk-nacks here can go to charity, unless…'

'That is fine,' I said.

She came over to the kitchen and started opening the lower cabinets. 'The pots and pans can go too.' I looked at her standing with her hands holding some. They looked as if they had come straight from a shop. Then she opened the top cabinets, looking through sets of plates, bowls, cups and mugs. One would think that a family lived there. I recognised the plates and cups with delicate flower patterns. I had eaten there twice over the six-month period that I had known her more intimately. It was getting cloudy outside judging by the light coming from the window.

'Do you mind if I took the plates?'

I wondered why she asked me that.

'Not at all,' I said.

'I will organise for all the things to be taken away. We might spend a bit longer in the other room. She couldn't say bedroom. I wondered what she thought about Kate and me.

The bedroom hadn't changed; a single but large bed with a pale bed-cover, slippers tidily sitting on the floor by the bed, a small bed-side table with a lamp and a book. I couldn't recognise the book: *The life and times of an Andes flower*. The South American author was unknown to me. She had a bookmark on page 202. The book had 231 pages. I started flicking through it. The telephone rang. It was Elizabeth's mobile. She moved her hand into her bag and took the phone out immediately as if there was a particular, well known, easy-to-access place for it. She listened, but in silence. Then she said, 'it is rather awkward but I will be there, OK.' She looked at me with disappointment. 'My daughter has had an accident in the school, apparently not serious but she is in Casualty. I have to go. I am so sorry for this.'

'Oh, no! Is there something I can do?'

'No, no. I'm sure it is OK; one of those things and of course it had to happen now. Do you mind continuing here without me? Just shut the door behind you as you go. Of course take whatever you think you have a need for. I am sure she wouldn't mind.' I stood there: 'But perhaps I should come with you.'

'What for? ... No need, really. It will be a great help if you could look through the whole stuff and get this business over and done with.'

'Don't worry, I'll do my best.'

She took her handbag and left.

I had the book in my hand, looking at the window the other side of the room. It had started to drizzle. Suddenly I had the urge to leave the place. What was I doing there? Why did I agree to go there, to look at someone else's personal belongings, and more than that, to decide what to do with them? I sat on the bed. The book was still semi-open with my finger as a bookmark. I opened it again. I had no wish to read it but started to flick through the pages. There was a white piece of cut paper in it, with something written. It was Kate's handwriting. I read: 'to include in my diary.' I closed the book and closed my eyes. I wanted to be somewhere else, anywhere. There was some noise, two people quarrelling in the top flat. I left the book on the bed and began looking, starting from the large cupboard with sliding doors and two drawers at the bottom – perhaps the biggest item in the flat. Inside it there were six or seven items of clothing hanging, five jumpers stacked on top of each other and three ironed and stacked shirts. Three pairs of shoes were sitting on the floor of the wardrobe. On the other side of the wardrobe there were perhaps 200-300 books stacked and arranged carefully by authors' names. I thought perhaps she would like these to be donated to the university library. It was easy to do. I felt I was somewhere miles away not know how to get back. I told myself I'd better be out of this place soon. I should catch a taxi to my office, see people moving around me, do a bit of filing…then go for a relaxed drink.

I wouldn't need to look in the bathroom. Here would be a glass with a pink toothbrush and toothpaste, a bottle of liquid soap, a longish white towel, a hand towel, the shampoo…the usual. All those items would have a different meaning for me now.

I opened one of the drawers in the cupboard. It was for her underwear, white, light colours, blue, pink, yellow. The other drawer was untidy, the only untidy place in the whole flat. There were loads of pictures of all sorts in it: family pictures, pictures taken in studios with her father and herself alone when she was six or seven, an old picture of a young woman I assumed to be her mother, and a picture of a young man with a safety hat, taken in front of a factory, perhaps that of her brother who was working somewhere up north. Under the pictures, there was a notebook with a dark brown leather cover. I opened it. Only one third of it was used. I could recognise her handwriting, tidy, meticulous and feminine. Each page had a date on the top left-hand corner and a line was drawn after each day's entry. I read the first page:

'It is such a nice day today! What joy! It is sunny. Sun shines through the small window. A sunny Saturday. I shall always remember this day. Such a nice day to start my diary. I've always wanted to keep a diary since I was a child. I wonder why I haven't done it earlier. Perhaps I was waiting for a good start, for a truly sunny start. And today it is. But I am still shy. I feel embarrassed that I am writing this at this stage. Is it not too late? I tell myself that I have started writing because I have started seeing him. It gives a false picture of me. This is not a youngster's writing, excited after her first date. I hope it is not that. It is… how can I put it? It is about what happens in the air when I see him. All those talks of Nietzsche, Woolf, Schopenhauer! I smell the nostalgia hidden in the pages of dusty books. The way the conversations move! The way he moves his hands and I laugh. There is so much to read and then to talk about.

I will be seeing him this afternoon, a sunny restful afternoon with coffee and Danish pastry. I have a bunch of narcissus in the pot in front of me. The room smells of sunshine. I am happy after a long time. I am lucky!'

I continued reading. It was another date:

'Today, it is exactly one week since I started seeing him and he told me he is going to be away for a couple of days… a research meeting; I do like that sort of life. I think he has everything, so why would he like to continue to see me? I am sure he has healthy liaisons of an intriguing nature; a man alone and well off financially, he travels, he sees people and reads books (thankfully not the best sellers!). So he has to be content with his life. I think those who read best sellers are sad lonely people who have given up. Given up thinking, they go for cheap emotions to keep themselves satisfied with a sense of goodness, of sympathy, of lousy adventures and phoney imaginations. Romantic science fictions about an amazing stone in a far away planet that attracts emotions with a speed five times the speed of light! A humane serial killer, never to be captured, who sacrifices himself to save an unruly youth from dying under a high speed train, a young girl and her mobile phone experiences…well I see this one everyday, not only a young girl, but businessmen too with their Friday evening bunches of flowers going to their wives talking of their unyielding love. Sometimes I think I don't belong to this decade, or century, not that I like period costumes but I cannot see myself fit for any of these things. Ah, and that reminds me of our shared dislike, passionate dislike of period movies! This, I must say, I have to add to the list of best sellers. Now, this goes for those women with dilemmas about their chastity and those men with questions of honour too! This is the time we are living in, and what do I like? Yes, I like slow-pace books and I read them slowly. And I like him. More than like, I respect him for what *he is. I hope to keep, to continue seeing him more, even if for expressing our shared dislike of the best sellers! And it seems that it is going to be so. He asked me about my degree. 'History?' he guessed. And he was right. I suppose he was pleased with himself. He was correct in his first attempt. Oh, he wants to know about me. 'What are you doing in the science section?' I looked at him as if he had asked a silly question. 'Not that you shouldn't be,' he added. I suppose he is a charmer. I am in two minds about charmers! They attract you but then they overdo it all the time. They get so involved with their own image that they forget why they started to be charming! I have talked too much. Better sleep now!'*

I flicked through some more pages and continued to read from a different page further on:

'I feel ashamed. How could I behave like that? It was as if I was haunted. I am not on those terms with him. I talked too much and then suddenly erupted angrily as if I had known him for years, and yet he didn't seem to mind. He did leave soon. He did leave soon after though. He didn't say goodbye but there was something in his eyes as he was leaving and then I knew he wasn't angry with me. Perhaps I want to believe it that way. I haven't heard from him for three days now. Maybe he is annoyed; maybe he doesn't want to know. After all who am I? What am I to him? If he hadn't minded my anger, he would have contacted me by now. Why should he, even if he is not annoyed? We are not on those terms to contact each other every day. The point is that his office is not on my way and it is awkward to go that way just to see if he is in. But why shouldn't I call him? What is wrong with that? Yes. I must do that. I can apologise for the way

I behaved. It was so uncalled for. He wanted to have a coffee and what he got was a barrage of insults. I shall call him tomorrow. I must call him even if we are not to see each other again.

Another page:

I phoned twice in the morning, there was no answer and I didn't leave a message. I phoned again after lunch. It was him. He was surprised. He had just come back, literally as I phoned him. He said he had left for an unexpected meeting on a project. He seemed happy, things had gone well. Then he asked me what I was doing tonight. He asked me out to The Glass Cabbage.

Raindrops were hitting the window. I remembered the restaurant. We had a pleasant night. The restaurant is a furniture shop now. Strange how fast it was turned around. I couldn't continue with the diary. I took it with me and went to the kitchen.

My throat was dry. I went to the sink and turned the tap on. I let it run for a time and drank from it. Then I left the flat for the office. I don't know why I went to the office, could have easily gone home. It was late enough. As I arrived, I phoned Elizabeth but she wasn't in. I thought it was stupid of me to think she would be back that time of the day under the circumstance. I did a bit of tidying up and went to the pub. It was dark and empty. I had a large beer very quickly and then left.

I decided to walk home. It was raining but I needed the walk. The streets were deserted; a rainy Thursday night around ten wasn't that attractive. I decided to go faster.

My mind was racing and now I wanted to be at home. I thought it had been a long day although I hadn't done much. Kate's diary was in my chest pocket and I was pressing on it with the inside of my arms, my hands in my side pockets. I remembered the drawer with the pictures. The collection was odd. And the way she had put them all together was untypical of her, she was so tidy. There were some official pictures, some pictures taken with her colleagues by the book shelves and at the desk. Then there were old pictures with her parents when she was little, then pictures of her as a very young girl with her father. And among all these she had empty postcards of Himalaya and South America. There were also two pictures that I knew well. They were pictures of a river as water was splashing onto its stony bank. There was nobody in the picture. She took the pictures when we went to the countryside for a weekend. I had forgotten about that trip. It was the only time we went somewhere together for that long. I felt the thickness of the bundle of pictures in my pocket. I had taken some of the pictures with me thinking that I could give one for the memorial to be printed in the university magazine. But I had more pictures with me and thought that I was making excuses for having taken the pictures. For whom did I need to justify my action though? After all I had her diary in my pocket. I could not sit there in the flat and go through all the pages. There wasn't much written but I had to read them slowly, very slowly.

I was now almost running and was close to the flat when I tripped and fell. One side of me was completely wet from the rain water in a puddle. I wasn't sure whether it was better to take the diary out of my pocket or to keep it there until I went into the flat. I kept it in and started climbing the stairs. As for the pictures, they could be dried later if they were wet. As I started to go up I felt a sharp pain in my upper thigh. I opened the door.

'So you are home eventually,' Carol said. I just ignored her and went quickly to the radiator, taking the diary out of my pocket. The radiator was cold. 'This is cold,' I said.

'I know. It was too hot in here. You know me!'

I left the diary open face down on the radiator. The pictures seemed to be OK.

I went to the boiler and turned it on.

'What is the urgency?' she asked.

'Nothing of any importance to you.'

'So you mean none of my business? You are a rude man. Come here and make your love happy!'

I said, 'I am going to take a quick shower. Have you eaten?'

'What do you think? Should I waste my youth waiting for you? I had a quick bite with friends.'

I turned on the shower. I wanted to stay under it for a week or two!

When I came out of the shower, Carol was in a deep sleep. The flat was warmer now. I went to the radiator. The diary had dropped on the floor. One page was folded under the weight of the rest. I opened it and straightened the pages, put it back on the radiator and went to the kitchen. I sat there. There was some ham and cheese and a stale baguette. I had the meal with a bottle of beer.

11

Next day, the morning was bright and it stayed sunny for the best part of the day. When I came back to the flat, Carol was singing away walking naked into the bathroom and back.

'So it seems that you have something going tonight.' It was just a manner of speech from me.

'Yeah, it's my Salsa trainer. You must see him. He is gorgeous.'

She was wearing a dark red skirt and a white shirt with the top buttons undone. 'I might go to Brazil you know. He is going back. He is on short term visa. He works in the dancing class just for fun. Nobody wants him to leave but he is going and I think I will go with him. He'll be gone within a couple of months. So I don't need to look for a flat here any more! You don't mind me staying for a little bit longer do you?'

'I am not particularly keen on you staying here. I am sure you feel the same, it is not comfortable.'

'Oh, come on! Don't be like this.'

'Look! You have stayed here long enough! After all your Brazilian will be upset to see you sleeping somewhere else.'

'Who's going to sleep somewhere else? I shall be here sometimes. It is a pity because he is staying with a friend of his as he is not sure what to do next.'

She was doing her make-up.

'I thought he wants to go back.'

'Yeah! That is an option. He might yet be convinced to stay. He can stay you know. He is a very well known artist. The Home Office will be only too happy to offer him a visa. It is just that, oh why am I explaining. You can't understand. He is an emotional man. He is volatile. He loves living.'

'Well I am happy for you but I really want my space now.'

I went to the kitchen. I wanted to be alone. I didn't mind eating alone; actually, I preferred it but I had no energy to go out. I took out a box of ready-made food from the fridge and looked at the thin metal-looking box with the pasta inside it. I put it in the oven. Soon the oil would come out of the food, light yellow at the edges of the strings of pasta, looking heavy. I opened a bottle.

'Be a good boy and pour me a glass before I go! You will remember these moments and regret having been so awful to me.'

I poured her a glass, sat at the table waiting for the pasta to warm up. She came towards me with the glass in her hand. 'Don't be stingy, give us a kiss!' Her face was near mine and I could smell the make-up. She stayed behind longer than I expected. I surprised myself. How could I after that exchange of words only a few minutes ago? And how could she? She was going to see the Brazilian shortly, all made up for a long night. But her motive was clearer to me, somehow cheap. As for me, it was, I suppose, a question of ego. No matter what her motive was, I was chuffed to see her stay and show such interest. Perhaps all she did was to make me jealous; perhaps she really wanted me and was going out of her way to reignite my waning attention.

She straightened her skirt. 'I really have to go now. I am too late.' The plate of unfinished pasta with the aluminium container was sitting on the kitchen table. I poured some water in the kettle to boil. It was too humid in the kitchen. I opened the window. Cold air rushed in. I was looking forward to reading the paper, anything that could distract my mind. I was hungry now but had no appetite for the cold, oily pasta. While having the coffee, I pictured Carol getting into a taxi, tidying up her hair, pulling her stockings up revealing her thighs. Which one would she do first? I thought she had lost weight. She was really quite thin now. Perhaps she could be a good dancing partner for the Brazilian. Oh, by the way, if the boy was so important to her, why didn't she mention his name? The kitchen was getting cold. I closed the window, sat by the table and opened the broadsheet.

I kept on reading the headlines. There was a flag of a country with some odd comments under it. I could not find the relevant line quickly to see the significance of the picture. I couldn't concentrate. Now I kept on thinking of Kate and hospital food. Eventually, I stood up, took the pasta box to the sink, threw it into the rubbish bin and started washing up in silence.

12

It was a university-based staff-student committee meeting with a three line whip to attend. I arrived a couple of minutes late but the staff were still coming in. There weren't enough seats. I squeezed myself into a seat at the corner. It was going to be a long and useless meeting and I thought that I had secured a good corner to doze off. A piece of paper went around with our names to sign. After the usual introduction, the Dean of the faculty started with the way things had changed and that we were now much more accountable both to our colleagues as responsible individuals and to the students who were our customers demanding attention, and deserved it because they paid. Then he laughed: 'And remember, the customer is always right!' I felt claustrophobic. His comments reminded me of a corner shop near the university. The shopkeeper had a handwritten piece of paper with the same sentence stuck next to the till.

The room was already stuffy with closed windows and steaming wet raincoats that the staff had hung or left on the floor next to their seats. I was struggling to keep my eyes open.

'…and I'm not saying these things just to fill a gap, we are all busy and have loads to do and this is the last thing I want to say but it is quite worrying…'

He brought out some papers from a folder and calmly waved them:

'I have had a series of complaints from a student…it is like a story, a boring one but alarming. I wonder why we should ignore students and give them the excuse to complain. What's more disturbing is that apparently the line manager had cautioned the person in question about his treatment of the student. Was there a positive action from the staff in question? No! I have to say that I am very disappointed. This sort of behaviour will not be tolerated in the future. Let me make it quite clear,' he was getting quite animated, 'of course we want to maintain the quality work that we do but I should not have to remind you that it is the question of bums on seats. We cannot afford bad publicity.'

And he went on an on. I looked at Michael who was sitting next to the Dean. His eyes were looking at the piece of paper in front of him and he was scribbling on the paper. Outside the widow, I could see the trees bending in the wind. It was quite strong. Then I could hear the rain hitting the window. I thought it might stop by the time the meeting ended.

I rushed to my office after the meeting. It had gone on for too long and I had an urge to go home. I was pleased that I did not respond to the Dean's long speech on work ethics and responsibilities. I wanted to tell him, and for that matter the Chair and other colleagues sitting there being lectured at, that I didn't care a hoot about bums on seats and actually I thought fewer bums on seats would be better, that accepting whatever illogical demands the students had would and had affected adversely our education system, quality of service, and society at large not to mention our international standing. I wanted to say that imitating other countries' relaxed systems had created a sense of numbness in our youth and that our timid blind tagging onto fashionable untested ideas was not only irresponsible, but it was a betrayal. But I didn't utter a word. I needed to see Kate, sit there with her in the coffee shop and discuss all this with her, sort of nagging, get it out of my chest. But that was a dark joke now.

Richard was standing outside my office. I didn't have any desire to see him, talk with him, have anything to do with him. There was no need for that speech by the Dean to strengthen my feeling but there you are. He was standing outside my door. I said, 'was it useful?'

'I don't know. It didn't work.'

'What do you mean it didn't work? How come?'

'I am not sure, I couldn't make it work.'

'Oh, I am sorry. I hope there weren't too many numericals. I am sure you will do well in general.'

'I wanted to say something.'

'Yes? I was collecting my stuff, taking my coat to leave.

'I am sorry but I lost it....your calculator!'

I didn't say anything.

'I can pay you for it. I can do it in instalments.'

Pay back! Instalments! I could erupt. I just said, 'don't worry.' He was still standing in the office at the door. I had to practically push him out of my office as I was leaving. I started to run. I wanted to get away from it all. I couldn't understand people I thought. Did I expect a lot?

As I reached the street, the bus was just leaving. I managed to catch it, just. I was wet and the driver didn't like me as I was going through my pockets to find the ticket. So what if he didn't like me? Perhaps he didn't like my coat, or my face. 'So what?' I kept on telling this to myself as I went along the bus to sit at the back. The bus had braked harshly twice and I was lucky to have stayed on my feet without damaging my back. I wondered why I bothered to go all that way to sit down while my stop was only three stops away. Why didn't I stand by the door to get off quickly? But then it meant that I could end up having an argument with the driver.

And after all this, I missed my stop. I started walking back and it was pouring. By the time I got to the flat I was completely soaked. Carol was not in and the flat was cold. I touched the radiator, it was cold. I checked the boiler, it wouldn't start. I sat in the kitchen for a while. Still. There wasn't much in the fridge but I couldn't make up my mind to go out. I took off my coat, dropped it on the floor and sat on a chair. Kate's diary was sitting on the bookshelf. I took it, and sitting in the kitchen started reading:

I looked at him as he was talking to the students in the

corridor. There is something about him that I cannot place. I am not obsessed. I only observe. But I was curious to see what he was talking about. The students were laughing. He seems to me to be a serious man; a man of some discipline.

I moved to another page:

He wanted a book by Hegel. I wonder why? Not that it is an unusual request; it is unusual, though, coming from a scientist and during the term time. He couldn't find it. He was quite embarrassed when I went straight to the shelf and showed him where it was. It was right in front of his eyes staring at him! 'Sorry about this, sorry to have taken your time,' he said.

I wonder if he was sorry for his mistake or for losing his image. I would have been! But then maybe he was genuinely sorry to have taken me from the desk at the ground floor all the way to the end of the second floor. This was the event of the day for me apart from having to ask the security to come over and deal with some rowdy students and their mobiles. What a change. Is there a generation gap really? Sometimes I feel I am older than him! He seems to understand the students better than me, anyway…looks more tolerant! It seems that he is creeping into my mind and I am accepting it with pleasure. Calm down! I'd better keep calm.

The kitchen was very cold now but I didn't want to leave, continued reading. Another page:

I didn't expect to see him at that party. It was a nice surprise. It really wasn't a party; it was a university reception, some sort of marketing event. I wouldn't have gone myself had it not been for

Elizabeth not going. There was some sort of problem with her daughter. She lives alone with her and most of her time is occupied by her. I suppose it is not easy to live with a daughter in her early teens. 'It is not a good show if the library is not represented, would you be able to go? There are drinks and nibbles. I was going to buy some food on my way and have an early night,' Elizabeth said. 'OK, I don't have any particular plans,' I said. As if I would have!

I asked him 'I was pushed to come here, what made you?' I surprised myself by saying that. How could I say that? So out of place I thought. I suppose after the library episode, I felt self-confident. 'There was no one to push me so I pushed myself to come!' he said. He was smiling as if he was into some sort of mischief. 'Actually I came hoping to see someone. I have been trying to find him for a month now. But it seems I'm not in luck.'

We listened dutifully to the short speeches. Thankfully there weren't many. Then he said, 'perhaps we can escape from the plonk and have some decent wine.' 'Why not', I said. I suppose I was curious to know him; a science lecturer who reads Hegel. Who else did he read? It would be nice to enjoy a different but relaxed chat.

We ended up in this small restaurant, simple, with good food. And the wine was fine. We didn't talk about Hegel or students or colleagues though. He seemed to be somewhere else, totally. He talked about his experience when he was away to a meeting in another country; a boy on a motor-cycle was hit by a car. He went into the details, how the boy was thrown in the air, how he was crushed against the open gutter, and the blood. Then he started apologising. I was sitting there looking at him talking, watching the subtle changes in the skin on his face, how his hands moved,

78

and the way he stared into the air as if he was talking to an invisible listener. Then he asked about me. This was so embarrassing. What could I tell him? That I lived alone? Big deal, so? Tell him that my parents separated ten years ago when I was a young girl? That I have completely lost contact with my father? I thought that the night was not going well! I asked:

'Have you seen "Snakes never smile"?'

He laughed 'Do you think I should have seen it?'

I said 'Everyone talks about it.'

'Maybe we could go see it together.'

I felt, in a strange way, at ease with him. He makes me think about books! I should take out and read again some of the books I haven't read for some time. Have to say, the night actually did go well. We walked a bit and I managed to catch the last bus home. Oh, I just noticed, he didn't say if he had seen the movie.

I remembered her when she jumped into the bus that night. She got in as it was moving away and I saw her going up the stairs.

I couldn't continue with the reading. I left the notebook on the bookshelf, took my coat, grabbed the brolly and went out. The rain had turned into sleet. I had the corner bistro in mind. Its windows had steamed up as I entered but there weren't many customers, only one table with a couple having coffee. It was still early for dinner but it felt good to be there. I had hoped to see a crowded bistro but I was happy to be in a warm place anyway. The Polish woman came over. She had a faint smile. 'Good to see you again.'

'Yes, I have been too busy with things.'

'Would you like a coffee?'

'No, not really, could I have a large whisky please? I would like to eat after that.'

'Yes of course.' She didn't ask me if I wanted it on the rocks, with water or without. But she came back with a glass, a bottle, some water and some ice all separate. So I was in charge. I had never drunk there before. I poured myself a good portion of whisky and kept the glass in my hands to warm it up. The metal ice container had droplets of condensation on it which joined together and ran down its sides. I thought of the hospital where Kate was admitted. I started imagining as if I had gone there to visit her, the builders standing idle outside talking with their coffee cups in their hands facing the renovation work where a heap of cement, pieces of wood, some bricks and a cement mixer were spread out. I imagined coming out of the hospital there would be a small traffic jam because of the building stuff. I would wait there for a taxi. An old man would come out of a taxi slowly with the help of an old woman. His hands would be shaking and he would have a problem getting out. I would go closer but he would be out by the time I reach the taxi. He would look at me and smile: 'thanks all the same,' he would say. I would get into the taxi and say 'the University please.'

As she was coming over to my table, I remembered the Polish woman's name, Anita. She said, 'are you ready to order?'

'I love your soup.'

'Yes, and anything else after?'

'You choose something for me.'

She blushed.

'I leave the whisky for you.'

'Thanks.'

I still had some in the glass but I poured some more. The couple at the other table were laughing. I thought about the meeting and then Richard, the bus driver and then the flat and the coldness, the boiler. I had to do something about it. Then I thought of Carol and her Brazilian. Anita came with the soup.

The bowl was full nearly to the rim. I started to eat it as she talked:

'I shall bring you something I prepared earlier; I hope you'd like it.'

'I am sure I would.'

The couple at the next table were getting ready to leave. The woman was wrapping her woollen scarf around her neck. It was maroon with some small knitted woollen balls in grey. The man was tall, thin and had a flimsy dark blue jacket on. As they were leaving, she glanced at me with a satisfied look. The man seemed to be in a hurry.

Anita came with a plate of meat and boiled vegetable.

'I hope you like this.'

I asked her:

'Which town are you from?'

She said, 'Lodz but that was a long time ago. I have been here for a long time, nearly 15 years now. I have my daughter you know.'

'I couldn't imagine you have a child and are married.'

'Was. I left him and came here with my daughter. She was only one when I came over. I was lucky to find a job here in this shop. The owner is very good to me.'

I was relaxed after the whisky and the hot soup. I asked her to sit at the table and she did. We were now the only couple in the bistro.

'I must say, this place is very homely. It doesn't have a restaurant feel to it,' I said.

'I am glad to hear that….and John would love to know that too. If you tell him when he is in, he would be very happy. This shop is his life. For fifty years he has been running it, most of the time by himself with the odd help coming and going until I came. It was an afternoon and I just came in by chance; had no hope. Desperately needed a job having the kid and the money was running out fast. But it didn't take him long to take me on. And I think I haven't disappointed him. It is a matter of being at the right place at the right time don't you think? I have been very lucky, in a way. No job, a one-year-old child, a foreign country! I don't know how I did it, leaving my town like that. I think I was haunted.'

I looked at her as she spoke. I thought she was 35 but looked older with the wrinkles at the corner of her eyes.

'I couldn't have guessed that you had a 16-year-old daughter.'

'She looks older, wiser than her age too.'

'Has she got it from her mother?'

She blushed.

'I thought I was wise when I came here to study. But I couldn't. That wasn't wise.'

'But what happened?'

Three young men in business suits came in and Anita stood up.

'Sorry.'

And she went to direct them to a table. All tables were neatly decorated with a small glass vase and a couple of paper carnations.

Soon after that another couple and then another couple came in. Anita had put a nostalgic old song on the CD player behind the counter. It mixed with the hum of the crowd. I had another sip of my drink, put money on the table and left while she was in the kitchen.

13

Next day I had to go to my office early in the morning to finish off some backlog by 10:30 a.m. I left my flat at 7:30 and walked fast to the bus stop. Round the corner, Anita was busy talking to a customer. I arrived at my office at 8:30 and started working. I worked without interruption for nearly two hours. Then I thought to have coffee in the usual place and return to go to my research group meeting. I went through my movements for the day while having a rushed coffee as if having it was part of the 'dos' of the day.

It was getting late for my meeting. I paid for the coffee and rushed to the meeting. My group was already in the room. I sat next to a new researcher who had started in my team three months ago. She had long curly hair and a full face. There were six others around the table; two were away at a conference. I thought that with three more to come there will be twelve of them. It would be good to keep the numbers I thought; here's not a case of bums on seats, it is a group of people trying to discover something new.

'Who do you think you're kidding,' Kate would've said. I felt upset having that image in my mind. I thought, I don't need to apologise for my thinking, I have good intentions, I am enthusiastic about my team and if others have a problem with that then tough! Others? Do I consider Kate as others? Surely! If she doesn't understand what I say, what I think, then she is an outsider. But this defeats the issue! I am proving her right! I am sitting among my supporters – and that is debatable too – and I am saying that other people's opinions are irrelevant. This is exactly what she would have said about me, arguing about!

Our meeting went well. Reports were mainly on target. Some with short delays and some a little ahead. I went to my office, had a sandwich while working. I had four courses to teach and one was in ten minutes. I grabbed the transparencies and rushed to the lecture room. I arrived before the start and was pleased about it. I could have an informal chat with some of the students before starting. But there was only one girl sitting there deep into her lecture notes trying to extract something, and then they came in dribs and drabs and all late. I waited ten minutes as they were coming in. There were twenty-three students eventually.

It was a day of doing nothing in particular, there was no pressure but I was exhausted. As soon as I arrived home I went straight to bed. It had gone just after seven. I knew Carol would come in at some point and it wouldn't be a good sleep but I didn't expect not being able to go to sleep at all. Yes, it was unusual for me to go to bed at that time and like that with no food and no drinks even. But I felt low and I couldn't put my finger on the reason. I was uneasy, worried even, and there was nothing to be worried about. Then I thought about Kate, her pale skin and the way she talked, the way she discussed with passion. I got off the bed and went to the sitting room. It was cold. I took the notebook, sat on the sofa and started to read it:

We had an argument. I don't know how it started. I was ready for a good afternoon coffee with him, to relax a bit, just for a break. The air in the library was too stuffy and he had not phoned but as I was going for coffee by myself he rang. I was so happy to hear his voice! But from the start he was fidgety. I suppose he was in a bad mood and wanted to vent his anger somehow. He didn't say much about work but I knew he was irritated about something. I just don't know what I said exactly but it was something like: 'Sometimes one has to make sacrifices'. I wanted to console him. It was just an innocent remark. He interrupted me abruptly: 'what do you mean? Do you suggest to suppress what one really thinks, what one really desires, for someone else's satisfaction even if you believe he is wrong? How can you say that? If that's the case, then what is the meaning of your existence? You might as well forget about it, about your beliefs! Be one without any principles!'

'I just wanted to say…' I said.

'What? What could you say? That it is in the nature of Man to be forgiving? I am sick and tired of all that tripe! And we are fed it everyday…continuously. It is not even force feeding! We just eat it and feel satisfied. But this sort of junk does not alleviate my hunger. We are fed with this tripe by the sanctimonious and what they do in reality is something else. Just open your eyes to see what happens around you!'

I was in a daze. What was the big deal, why was he so animated, I didn't know. But I also liked him for it; his passion was so much in contrast with the sleepy stuffy library atmosphere. Then I felt a sense of mischief and I enjoyed it. I said:

'And what is the big deal? You think you have discovered something?' Suddenly I thought that if I continue on this line, I will enter a different phase with him but I had started and there was no stopping:

'Those books that you read are full of these sentences. They remain as sentences…rigid… and so do you! If you are so much against sacrifice, why do you spend your valuable time with a bunch of disenchanted boring students who don't know what they want in their meagre lives? Look at them with their mobiles, their outfits, their … I don't know what! Is it not a sacrifice wasting your days hoping for a change? If this is not a sacrifice then it is stupidity living like this with a heavy bag on your shoulder, practically! Is it your cross? Are you paying back for the sins you committed by being born?'

I was furious. I know I had gone too far but I could not stop myself. Maybe it was because I expected to have a good, relaxed coffee and that I had ended up with a man in a bad mood! Maybe I was angry with myself that I was unable to calm him, to create a good atmosphere; even worse I had inflamed the situation! He put his hand under his chin and looked at me. He had suddenly gone quiet. He had a sip of coffee.

'Do you know? Prometheus did not bring fire for Man because he was tired of Gods. He didn't do it because he felt sorry for Man's ignorance. He did it just because he liked to do it. The fire was not his cross, it was his extension!' he said.

Then he stood up with the cup in his hand, had a quick sip, left the cup on the table and left!

I sat there and looked at the pavement. The students were coming over. Their classes had finished. Soon the coffee shop would be inundated by them. I came out. I walked to the bank to cash some money. Then I went back to the office.

I poured some whisky for myself and continued from another page:

So this is it. Something I always feared. A fear I couldn't place, I was never sure of the reason for my unease and now, I know. The doctor was very professional. I saw him early, 8 in the morning, before going to work. I suppose he saw several more patients before he went for his coffee; like us. We see students coming with their requests and problems. We all gather in the coffee room unless we decide to go out for coffee as I have recently done. Such a pleasant deviation for me; only for a short period. And the period will be cut short!

The doctor said:

'I am afraid I have bad news.'

Do they practise for sentences to use? Do they learn them from TV programmes? They are so lousy doing it. But I only remember some of his words. I suppose he talked quite a bit.

'Still, all is not lost. There should be some time, you can enjoy life day by day.'

So it is just a matter of days, not months not years. Perhaps I should be grateful. The agony will be short.

I came out of the clinic. There was a cold wind. I didn't need to worry about catching a cold now. I had something superior! Now, how do I continue? I didn't tell anyone of the scare, that I had gone to see the specialist, that I had to go through the usual rigmarole of samples and tests and waiting. But it is over today. Now I have to think. What am I saying? Now it is the time to forget about thinking. I can do anything I want. It is a freedom to be cherished, not to forget! I can give my notice. They will say why! And I can give them any answer I liked. 'Oh, my rich uncle died!' A running joke for all to laugh at. I can go out and kill someone, Oh, not only one, several. As many as I can before I get killed or detained. 'Why did you do that?' they will ask, 'why does an obedient, silent, responsible respectable young librarian kill people?' It will be a hay-day for the journalists, for the newspapers. 'Oh, I just did it because I felt like it, because I wanted to experience how it feels, because I wanted to see what Albert Camus had in mind when he was writing...'

No, I haven't told anyone about it. Perhaps I should. Do I need people's sympathy? David talks about the miserable state of those who love to show that they sacrifice everything, those eternal martyrs, those who continue living just to see people admiring them for their 'courage'. But I cannot continue to live! I just see no reason to advertise my state! I don't see myself killing people either. And I still love my work! But there isn't much left of me now. The best way to accustom myself to having to leave is perhaps to go on a trip. I can get six months, a year off, go around the world. Yes! I might even be able to trick the trickster!

Another page:

Yes I was always afraid of a catastrophe. Now I am in it, I live with it, live! And now I am not afraid at all. I can be drugged; I will be drugged as they see me going through the procedure. It is like anything else really. Buy a ticket, cash or credit? Go onto the platform, wait for the train, wait for people to alight first, then get into the train; as you are going in, eye the seats, is there a seat available? Is there one that you prefer? And soon there will be the time to get off, prepare yourself for it, stand up before the train reaches the station.

So they will increase the dose as we go; now I feel the pain, now I don't. And then there will be the big dose as a matter of routine.

The basil pot in the kitchen needs water.

14

It was the semester break. There was a relaxed feeling walking with Kate knowing that we had plenty of time going to bookshops, flicking through books, going for a drink, seeing a light movie and being together without rushing. She saw a pretty clean, as if untouched, book: 'Death of the myth'. I didn't know the author. I didn't know the book. She bought it and we moved to the bar nearby. It was crowded with cinema goers, art lovers and tourists; now that I think about it, it was a strange combination. I got a couple of drinks and just before sitting down she said:

'The fact that someone claims the death of something, it means that it exists or at least it has existed at some point in time. And if time is an illusion… if time does not exist… then it means that that something exists anyway.'

I said:

'Then by your own logic, if you say that time does not exist, it means that it has existed, at least at some point! This means that time does exist. And if time exists, then we can claim death!'

It was a point of potential argument and serious

disagreement but we laughed. It was a rare occasion when we did not continue a discussion, we started looking at other people in the pub and tried to guess who does what and what each couple's relationship was, how they would behave in private and in public. Then somehow we started again talking about the death of heroes, the death of God, the death of ideas, ideologies, and it was all fun talking about a concept sparked in us by the name of a book, second-hand but shiny, revived after perhaps a long stay in an outdoors second-hand bookshelf.

Her face was cold as I touched it with the back of my fingers. We had walked leisurely by the river after the movie. As we were going up the stairs to my flat she said:

'Do you think we are taking things too seriously? Perhaps the film was real. Perhaps we have little time for comedy in our lives.'

'There is always a danger of assuming things are rosy, and then as you smile, the catastrophe hits,' I said.

'Yes, but thinking like this, there is a real danger of missing the laughter for an imaginary catastrophe.'

We were by the door of the flat. We stopped talking and as I took her in my arms, her shoulder was cold against my face. I thought, she feels the warmth of my face, and this gave me confidence. We didn't talk much through the night.

15

I didn't expect Carol to be in. She had a very thick blue jumper on and was curled on the sofa. Her hands were hidden under the stretched sleeves with her chin resting on her knees. 'I am freezing,' she said.

'Didn't expect you back tonight.'

She didn't answer. 'Why did you turn the heating off? It's freezing,' she said.

'I didn't.'

'I didn't either. Somebody must have,' she said.

'So why didn't you turn it on when you came in?'

She didn't say anything.

'It seems it is not working. I don't know what has happened. If you could stay in tomorrow, I…'

'You don't expect me to do your housekeeping for you do you?' she said.

'But you live here too you know.'

'I said I will be leaving soon. I am looking for a flat, you know that.'

'I have known it for a long time.'

'You are so insensitive. You cannot see other people's problems; you and your miserable little flat. Anyway I am leaving. I am going to Brazil.'

'Good! So we have some commitment here.'

She didn't say anything.

'So he proposed to take you with him, did he?' I said.

'He will, he will, you are more impatient than I am. I know you want to get rid of me, but it is a big commitment on his part.'

'Why is that?'

She was silent again.

'Is it so big a commitment to agree to take someone to his own country? He is not delaying his return for you.'

'It is not like that. Anyway you didn't stop me from going.'

'You decided to go, and you decided to come back.'

'Exactly! What was I in your life? What am I in your life anyway?' she said.

'Now it is me! You come back and sulk in a corner, God knows why, and it is all my fault. Get a grip! We didn't have a commitment. Now if you are disappointed with him, perhaps you had gone too far in your expectations,' I said.

I went close to her and she leaned her head against my thigh as I was standing next to the sofa. I sat next to her.

'Have you eaten?' I asked.

'No!'

'So you didn't go out either.'

'No. some of his Brazilian friends came and they were talking their language all the time. You know the lads. I didn't stay.'

'So what now?'

'Can you make me an omelette?' she said.

There was only one egg left in the fridge. I took my coat and went out. It wasn't raining but it was cold. There was a late closing supermarket near the flat. To get there, I had to pass by the bistro. It was even more crowded now. I wondered where Anita lived. I bought some eggs, milk and bread. When I came back, Carol was sound asleep in the bed.

I put the eggs in the fridge. I thought that tomorrow I must remember to call someone to come and fix the boiler. The kitchen was cold. I heated up some milk and sat on the chair at the table facing the fridge. The milk was boiling. I poured it in a cold mug and wrapped my hands around it. Kate would have loved this I thought. I took out some office work from my briefcase leaning against the wall and started reading. The new project was to start; new faces to go with it. Three more people. I started the laptop and began typing in the advert. The whole thing would kick off by the beginning of the spring. This was one of the last things I talked about with Kate. She was jolly and I knew she was in for a discussion. I knew she would challenge me no matter what I said that afternoon. I couldn't wait to tell her the news: 'I've got the project,' I said. 'Are you happy?' she said. It was obvious that she was looking for an argument and I fell for it!

'Of course I am happy! What a question to ask me!' I thought she was such a paranoid. She couldn't accept anything without questioning it. I was sure she would argue with that too!

'You think you are a scientist but are you really? All

you do is to have what you call '*research meetings*' and to fill supervisory logs; and the best you can do is to publish an article in this journal or that and show off.'

'You are such a cynic.'

She ignored me.

'And what if your results do not match your speculated outcome? Oh! Then it is too bad! You repeat the experiment; you can't accept that perhaps things are not that way oriented. You are prepared to say that you have failed to prove things rather than to accept that perhaps things are not rigid, the way you expect them to be.'

'Now this is a flimsy argument.'

'Ah! You see. This is where I say that science today is nothing but religion! You are the one who is right. If you are pressed, then you are reluctantly ready to accept that other, so-called, scientists are also *right*. But who am I, just a layman, to challenge the essence of your beliefs? My arguments are too soft, too shallow!'

'But listen, I just wanted to break the good news...'

'And I say I am happy for you! If anything, I am happy that you will create a job for a poor desperate graduate.'

'I cannot win,' I said.

'You see? You don't want to consider what I say as a possibility. You just look at it as an attack on your principles, dare I say lines from a holy book! Let me tell you. As far as I am concerned, at least those so-called scientists that I have seen are all tied up with their dubious ideas and they think those are the eternal laws, laws of nature! After all, wasn't he, that man, one of your gurus who looked for a formula to define the whole world? You are all trying to prove God and you so proudly consider yourselves atheists! You are a bunch of *employees* with different tags.'

She said all this with calm. She stopped in the middle of sentences but I didn't interrupt her. I looked at her, at her lips, the way her eyes moved while she spoke. Then I said:

'I didn't know you had such a high opinion of me.'

'Oh! Don't create a special position for yourself! There are hundreds of people like you out there. Look at your small team, you all think the same, different coloured pencils but all pencils. You cannot think of a world outside the paper.'

'Listen, I have to go back I have a meeting. Could we have dinner?' I said eventually.

'Yes of course, talk with you on the phone.'

I came out and rushed to the research meeting. My team was waiting.

16

I put the mug on the table and sat there for few minutes. Then I brought out Kate's diary from the bookshelf and started reading:

Now I know that is it. The verdict is given, whether David brings in his usual strong arguments for or against it, the truth is looking me in the face; every minute with each breath it comes closer. It establishes itself more and more in my blood, my flesh, my mind. I will be gone, silently and calmly one of these days. And what will I miss? These moments of talking with him, these moments that have come so late and are fading away as I sit across the small table and look at him with all his passion and anguish about his research. Sometimes I think he is a wrong man in a wrong job in a wrong century. But the truth is looking at me and telling me it is me who is wrong, my existence which is rejecting itself and has to go. Obviously I am not for the future, for the near future, not even for the next year perhaps.

What a wishful person he is. I see all his naïveties and still I love our chats. Perhaps I get some sort of satisfaction when I see him and his naïve arguments even; what I am writing is showing my arrogance! But he is naïve! Him and his research! He wants to change the world by a new drug! He writes research proposals, he becomes excited about it all, goes through the ups and downs of getting the funding, and to get it he promises the world to the funding body with specific dates and 'deliverables'. The sad thing is that in the course of the process, he convinces himself that he has the answer, that he can deliver all those fantasies in a miserable three-year period. And he tries to convince me too! Me, who is sitting across the table carrying the 'truth' listening to his argument about the promise of new drugs! He even wants to defeat ageing now! Oh, good. I do like to get old. I love the experience of getting old, I do want to walk slowly and look at the whole world with a different eye. But what is my right? I cannot get old, can I? I am one of the fortunate selected people who will have a short-cut. Yes I had imagined myself, sitting by the counter at the library in silent summer afternoons reading a book, I had imagined myself in the pauses between reading pages when you take your eyes off the page and look up but you are not looking at anything, I had imagined myself old with wrinkles, with hair gone grey, mousy hair gone grey and I had liked it. But sorry I don't have time for it now, I have to let go. What will I miss? I will miss life, simple! But how could I miss it if I don't exist any more? I am not there to feel sorry for not having those moments with him, not having the reading moments, not having the excitement of going for a walk talking about Socrates and Nietzsche and their differences.

He says, 'yes I am happy; I got the project eventually… what a question you ask! Of course I am happy.'

'This is like a priest being happy by being offered a parish. Now you can go and start your sermon.'

'Why are you so bitter? I am just sharing my success with you, that's all.'

'And I am happy for you! You cannot deny that the whole thing is a farce!'

'Oh, come on. Obviously something is wrong. Let's have a drink. Let's celebrate.'

We had a bottle between us and both were hungry. I looked at his face and liked the freshness of hope in a middle-aged man!

'Let's go home.'

'What about food?'

'That can wait,' I said.

It is just that his passion in discussions excites me. Yes, there is a naïvety but there is also a stream of energy that flows towards me and suddenly I don't care. I don't care about the truth! The coldness of mattress and the warmth of his skin after the wine and the afternoon sun outside was all that I wanted then and I had them all.

17

It was one of the last lectures of the semester.

'Why do you bother?' I said to myself. Some were talking, some were taking their notebooks out, and some were just looking. But there was no response to my question. I couldn't be bothered continuing along that line. I was bored with my own sentences now. Did I still, after so many years of teaching, hope that what I said could make a change? Did I believe in miracles? How could I make any change in a university student old enough to run a business? I was giving lectures to a bunch of disillusioned, disinterested youth who didn't even know why they were there. I wouldn't have minded if they protested by not attending the lectures, by coming late trying deliberately to disrupt the lectures. But they weren't late for the lecture to be rebellious, they just didn't care. Was I wasting my time teaching them? Perhaps Kate was right. Whatever she said earlier about scientists and research could be valid for lecturers and teaching too! And what about other professions? Oh! That's great. What a picture of our society, but then, isn't it a negative way of looking at things? If she was right, then how come we had progress in science, effectively, on a daily basis?

Then I thought how come I hadn't noticed Kate's comments being so negative while she was usually a positive person. Should I leave the whole thing? I didn't need to keep the job to sustain myself so why was I standing there in front of the disenchanted gang? I was tired. I sat down and continued with my lecture. A student was sleeping in the corner and another was sending a text message on his mobile. Had I failed?

I finished the lecture and went back home. I just didn't feel like doing more work in the office. It was early afternoon. As I got out of the bus, I saw Anita coming out of the bistro with a young girl.

'Already finished?' I asked her. She looked tired.

'Today I've had Hanna with me. It is the half-term. She helped me in the morning so I have the rest of the day off.'

'Doing anything special?'

'No. Not really. There isn't much time left to go to a gallery or something.'

'Do you like arts?'

'I don't mind going to galleries sometimes but Hanna paints and likes it.'

I looked at Hanna. She was tall for her age. She looked serious.

'Do you want to come up for a coffee? It will be different from the routine!'

Anita blushed but there was no impression on Hanna's face.

'Thank you but we must go home.'

'You can do with a cup. It is still too early.'

'In that case…that would be nice, thanks.'

We went up. As I went in, they stood by the door.

'Come in, come in!'

We went to the sitting-room.

I don't know why I invited her to my place. But they were in now. I asked: 'Coffee?'

'Yes please but actually, Hanna doesn't drink coffee.'

'Tea then?'

'If it's not too much trouble.'

'Not at all, my pleasure to make tea for the young lady.'

I came back with the drinks and some biscuits. We sat around the coffee table. Hanna was looking at her tea all the time. She had a very pale face, a narrow nose and small eyes. I could never have guessed they were mother and daughter.

'So which painter do you like?'

'I don't know. All of them I guess.' She spoke softly and with a very low voice as if she was whispering something. Anita said: 'She has seen a couple of exhibitions recently; one of Picasso and one of Rembrandt.'

'So, which one did you like better?'

'Don't know, both of them I guess.'

I stood up and went to the window. It was windy outside. Anita said, 'are you very busy at work?'

'Oh, yes; but this is not something new.'

'Yes. I am sure. I see you rushing to work sometimes.'

'It's because I love it so much,' and I laughed.

She said, 'I know you love your work.'

'But how do you know?'

'I just know. When you are a waitress you understand many things.'

'So what else you understand about me?'

She didn't say anything, but blushed. Then she said: 'You like whisky.'

I laughed: 'And I know you are a very hospitable person.'

'Do you really mean it?'

'You are generous with your whisky.'

'But that is work.'

'It is not only the work. Is it?'

She blushed again. 'We really should go. It takes us some time to get home.'

'Do you live far away?'

She did. It would take her 1-1.5 hours to get home on a good day. I noticed that Hanna hadn't finished her tea. Anita stood and started to take the cups to the kitchen.

'Don't worry about those. This is my territory!'

She took the cups to the kitchen anyway.

'Thanks very much. We really enjoyed your company.'

'You should do this again.'

She didn't say anything. I looked out of the window. I saw them as they were walking to the bus stop. She had taken Hanna's hand. They were walking slowly but weren't talking.

I was walking home from school. My father was walking next to me. I had my school bag on my back.

'Walk properly!'

He used to take me home only some days of the week.
'How was school today?'
'Fine,' I said.

It would take an hour to get home. We used to walk for a few minutes, sometimes longer, to get to the car. Then he would drive away from the busy streets through the suburbs and then country lanes. He wouldn't have the radio on. The air would change as he drove close to the countryside. He drove silently and I would look outside through the windscreen thinking about homework, my friends at school and next day's classes. He would drive slower in the winter.

The door opened and Carol came in.

As she was coming in, she called me. Then she walked in to the room with a man.

'This is Fernando.'

Fernando was a well built tall man with a big face and big hands.

'I told you about Fernando. He is going back to Brazil to take the main role in Carlos Dance Company. He is taking me with him.' She squeezed Fernando's arm as she was standing next to him.

'That must be exciting for you, when are you leaving?'

'We are going next week.'

Fernando was silent but said:

'I have spent enough time here.'

'But you want to leave so soon,' I said.

'Oh yes, it is quite late if you ask me.'

'But it should be exciting for you to go together,' I told him.

'Oh, no, Carol's not going with me.' Fernando said.

'No?' I said.

'There are three of us who came here and we are going back together.'

Carol said: 'They are inseparable, in dance… and in life… I will join him later. I wanted you two to meet; my old and new friends. Is there a drink going? I can see you've had friends here.'

'Of course; Whisky perhaps?'

'Now! I like it here,' Fernando said.

'And the usual for you?' I asked Carol.

'Yes darling.'

I poured a large whisky for Fernando and for myself and a Bailey's for Carol. It was the bottle's last serving. I took the empty bottle away. As I turned back Carol was sitting on Fernando's lap. 'He says he wouldn't have me in Rio if I am not a good girl,' she giggled. I noticed she had changed the way she laughed.

'And what does that mean?' I said. 'Surely you can't help it, not being one!'

Carol giggled again. 'Tell *him* that. He's such an awful man.'

Carol had already finished her drink and Fernando had the last gulp.

'I must get going,' he said, 'thanks for the drink.'

'But surely you can have another?' I asked Fernando.

'I'd love to have one but I really have to get a move on,' he said, 'but I'll keep in mind your invitation.' He blinked.

Carol followed him to the door. I poured another large one for myself and sat deep in the sofa. Then Carol came back and sat next to me. I could smell her perfume as if she had applied it just now. 'I like you David.'

'Yes I know!' I said.

'But it's true. You are horrible and I love you.'

'So when are you leaving for Rio? I expected you to go with him.'

'You know how artists are. Disorganised, temperamental… Ooo, I don't know… I am not sure if I ever do.'

'But I thought you were committed.'

'I am. But am thinking about it.'

'I need to get my flat sorted. I cannot live like this,' I said.

'You are starting again. I told you I'll be going soon. Who knows, I might follow Fernando.'

'But I cannot wait for your whims, one day you might…'

'I have been looking. You know that. I haven't come across a reasonable flat.'

'And if you don't?'

'You are such a pessimist. Come on. You've changed so much. You weren't like this before.'

'I am now!' I had another sip and stood up to take the glasses to the kitchen. 'By the way, no Bailey's left.'

'I should remember that. What should we do for dinner tonight? Let's make it a good one, we both deserve it.'

'OK, but I wonder why!'

'Do you have to philosophise about everything all the time? Let's have a good time, no discussions OK?'

She had her low-cut red outfit on. We were sitting in our busy restaurant with a bottle of wine and each had finished one glass already. The waiter came to us and took our order fast. We knew the menu and we knew what we wanted. Carol was in a happy mood. I asked myself why but I had no answer for it. It was obvious that Fernando had no plans to take her to Rio. I had asked her to leave the flat and she didn't have a source of income to fit her whims. She left her job as a receptionist in a 'modern' small gallery when she decided to leave the country and now had no work; yet she was jolly. She put her hand on mine. Her fingers were cold; the fingernails were long and red.

'Tell me David, what is your ambition?' she asked.

I felt awkward. What a question. What was she thinking about? In any case, whatever I would say would be beyond her.

'I'm ok as I am.'

'No ambitions then?'

'Not really. I do things as I like them and I challenge things as I face them.'

'Oh! You are a defensive man! Look at Fernando, he is a go-getter. A real man, all flesh and bone alive, he will make it.'

'I am sure he will. Good for him, and for you. Are you following him?'

'Yes. He needs me. He cannot make it there without me.'

'What makes you think that?'

'My feminine intuition!'

'In that case you should have guessed my ambition. Anyway, what is yours?'

'I want to be in a big dance company… a modern one. I don't mind if I don't dance but want to be part of the whole thing.'

'I didn't know about this passion of yours. It is a recent acquisition I take it.'

'Not really. I have always wanted to be there. When I was a child I wanted to become a ballerina. I am artistic you know.'

I looked at her. I could feel her skin. She was eating fish and salad. I tried to imagine her on a hot afternoon in Rio in a big hall, wearing a long red dress, changing the music but the picture was too remote. She started again:

'You don't have any ambitions because you are surrounded by your students, the kids. You love this feeling of being wanted all the time. When you are hassled, you love it. I've seen you with your papers. Take the students away from you and you are dead.'

'So is that why you don't let me be? You are so concerned about my life!'

'I am really hurt now! Anyway, thankfully I am not your student.'

She left the fork on the plate and took my hand.

'You are cruel! But you are not one of those who want to show their power to the kids. You love yourself so much you don't have time for anything else,' she said.

'I think you are upset about something. What is this? So much inside information about me!'

'You cannot accept it; it is too much for you. But let

me tell you. Is it because you loved that librarian of yours so much or is it that you didn't care a hoot for her when she was dying? I remember we had the best times together just then!'

'I thought you wanted us to have a relaxed dinner without any discussions,' I said.

'Yes, I am having a relaxed time. Very relaxed! I am not sure about you though because it will need extra effort to make you more relaxed than you are anyway!'

She was eating the salad and I poured some wine for her and myself.

'You don't need to be sarcastic. You have made up your mind… very tidily too… you know me so well I should apply to you to know who I am.'

'Perhaps you should!' she said.

'No thank you. I am quite alright the way I am.'

She started laughing.

'You see, you can be made fun of so quickly! Take it easy. I was joking all the time! Couldn't you guess? Where has your sense of humour gone? This is all because I have ignored you. Is it because of Fernando you are so serious? Could I have a bit more please?' She brought her glass towards me. Then she told me about the movie she had seen with Fernando. An action thriller. I could imagine her in the cinema with her big bag of popcorn, eating away, leaning toward Fernando.

We had a long night eating and drinking. And then we were in bed with full stomachs. There was no point sitting on the sofa in the flat. As Carol moved in the bed I thought she had lost some weight. Soon I could hear her going to sleep but I couldn't go to sleep. I was thinking of my day: The students, Anita and her daughter, Carol and Fernando and then our dinner. I went for a relaxed night as she had suggested but as it happened, she started giving me a piece of her mind. What if whatever she said was right? So what if my world was centred on myself? Isn't everyone like that? But then, am I everyone? I always had high expectations of myself....where are those standards...those codes of conduct to ensure I was different? Carol's breathing was deep. I couldn't place her; a near fight in the restaurant and what they call intimacy a few minutes ago... for a few minutes. I though she was a confused girl getting old trying to find a secure life for herself. Again, I suppose everyone does that. I got up carefully and went to the kitchen. The light from the street lamp was shining in. I sat by the window, the rain had started again and drops were hitting the window. Did I want her to come from behind, put her hand on my shoulder and say '*what are you doing sitting here alone, come back to bed*'? Then I thought about our early days. She used to smile from a distance as she came close. Red, smiling lips! There was something in that approach that would move me. I always tried to avoid talking sense with her, not that it was difficult. But then tonight, she was different. My expectations from her were quite obvious. I suppose hers was the same. But what if she had something else in mind all the time. What would I care! Ha! I was behaving exactly as she had said. I was self-centred, conceited! But should I have behaved differently, emotionally, sensually, considerately? Wouldn't that be lying to myself? Putting up a good guy image! But what about Kate? Carol was right. I didn't go to the hospital. Granted, it was only a short period. She was in the hospital only briefly. But was that a justification for me not going to see her? Not even phoning?

The rain was hitting harder and I was cold.

I thought about reading Kate's diary but suddenly felt so weak I dragged myself to the bed. Carol turned in her sleep and now her back was facing me. Her body was warm. And I went to sleep soon.

18

Next day I went to work early. It was midday when I had a call from Elizabeth.

'Hello David, been trying to catch up. Have a minute?'

'Yes. I meant to phone you myself. How is your daughter?'

'Well, OK now.'

'Good to hear that, and how are things going with the flat?'

'Oh, that's done. But I wanted to talk with you about Kate. Here in the library, we have been talking about it... you know she was very much loved by all here, they want to remember her... I thought about you. Are you interested in participating?'

'Sure, when is it?'

'Haven't set the date yet, waiting to confirm with you first, but would you be interested in saying a few words?'

'Who? Me?'

'Actually, everybody here thinks you are the right person to take the lead; say something about her. After all, you knew her best... that is, if you feel like doing it of course.'

'I... I just don't know enough... what could I say? I am not sure if I am good at these things.'

'You are too modest David! I am sure you are the best person. It doesn't need to be long.'

'Let me think about it, but I don't promise anything.'

'It can wait a couple of days! Just let me know. We hope not to let it get too late though, it is already late.'

'OK I will come back to you soon.'

I went out for a coffee. The café was too crowded. I decided to walk to the one further away. I sat in a corner. The coffee was too weak and cold. What could I write? How presumptuous people are. Why should I write? I took the coffee to the counter. 'This is too weak and too cold.'

'I will change it for you sir! I will bring it to your table.'

I went and sat there. I deliberately tried to think of other things. What would I do after work?

The coffee arrived. It was hot but weak. I had it and went back to work. There was a phone message. It was from Fiona. I had forgotten about her after my last phone call.

'David! I am coming up on Wednesday for a short meeting; can we spend half a day together? Staying at the Royal Bell, give me a buzz if you can.'

I phoned back but there was no reply. I was furious to have missed her call. I left a message for her saying it would be great to meet and I look forward to that.

On Wednesday, I started early to clear my desk before seeing Fiona. We had a pleasant late lunch. The sun was out all morning and the coolness of the day disappeared under the warmth of the hotel restaurant by the window where our table was. When I arrived, she wasn't there yet. I ordered myself a whisky and sat in a comfortable chair. I didn't wait long. I saw her coming in with a couple of large colourful bags. She came over. 'You haven't been waiting long, have you?'

'Not really, you look refreshed.'

'It's the shopping! Be with you in a minute.'

Then she disappeared in the lift around the corner. I had a sip of my whisky. I couldn't think about anything. I looked around the hotel lobby as I was sitting. A couple of old gentlemen were sitting a couple of tables away with a broadsheet in front of them, a waiter was walking towards another table with a single middle aged-man, there were two large green plants by the two columns. Then I saw her coming over wearing a red polo neck and a grey skirt. We hugged. 'Let's have something now, I am famished.'

There was a pink flower on the table, large plates with small flowery patterns and heavy cutlery.

'So how was your day?' I asked.

'Efficient! As you may expect from me David!'

'Perish any other thought!'

'It has been a very early day for me. We had an early meeting which was thankfully short, just signing some forms. We are trying to submit a proposal. I am not that hopeful really but it is exciting. I went to do some shopping straight after. Anyway, what have you been up to?'

'Nothing much... nothing exciting! Mainly work.'

'No debauchery then?' she smiled.

'Not really.'

'How boring! Now you have your chance!' and she laughed.

'And when are you going back?' I said.

'I have this afternoon! Tomorrow morning, I am off early.'

Her room was bright with the sun and she looked spirited. She smiled as if she was looking at an imaginary figure. Then she started taking things off, elegantly.

'Are you going to sit there all the time?' she asked with a smile.

'I was just admiring your clothes.'

'And what makes you think I am satisfied by that? You had plenty of time to admire them while we were eating!'

I thought that her words matched her, matched the way she dressed and the way she walked.

'I have no long term plans to be frozen in admiration,' I said.

'Now! That is reassuring. I don't wish my name recorded in the criminal history as the woman who killed people by freezing them.'

I laughed: 'But people would write and talk about that fixated glance of admiration in your victims' eyes, and there will be many of them.'

'And how do you know that?'

'I have inside information.'

'The inside information is what you will have soon, but only if you do something about that admiration!'

Her movements were relaxed, her warmth seeped

slowly as our skins met and it stayed. It lingered like a sentence remembered from a pleasant conversation. We stayed until the room was dark.

'Should our meetings always be so short?' I said.

'That's why they are pleasing!'

The hotel lobby was busy now. We had a drink at the bar.

'So when are you going to be here again?'

'Have no plans.'

She was drinking her wine.

'And would you come over?' she said.

'I doubt it.'

'So, it would be sometime somewhere.'

'It will,' I said.

As I left the hotel, it was cold again. I passed by the bistro near my flat. Anita was serving. Her back was towards the window and her hair was tied back.

I opened the door to the flat. Carol said: 'Hello David.'

She was on the bed with a big brown teddy bear.

'Look what I've got.'

'How can I miss it?'

'Fernando gave it to me. He wants me. He wants me there. As soon as he settles, he wants me there.'

'Well, I thought that was the case.'

'No, you can't understand. You are such a matter of fact person. Can you understand someone sensitive, emotional?'

'OK, you've got a teddy bear, what's the big deal.'

'Do you know? That's the problem with you. You

think that you are the centre of the universe, that your opinion is the only one; it is only you who has emotions. But you don't understand people.'

'Obviously you have eaten,' I said.

'Oh, we had a lovely time. He is leaving tomorrow. I will follow him soon. I shall miss him like mad.'

'He leaves tomorrow? That's some news. So why didn't you stay with him tonight?'

'His friends are with him aren't they? He is so wise. We can have all the nights we want when I join him in Rio.'

I watched her as she moved about in the flat. I started thinking, should I write something for Kate's memorial? I needed a large whisky. I finished it quickly and poured another but I couldn't think. What could I write? Something to suggest that her friends cared? Did we? What did I do when she was alive? And so what if we did care? What did it matter now? And it was not that she was a world renowned figure. *'Now we have to acknowledge the loss of such a loved person. She is in our hearts'* and all that crap! If the event was meant for remembering her, she was nowhere now to be pleased about it. Even if she were alive, I wondered if she would have liked a party in her honour, let alone to be acknowledged in a particular way. Was there a tendency to use the event to boost our own egos showing how good we are, how generous we are, we are taking time from our busy life to devote some minutes to our beloved colleague who is not with us any longer? I am sure she would have loved the discussion! She would say, *'you claim you are an admirer, no, a devotee of Nietzsche and now you are doing this benevolent act of sacrifice and pity. Nietzsche would be turning in his grave!'* How could I answer her?

I had another large whisky. I dozed off on the sofa as the light, the dim light of morning, was coming in through the gap in the curtain. It was a strange feeling. I wasn't sure if I had slept or not. It was as if I was continuing with my thoughts without a break. Then I knew what I was going to do. I just knew that I would write and I would give a speech. I didn't need any reason for it. I wanted to do so... to say I loved her.

I felt sleepy. I walked clumsily to the bed and quickly fell asleep. When I woke up, it was midday. Carol had gone. There was a note on the table: 'Be there for me tonight, I shall feel lonely.'

19

It was early evening when I arrived at the flat. I poured myself a large whisky and put on an old album of songs. I suddenly thought I could not continue with things the way they were. I wanted to be somewhere far away, somewhere where I didn't know anyone, somewhere where I could start with a clean sheet. But I couldn't put my hand on anything particular that I wanted to escape from. I thought about the boy who couldn't find his exam timetable. The disillusioned gang of boys and girls with their frightened faces standing outside the exam rooms. Carol and her teddy bear. I was tired of them all but how could I condemn any of them? It wasn't condemnation; it was as if I wanted to migrate to a different life-style. OK, the girl was in search of a partner for life! As for the students, was I kidding myself trying to put down rules and regulations to 'assess' their abilities, their knowledge, their potential? I am the clown and they are the audience and I can only continue if I assume such an authority for myself. I am the system! I repeated the old songs and poured a larger whisky. I pictured Kate's flat. She had left her diary under her old photos. I didn't have old or new photos!

Only those that students took in ceremonies and sent them to me and I always left them somewhere in the office, never remembered where, somewhere where they would disappear with old papers without me knowing it. I could never understand those who displayed their pictures in their office, the picture of themselves standing on the steps of a conference building together with too many delegates to fit in. Pictures taken with a fish on a fishing holiday, probably the holiday of their life since they don't normally do such things as university lecturers! And what about the diaries they keep? The books they read? I felt that I had double standards. I criticise people for what they are, for what they do…and yet I tell myself that people should behave the way they want to be. I talk as a liberal but I am harder than a religious figure surviving on people's guilt! And who is the guilty party here? What guilt? It was as if I was I carrying a court in my head. A court complete with the innocent, the accused, the guilty, the jury, the defence, the audience…. Should I let go? Let go?

As the whisky was working on me, I thought that perhaps I should work on myself to let go. Everything was a struggle a minute ago! Now, everything was progressing, moving at its own pace! There was no need for me to push! Perhaps it was my interference that slowed the processes? I asked myself again, am I the guilty party? Could I escape myself? Ever?

I dozed off. When I opened my eyes, Carol was standing next to me. Her eyes were tired. She smiled:

'I thought you were going to put me in a good mood. But it seems that it was wishful thinking?'

'No, no, I just dozed off.'

'It looks like it! We need to buy some drinks. Some fun ones for me and some serious ones for you!'

'We shall forget about everything. We are going to have a good dinner. And you should promise not to be too seductive! I am vulnerable!' I said.

'Ooo! What a transformation from a sleepy-head! At last I am getting somewhere!' she laughed.

It took me some minutes to stand up and take a shower. As I was going to the bathroom, I saw Carol sitting on the edge of the bed. She had her head in her hands. I couldn't see her eyes.

20

People call it 'The Snail'. On its door, a thick timber, there was a small plaque: 'The Slimy Snail'. I rang the bell. The door opened. 'Good evening Prof. Hardag.' We went in. There was a small landing. A tall ceramic flower pot was standing in the corner with a single long-stemmed yellow South African flower and a long, wide leaf supporting it. Our table was in a corner. Carol sat on a chair facing other tables. I sat on a chair next to her facing the window with a long beige curtain, drawn. We started with champagne, went quickly to white wine and asked for the menu. Carol had lost some weight for sure. I could see wrinkles emerging around her eyes and these were permanent ones. I thought that she had changed even from last month. It was a couple of months since she had returned from the airport aborting her journey and now she wanted to leave again.

'I am going David. I am going to follow him.'

She said it as if it was a threat. Did I care?

'Are you sure about this? Do you know what you are doing? This is not a case of coming back a week later, you know.'

'What makes you think I will come back? Fernando

wants me. He wants me there.'

'And do you want him? Do you want him there?'

'Do you mean I shouldn't go?'

'I never said that.'

'But you mean it don't you?'

'I am concerned for you. I want you to have a good life.'

It was difficult for me to say that. Was I really concerned?

'Come on, you want to convince me not to go!'

The waiter came with the starters.

'What do you plan to do there?'

'I told you, I'd do anything in his dance company.'

'So he is employing you?'

'What do you mean employing you? We are much closer than that. My God! Haven't you got it into your head?... OK, OK… me and you…we are together but him, he is a serious man. He is a man of commitments and he wants me there.'

'So you are getting married or something?'

The waiter came over and started serving the red wine.

'Well…he hasn't said it in so many words but if you want to know, yes. He said he wants to introduce me to his mother. His mother is quite old. His father died last year before he came over.'

Now the main dish was coming.

'I am happy for you.'

I wasn't. I wasn't happy or sad. I thought about the flat and her not being there. I thought that I would have a big clean-up and that it would be good to go on a long holiday; a long holiday with a short holiday after that, immediately, to ease me back into work.

'So you'd keep in touch, would you?' I said.

'What do you mean? You must come over. You should be there for our wedding.'

'I am sure the place will be very exciting.'

'Exciting? I am already thinking things.'

'Don't tell me you have already planned how many children you will have too?'

'I haven't but why not? Perhaps I should.'

We decided to go for a long walk after dinner before we took a taxi home. We walked through the dark cold silent streets. When we arrived at the flat, it was really cold. The boiler man had not come during the day and I had to chase him up the next day. At the time, it was a case of going to bed.

21

The flat is calm. I am waiting for the boiler man to come. I have finished my breakfast; actually I just had a strong black coffee. Earlier on Carol had her breakfast slowly, toast and peanut butter, and left. I assume for the day. She was jolly and moved around in the flat. Now that Fernando had gone, she had all day to idle away and she seemed animated when she left. I thought it was best to work from home. A new project was starting but I was already working on another proposal.

I waited for the boiler man until 2 p.m. He was supposed to come first thing in the morning. I was hungry and had done a good chunk of work on the proposal and needed a change of scenery. After some hesitation, I decided to go out. I thought to have a quick meal at the bistro.

The place was crowded but was getting quiet as people were gradually leaving. Anita wasn't there, the owner was serving and he was rushed off his feet. He got the order with a friendly but firm smile. I was having a beer, watching the place getting empty fast and then Anita came in in a hurry. She went straight through the swing door while she was taking her thick red scarf off and starting to unbutton her coat. Now there was only one table occupied when she emerged with my plate in her hand.

'Hi!' I said, 'you seem to be in a hurry!'

'Yes. Hanna fainted again, had to take her to the hospital.'

'What fainting?'

'Well. She just faints sometimes. It is happening more often than before. She had that when she was a child and now it has become more frequent.'

She had kept the plate in her hand while she was talking. She put the plate on the table.

'But what does the doctor say?'

'Her GP doesn't think it is serious. He says it is normal for a girl of her age.'

'Normal?'

'He says he has many examples of young girls like her.'

'So what's there to do?'

'Eat well and exercise! She has never been into sports, but I make sure that she eats well. It is just that she fell and wouldn't come round.'

'So what did you do?'

She laughed, 'well, got a taxi and took her to the casualty ward. By that time she was fine so we came back. Otherwise, I am not sure what would have happened had she remained like that.'

'Why don't you sit? Would you like something to eat?' I asked.

'Oh, no. Thanks. I have been late and there is chaos in the kitchen. Poor John has panicked.'

'Where is Hanna now?'

'At home.'

'Alone?'

'Yes, but it should be OK She is lying down and she has some homework to do.'

'How did she take it?'

'OK. She doesn't talk much. You noticed the other day, didn't you? She is like that. It is not only with people she doesn't know... Sorry.'

Then she left for the kitchen.

I paid the bill and went back to the flat. There was a note from the boiler man. It was a small card:

Time of call: 2:15 p.m.

No answer.

It was 3:10 p.m. I went in and sat by the kitchen table then phoned the boiler services company.

There was an irritating young voice on the other side.

'The service engineer was sent to you sir.'

'Yes I know he came. But he was late. He came after 2, he was supposed to be here first thing in the morning.'

'We don't guarantee the time of visit sir. If there is another big job, the visit can be delayed. But he came and nobody was in sir.'

'But what is the use of giving us a time?'

'We make sure that the visit happens on the day. We cannot guarantee the time though. We do our best sir.'

'So when can he come again?'

'It will be another engineer sir.'

'I don't care as far as someone comes.'

'We don't have a free engineer until Thursday sir.'

'Well I have to be in the office that day. What about Wednesday?'

'Sorry sir all our engineers are busy. The only possible time is Thursday.'

'OK then. It will have to do.'

'So you want to book the slot then sir?'

'Yes please.'

'Could I have your name sir?'

'You have all that in front of you.'

'Sorry sir. I have to ask you again.'

'This is David Hardag.'

'Could you spell it for me please sir?'

I spelt the name and the address and other details and then I had to describe the problem, the model of the boiler and the year I had bought it. I put the phone down. I went back to the proposal. I worked uninterrupted for nearly two hours. As it got dark, I stopped and cleared the table.

The work on the proposal was nearly complete. I had worked on it on and off for three months now. It needed a week to deal with the details for the final draft but I couldn't do any more work on that day. I made myself a coffee and hot milk. I had some biscuits. Obviously I needed it after the boiler saga.

'What saga?'

I started at myself.

'What saga? Why do you always make an issue out of everything? So what if the boiler man didn't come on time? You say you don't believe in rigid disciplines but in everything, any small matter, you seek it. Are you a spoilt brat grown up in size?'

'But can you believe the way that woman answered my call? Obviously they don't care whether they have a job or not.'

'As far as that is concerned, you can go and hang yourself! After all, she was doing her job. If you expect Oxford English, then you are seeking it from a very unlikely source.'

I am spending my days like a person waiting for some amazing news that will change his life, meanwhile, without saying it, I am convinced that the way I am leading my daily life is good. But where is the thrill? What is there to excite me? OK, there is the research and the odd student. But what about home? What do I do when I come home? A bit of reading, a few drinks, and then what? Dinner with Carol or someone else? Even the sex is becoming part of the daily routine…this is frightening. Yes, I have decided that the life I am leading is fine. I am certainly not going to limit my days, my minutes to one person only. It is OK at the beginning but it gets boring fast and then what? Things that once you enjoyed doing together become a chore; then comes the catastrophe of kids, something mostly inevitable… and decisions to be made. Goodbye to your days, your own days, to your nights of course, to your moments free from unwanted obligations. Perhaps it is OK if you like it as a job! But look at the hordes of people: it is a culture in its own right: the ritual of buying nappies, the changing of nappies, entertaining the brat, the baby language you adopt, the culture of a benevolent family. Then you begin to think about the church, the hungry masses in Africa. Have you ever looked at the way a first time pregnant mother looks, walks, with the aura around her? *'Look at me, Ah, I am the personification of goodness, forgiveness, sacrifice! Look at me; I have my cross in my belly.'* And the father? Look how his dress code changes, how his hair and his shaving pattern change, forget about the frequency of his going to the pub. All obvious? Fine, I am not up for it. So what do I want? Do you know? I can never be satisfied. So what's wrong with that?

Nothing really, this is your life, if you want to spend it as a critic, then good for you. Pour yourself a whisky; it is time, dark enough to drink. But when you are young and dissatisfied with things, it is somehow acceptable. They put it down to your hormones, but what about a middle aged man edging towards old age? What if he is not satisfied with his life and with alternatives he sees around him?... No! I am not for dramatic gestures and I do not need sympathy. Anyway, even if I wanted it there is no one to feel sympathy for me. There will be no memorial day for me in the office. Perhaps Anita would wonder what happened to the man who went there for a cup of coffee, a quick meal or a glass of whisky every now and then. In her final analysis, if the thought occupied her that much, she would think that I was a rude man who didn't care to say goodbye to her as I moved on.

I poured the whisky. What sort of a life was I seeking? I needed a change but didn't have a clue. Should I become more involved in the office and its politics? It will be going back a step, so demeaning submitting to the illusion of power. I couldn't do that now even if I tried.

So what am I to do? Was there anything attractive enough?

No, I wasn't depressed or anything. I was just thinking of a change but that was all, I couldn't go any further. It would remain as a mental exercise. I went to the drawer and took out Kate's diary and the pictures I had brought back from her flat. I wasn't sure why but I was drawn to that diary and the pictures. Was I trying to escape my thoughts? Perhaps, on the contrary, by looking at the pictures and reading the diary I wanted to encourage those thoughts. A picture of South American desert! I wondered where she had got it from. I felt uneasy. I put the picture away. I looked at another one. Her brother, I assumed, standing in front of long pipes criss-crossing over each other. I could smell the crude oil, the summer heat. Then there was a worn-out picture of a middle-aged woman.

Sitting there with the diary and the pictures I wondered whether that was all that had remained of her life; a diary and some pictures.

I went to the coffee table with the long table-cloth. My own old box of pictures was sitting under the table. I pushed the cloth to one side, took the box out as if I was haunted. I put on a CD, sat with the opened box; with the pictures all around me on the floor. The pictures were small. The few that were large were stained or blurred. Now I was far away in complete silence. Kate's pictures were spread further away in a corner next to her diary and my pictures were surrounding me. I took a small picture with corrugated edges. I was seven years old, standing under a tree with deep shade from a harsh sun. I could feel the heat of the sun coming out of the picture. I remembered the day…I remembered that my mother was sitting on a bench facing the sea. Her face was sad. My eyes were fixed on her. My father took the picture; did not tell me to smile, to look presentable, to lean my hand against the tree. It was a record of the trip to the seaside; a childhood holiday.

I collected all pictures and put them in their boxes. I looked at Kate's diary next to the box. I took it and started reading from it arbitrarily:

'I get tired excessively these days. Maybe it is because I think too much! My mind is obsessed with what I read and with my chats with David. In fact, I should be less tired. I get excited with us discussing the books… the arguments… and that makes me tired! I can never live like the magazine characters… chocolate and warm baths. I feel dirty if I sit in the bath. But how is it that most people follow these recipes? They feel relaxed. For me, this is a state of stupor. Today, Mary came and showed me a picture of her wedding dress. She was so excited. I was amazed, can you imagine? A picture! How could one be so happy to lose her freedom? OK, it goes back to security. But even then, what guarantee is there? More than half of marriages end in divorce. But why shouldn't they feel happy? It is good for them to feel secure, even if it is for a short time. What is wrong with being happy for wearing a new dress? A white dress with the scarf wrapped around the head and all that… walking down the church aisle to get to the moment of promise. How many times has one seen it? Don't they get bored with it? Don't they feel stupid when they themselves do it? Obviously not! They look forward to it. I should remember to talk about it with David. I am sure he would love it. I am getting tired and feel weak. Perhaps neither David nor I are social creatures. Perhaps **we** are boring, not all those who read the popular magazines and follow examples. I know it is impossible for me to live like them. But I shouldn't feel rejected for this. And I don't. There are loads of people out there like me. Like us. What about this one who went around the world on foot? Or the other ones who had their group wedding in a cave in that obscure mountainous place? They took their close friends with them too! But they do it to prove they are different. I bet once they settle down and get the first invoice for their kitchen table and fridge, they will start behaving differently. I think they behave differently because they want to create a certain position for themselves. The man probably wears a bow tie with a striped pink shirt and the wife buys her dress from a charity shop. They go to the park in the summer, take a bottle of wine, have a picnic. The wife looks at her man with such admiration when he talks about the faults in the architecture of such and such church. Then, as they sip their wine with the cheese that she has bought on strict instructions from the man, she takes his hand and starts stroking it. The man continues with the wine and goes on with his insight into architecture. A picture of love and admiration in a park with cheese and wine! So what happens if I visit them four years, perhaps ten years later?

Who cares? So what if they continue with their picnic in the future with one, two or three kids, or if they become each other's sworn enemy?

Now I have to stop. I am too tired.'

I sat there for a while with the diary in my hand. I looked at the window, the bookshelf, her box of photographs.

Then I put the diary on the box and left the box under the table again. It wasn't late but I went to bed. I needed to close my eyes. I hoped to go to sleep soon.

I woke up at some point in the night with Carol's hand on my chest. Her feet were cold.

'Did I wake you?'

Then she continued as if we had been just talking for a while over a coffee. 'People tell me I shouldn't go. Do you agree?'

There was no escape from it now, I had to answer her. I rubbed my eyes and said, 'I think you should do something you feel good about.'

'I don't know what I feel good about. At the moment, I feel good about your warm body.'

'But don't worry; tomorrow you will start thinking about Rio,' I said.

'Yes. You are right. But you always tell me to live for the moment. I am very confused.' She sighed and pressed herself to me.

'Why don't you sleep on it? You are not flying out tomorrow, you have time.'

'But what about Fernando? He is waiting for me.'

'Are you sure?'

'What do you mean?' she raised her voice, 'you are such a cynic!'

'In any case he needs a few days to himself to get organised.'

'Yes. He will phone me anyway. We can get organised.'

'Exactly.'

Carol wasn't in the mood to sleep now. I was wrong to hope for a good night's sleep.

22

My office was warm and cosy. I could easily go to sleep!
I made myself a coffee and made some phone calls. One
was to Fiona.

'I am surprised to find you in your office,' I said.

'I am not! I am dashing to the school. It's my
daughter. I don't know what they want.'

'I suppose teenage problems.'

'Maybe. But these are young people. They *need*
problems!'

'I see you are in a joyful mood.'

'As ever.'

'As ever of course!' I said.

'The problem is that I am stuck here, with trees all
around me for miles. For miles! I love them but they
don't have a sense of humour. That's my problem.'

'Same here, but I am surrounded by vegetables! And
do you think they have a sense of humour?'

'They can be juicy!'

'You must be joking! Not these ones!'

'Maybe you don't take care of them enough.'

'My dear friend, you know what a caring person I
am.'

'Oh, yes. I had forgotten. Perhaps you should remind me.'

'I would love to!'

'Must go, talk to you later.'

Now I was in a good mood. There was a knock on the door. One of my researchers came in.

'Ana, is all OK?'

'Do you have time? It is confidential.'

'Yes, of course. What is it?'

'I have had enough. I want to quit.'

'What? Why? What has happened?'

'It is personal.'

'But perhaps I can help.'

'Thanks but don't think so, really.'

'Your research is going so well. You've worked so hard in a short time. Don't you like your work? Perhaps you don't like it here?'

'No, no; it is not that.'

'Has anyone in the team done something?'

'Oh, no, no! I enjoy it here.'

'So what is it?'

'I am so ashamed. It is my boyfriend. He wants me to quit.'

'But why? How strange! Perhaps we can solve the problem together?'

'He thinks that I ignore our relationship. He says you are a different person now. He thinks I was not like this before I started my PhD.'

'How long have you known him?'

'Two years and a bit.'

'I find it very disturbing. And you want to leave the

work you like just because he says you have changed? Do you think you have changed?'

'Yes. I have changed a bit. But he thinks I am arrogant and we cannot continue like this. He says if I don't stop he will leave me.'

She was white in the face and her thin lips were dry.

'But one changes in life anyway. I am sure he has changed as well.'

'I don't know. He wants us to get married this summer but he says I have to stop my work before we get married. He says this is no life. He says if I continue like this nobody will want me.'

'What rubbish. So, all those researchers are left alone, they have nobody?'

'I don't really know. I don't know what to do. He wants me.'

'I am sure he does. But what about your needs? Wouldn't you blame yourself for the rest of your life if you leave your study? Does he know how much you like your research?'

'I guess.'

'Well why don't you have a good chat with him about it. Surely you can come to some sort of arrangement. After all, how can he be sure that you would pay more attention to him if you were miserable because you hadn't carried on with your research?'

'He says I don't know what life is, I don't know how to live.'

'And what makes him an expert in these matters?'

She remained silent. Then she thanked me and left. I didn't want to pressurise her into any decisions. I went silent and watched her leaving the room. Yet, I was feeling responsible for a researcher who was doing well, was enjoying herself at work but was practically intimidated to leave her work. For me it was an absolute case of the selfishness of her boyfriend. I had the whole afternoon to devote to work. I kept on working in the office until late. It was after 8 p.m. when I came out. I thought of going to the pub for a drink. It was crowded and smoky and I decided to leave but someone waved at me. It was Ian. I didn't mind seeing him; actually I was quite happy to spend a bit of time with someone else.

'What is yours?' I asked him.

'I am OK for the moment.'

I got a large whisky and sat at the small table.

'So, how are the in-laws?'

'Oh, they are gone.'

'So you have normality back in your life?'

'Except my wife! I wonder why I decided to ask her to marry me. We are so different.'

I was shocked to see him talking so openly about a very intimate personal matter. I felt embarrassed.

'Some say that's the secret of a long happy marriage,' I said.

'Well they have a dry sense of humour,' Ian said.

'But I am sure many at the office envy you, the lucky old chap they say.'

'Yeah, she is a lovely girl. It is good when it is good. But then, I need my space, I can't be at her beck and call all the time. She needs constant attention.'

'And you don't like that? It's great to be wanted.'

'But not always, it might look silly but I tell you…

She is jealous! She phones me at least five or six times a day asking what I am doing, who is there in the office, what happened in my lecture.'

'But you should be happy about that. She thinks about you. Perhaps she is lonely. You've got to watch it you know!'

'I don't know. All I know is that I need time to think. I need time to spend with my collection. The stamps are all over the place. It seems that she cannot see my needs.'

'Surely you can see her needs. But are you sympathetic to hers?'

'I do as much as I can.'

We drank our drinks and repeated them. It was around 11 p.m. when I came out. I decided to walk home. The air was fresh and it was dry. Walking down the long street, I started thinking about Ian and then about Ana, then about Carol. It seemed to me that there was something similar among them. Was it their involvement with their other halves? I never liked this phrase 'other half' and now I was using it. So what was wrong with that? It was too easy for me to consider their lives boring, mundane … there was a sense of instability in that, it seemed almost transitory, but what about my life? And whose life is stable? People lead their lives without thinking about these things. They are happy, they are sad. They just live their lives! They take it as it comes. They cry, they laugh about things I consider mundane but for them, those things are important. And who am I to evaluate the events? Who am I with my broken boiler problem? There was a temporary lull in my mind. Then I thought about Kate. The short period we were together…if one could call it being together. That short period did have something. It existed. It existed in me. My daily dialogues were based on those moments. In my mind I discussed events with her. I described to her my days, my interactions my discussions. So what do I have to say now? *Listen, my days are getting longer and longer? Listen, I saw a man who collects stamps, I don't…I don't collect anything?*

I was getting close to my flat. From the other side of the road I looked at the bistro. The lights were off. It was strange. Usually it was busy with the locals at this time. I got to the flat. Carol was asleep. Her breathing was heavy. She had had a few drinks. I went to bed, careful not to wake her up.

I dreamt that I was running on an undulating country road. I was escaping from something. It was sunny, a Mediterranean countryside. I got tired and stopped under a tree. I didn't have the desire to run any more. I sat looking back at the road I had run along. Nobody was in sight. Leaning against a tree I went to sleep.

Carol said, 'don't you want to get up today?'

It was nine.

'I am staying home waiting for the boiler man to come,' I said.

'When is he coming?'

'Anytime today! Hopefully in the morning. I would like to get this over and done with.'

'If you are a good boy, I will stay in and keep you company.'

'Only if you don't have anything else to do,' I said.

We had breakfast together without much exchange of words. There was a hazy sunshine outside and the flat was cold. But at 10:15 the boiler man came; a young boy with a pale bony face. He started with the pump.

'It is no use,' he said.

'Can you change it?'

'Yes, but I have to see if I have one in the van. There should be one.'

And there was one. I thought it was my lucky day.

'Would you like a cup of tea or coffee?'

'Tea, milk, no sugar please.' I thought there was a time when they wouldn't accept anything with less than three spoons.

'I am diabetic. My sugar level plays up,' he laughed. A young man of 25, I thought.

'My wife is diabetic too. We have a couple of kids. Seven and three. I am not sure about them.'

'Is the work tiring?' I said.

'Not really; better than college. I have a degree in physics. But then this job was the best opportunity. Pays well! Found it three years ago. I was very lucky.

'Don't you feel cheated you cannot use your degree?'

'Not really. I could be a university or a college technician which would be fine but this is good. In a way you are your own boss and the pay is much better. I see all sorts of people. You get to know so much about them; how they live, how they relate to each other, most of the time they fight.'

Carol said, 'do you ever come across anything exciting?'

'In a way, but they are the usual ones. Couples

fighting, most of the time if they are in. I prefer it when they leave a key for me. I don't need to bother about talking with them and have them poking into what I do. It's good to see people though. Individually, all of them are good.'

He paused and wiped his forehead. He was sweating in the cold. He had a sip of the tea. Then he said:

'But really, if you'd asked me, I wish I were an actor.'

I thought, here is a man who wants to be an actor, studied physics and is a plumber!

'I guess I can become one if I put my mind to it. But I don't feel like it as much as I did when I was younger. Anyway I wouldn't be able to support my family with an actor's salary. Not if you are not Sean Connery! We make it, just, with this job and my wife's wages as a teacher.

'Your wife is a teacher?'

'Yes,' he laughed. 'Guess what? Physics!'

We laughed and he was finishing his job.

'Do you want another cup?'

'No thanks I'd better get a move on. There are three other jobs to do before lunch.'

He cleaned the floor where he had worked and left. Now I could hear the sound of the boiler with a sense of satisfaction. This was the noise I always complained about.

Carol said, 'do you have time for lunch before going to work?'

'Yes.' I was thinking of the plumber with his oily hands yet clean with his work. I thought, he probably scrubs his hands when he goes home, there might be a ritual!

'Great!' said Carol.

I had the bistro in mind when we decided to go for lunch, but it was still closed. I thought it was Carol's good day. She suggested walking to another restaurant near my office. It was so helpful of her choosing a place near my office. We walked with some vigour, talking about the shops on our way, the new restaurants and the new fashion. When we reached the restaurant it was nearly full, we were lucky to get a table near the kitchen. The swinging wooden door opened and closed continuously giving way to the waiter with Italian dishes in his hands. We remained jolly. We were both in a funny mood and surprisingly the waiter came over quite quickly.

I thought he would appear around 3 if at all!' I said.

'I knew we would get a table and we would have good service. It is just because of us two being together. We are in luck together today. I can desire anything and I would get it,' Carol said.

'So that's why you offered to accompany me?'

'You are such a cynic. It was just out of love that I accompanied you.'

'I can imagine, how stupid of me to think otherwise!' I laughed.

'Exactly!'

We had a bottle of wine and the food was delicious.

'I noticed you didn't mind the young plumber,' I said.

'I have no complaints.'

'Maybe that's why you are in a jolly mood!'

'Maybe, maybe it is just the thought of having lunch with you!' Carol said.

'You can be so kind to an old man.'

'With a small snag, I regret not having taken his number.'

'Still not too late, I have the number.'

'What, a man with two kids? You must be joking. In any case, he was seven years younger than me. You know I like older men.'

'I thought you liked Brazilians.'

She had a sip of the wine.

'Had a call from him yesterday.'

'Oh, great!'

'Not that great.'

'What do you mean?'

'I don't know. Something doesn't sound OK. I can't put my finger on it.'

'You think he might have problems over there?'

'I am not sure. Don't think so. Perhaps there are no problems there at all. Perhaps I am the problem.'

'Oh, come on. Now you are a cynic.'

'Perhaps, let's talk about boiler men.'

'But he is married with kids.'

'And too young! I wonder though how someone that young could be married with two kids; one 7 year old,' she said.

'You should know. It is physiology!'

'I mean how do people decide so quickly and act on it too?'

'You shouldn't ask me! I am not an expert in this. I am nearly twenty years older than you and have none of that.'

'And you carry on like that. That's your problem.'

'I don't see a problem in this.'

'You will see one day.'

'Well, I prefer to enjoy it now.'

'Do you know? Sometimes I think you are a miserable old git.'

'I get it, what about other times?'

'Only miserable!'

We laughed.

We came out and I went back to my office.

The lobby was crowded as I went in. Students were chatting away in their coffee break. Some were standing in a corner with their mobiles tapping away sending messages. This was a picture that I was used to; going through batches of students chatting away, going to my office, turning on the computer and starting to work. But that day I felt idle. I felt that I had the time to relax and spend as I wished. I felt I was on holiday. I stopped as a student approached me.

'Sir, could I have an appointment to see you?'

She was putting her mobile into her bag. It was a big piece of rug.

'Yes of course, what is it about?'

'It is my marks.'

'Ah, non-negotiable.'

'Yes, I know. It is not that. I want to talk with you about my course, my marks,' she laughed, 'just about everything.'

'Come over to my office and I'll check my diary.'

'Now?'

'Why not?'

We went to my office. It was tidy. I was surprised at

myself. Somehow I had managed to keep the paper junk out of reach.

'What about next Thursday 3:30?' I said.

'Just like now?'

'Yes.'

Her phone started ringing. She began a long search into her bag.

'I'm sorry,' she said, and continued the search. I looked into my bookshelf for a text. She found the mobile, looked at it and turned it off.

'Sorry,' she said.

'That's OK; at least you didn't answer it!'

'I am sorry. I forgot to turn it off.'

'Do you mind me asking you a question?'

She looked alarmed. 'No.'

'What is the attraction of this? This gadget?' I hinted at the mobile.

She was relieved, 'I don't know.'

'What is this endless toing and froing of messages? Can't you people see each other? Meet, Communicate over a coffee?'

'Yes, but not always, that's different.'

'And what do you have to say to each other, always?'

'I don't know. It's fun!'

'See you next Thursday,' I said.

She left. There was a ray of sunshine coming in. I thought of the girl, her mobile phone and her bag.

Am I becoming irrelevant to young people's lives? Am I part of a boring stage in their lives as someone whom they have to face irrespective of their real interests? If their issues are becoming alien to me, perhaps it is me who has gradually lost something in the process of getting old? But have their issues ever been part of my life anyway? And, is what I see a real part of their lives? The time they spend with their mobiles, computers and other gadgets? As we get involved in this life of keyboards and screens, are we distancing ourselves from flesh and blood? What does it mean when we see all those famous video clips of peoples in hunger, war, natural disasters? Do they remain as a picture on a screen, on the cover of a fashion magazine with an "artistic" angle and expert rendition of light and shade?

There was a knock at my door. It was the same girl.

'Sorry sir.'

'Yes?'

'I am sorry but I have something to do next Thursday. Can I have another appointment?'

'I am busy now, come over some other time, we can arrange a meeting then.'

She left. I crossed her name out and dialled my lab to see how my people were doing.

As I was walking up the stairs to my lab I felt a sudden sadness. I couldn't think why. Was it because of the short meeting with that student? The girl was confused. But why should that affect me? Did I care a hoot if she was confused going around with her rug bag and the mobile? I might be affected by someone busking in the street, not by a youth playing with her mobile! Yes, I think this is what they do. Their mobiles are their busking bowls, their texts their begging statement; begging for affection, begging for words of comfort. Just look what they type in! They have developed a simple, fast language for begging!

I entered the lab. Two were pipetting away. 'Where are the rest of the gang?' I smiled.

'The other lab. Ana is not in, she's ill.'

'Oh, what's wrong with her?'

'Food poisoning, her boyfriend phoned to say she won't be coming in.'

I had a chat with the two, checked their results. They knew their stuff. That made me feel good but I remembered Ana and her problem. Why did her boyfriend phone? If he didn't want her to study, then why should he bother phoning? Was she really interested in doing the research? If so, then why should anything, anything, stop her. Was the boyfriend an excuse? *'Oh, life is not that black and white David,'* I started telling myself.

'You say that but there is a point in what I'm saying' I responded.

'Yes, but you can't generalise. As a lazy scientist, you crave for a generic solution to all problems. Yeah! You are a sucker for the Theory of Everything!'

'Why do you make everything so difficult? You make an issue out of everything,' Carol would have told me. 'Just relax. Who cares if students cook their brains with their mobiles? Is there a brain to begin with?' She would have laughed. 'And as for your PhD student, she might or might not continue. That's her problem.

She always thinks like that, basic. Perhaps she is right. I don't think that way though. Kate, strangely enough, would have agreed with her. But for a different reason: 'You love it David, you love it when they come to your office with their problems and you give them advice. It boosts your ego no end. You claim to have the robustness of Nietzsche but in reality you are soft like a jelly and they know it. This is the morality in you: morality of being good, being helpful, going out of your way to help! You love to feel that you are wanted. Your ego is submerged in it. And you even convince yourself that it is your job, your duty to be helpful. Sometimes I get so angry with myself because I think you are a hypocrite! But look at yourself. You are really a priest in nature! The only thing is that you teach science and your cell is your office!'

Suddenly I felt alone. I needed the coffee and the chat with Kate at our usual café. Who was I to criticise the youth for their mobile phone habit then? Perhaps they sought some consolation for their unease, perhaps they sought some moments of stupor. But what about me sitting in my office? What would I do when I left my office? Anything exciting? Anything creative?

23

The bistro was still closed. I was relieved to see the flat was warm. I sat on the sofa. There was a calm moment. No traffic noise, no noise from the fridge. I had no plans; I didn't feel like reading, listening to music, having a drink, going out. So I sat there doing nothing. I didn't even go to sleep. How long could I continue like that? Maybe 30-40 years? Of course there is the possibility of following Kate's example. Is there a problem with me not craving for things and situations as other people do? I like reading what the philosophers write. It is good to be able to discuss them with someone. But then what? I am not meant to write my views on life. Look at me right now, not knowing what to do, sitting here thinking about my dilemmas and doubts. And for what? For whom? For those "mobile" addicts? For women in search of security travelling the world to settle down and produce a couple of kids somewhere in suburbia? As for men, they easily demean themselves for a higher post, for a bit more in their pockets.

Now, listening to this Kate would have come down on me like a ton of bricks! 'Ha! Why do you think about the usefulness of your work and its effect on people?

You are too full of yourself to be good. You think about your influence on people, so much so that you forget to enjoy things. You want to have the right influence? If Galileo had thought that way, his work wouldn't have been acknowledged.'

Then I thought, is it not attractive to go somewhere, spend your days reading, writing, doing nothing special? Somewhere tucked away, somewhere I could have a cup of tea with the locals and live with my thoughts. But then that's exactly what I do here! I live with my thoughts, I talk to locals too. I invited Anita and her daughter to my flat. They are my locals aren't they? Oh! What had happened to the bistro?

It was Saturday. It had snowed the night before; unexpectedly and heavily. I went out to buy milk and bread and noticed the bistro. It was open now and a customer was coming out. Nobody else was inside. I decided to have breakfast there. Anita had a dark dress on, with a large black flower in her hair.

'Hello.'

'Good morning David.'

'What has happened? You were shut for some days.'

'Yes,' she paused. 'John had a sudden heart attack. It was fatal. It was terrible. He went so suddenly. He had no family. He died alone.'

'Oh, I am sorry; he wasn't that old was he?'

'No, he was only 61. Last month was his birthday. He was such a nice man.'

'I think he liked you and your daughter,' I said.

'He was like a father. When I came over, he was the one who really helped me. And now too, even after his death.'

'What do you mean?'

'He left his shop and his top flat for me.'

'I don't know what to say. What a great thing to do.'

'It is just like him. For me, he is still here with all the things he has done.'

'Still it is amazing.'

'Over the last few days I couldn't deal with everything and keep the shop open too. I am sorry. I am sure he would have wanted the shop to remain open. But I just couldn't cope with it. I have now moved to his flat above the shop. It makes life much easier. I have dealt with most of the necessary things now. They were really helpful in Hanna's school. She will move school to one near here soon. It is odd not to see John though. We were together all day every day… Such a lovely man. She paused, 'anyway, what can I bring you? Coffee and toast?'

'Yes please.'

I sat there and read the newspaper, with snow starting to come down again, this time fast and heavy. Soon it settled well on the pavement and the parked cars. I thought she would have mixed feelings, to suddenly have a home of her own, a business of her own, but losing someone she clearly cared for.

Anita came with the coffee, toast and jam. Nobody was in the bistro.

'Why don't you sit for a moment?'

She sat at the table. 'What do you think I should do now?' she asked.

'What do you mean?'

'I mean, now that I have the business, should I keep it?'

'Well of course. Why not?'

'Yes… why not?' she said and stood up.

'Perhaps you could come over to my place again, we can talk.'

She smiled. She looked tired. 'Yes… why not?'

24

The train trip took nearly four hours. I expected to get there before lunchtime and now it was a bit after. I could still make it to Fiona's office and have lunch before the meeting at 3 p.m. I had a useful couple of hours working on the train and felt upbeat about ideas to put into the proposal. As I looked out at the countryside I thought the winter was giving way to spring. At the station, there were no taxis. I had to wait another twenty minutes before I could find one.

Fiona was in a rush and, atypically, not in a happy mood. 'We don't seem to be able to have a relaxed lunch, ever!' She took her coat and bag from the hanger. 'I had plans for us but now the self-service should do.' We went through the pedestrian route through the campus. As we entered the self- service, there was a smell of boiled vegetables. The place was very busy. There were some thick pieces of pizza, fish with a creamy sauce and cold bits. I took a cold chicken salad and Fiona took the fish. We found a free table somewhere in the middle. She was still in a bad mood. 'I was really looking forward to spending some time with you today, to get away from all the crap.'

'We still have some time.'

She looked at me as if I was stupid.

'The others are already waiting,' she said.

'Well that's their problem. The meeting is at 3 p.m. and we have half an hour left.'

'Oh, great!'

She was already finishing her fish.

'There is coffee there, at the meeting,' she said.

'Fine!'

We put the trays on the racks and went out.

'I had forgotten what a nice campus you have here.'

'Some cold comfort! I am not a student you know! I just use the parking, and pay for it too!'

'I think we have good ideas to put together for this proposal. I liked your suggestions,' I said.

She smiled. 'Really?'

'I am sure you will be happy with the outcome too. You are just terribly unassuming,' I said.

'You always have a high opinion of me. It is good to talk with you, it boosts my morale!'

She laughed again. She was feeling better.

We entered the building. The meeting room was on the first floor. Already there were three other colleagues in the room. I knew one of them, with his small eyes. He was skinny and balding and wore glasses.

'Hello David,' he said.

'Hello Malcolm.'

Fiona introduced me to the other two.

'Juan has phoned. He had some problems with his flight but he is on his way. We can start and he will join us later.'

The meeting was unusually efficient, I suppose partly because we felt that we were late. But in reality we started a bit earlier. Juan arrived quite late. He seemed to me an energetic middle-aged man. He had a good reputation in the field and was quite successful. He apologised with his Mediterranean accent; the plane had taken off late. They had been sitting in the plane for more than an hour before it finally took off. He went straight to the table by the wall, poured himself a coffee and sat next to me, joining the discussions as if he had been there from the start. We covered most aspects by 7:30. They suggested going for drinks and dinner. I was in a rush to go back. Juan was going to stay there for a couple of days to have other meetings. Fiona said she would take me to the station.

'It is so decent of you! You are an angel!'

'I can be anything for an old friend.'

We were going to leave when Juan came towards me.

'I wonder if I could ask you a favour.'

'By all means.'

'We are organising a conference on science and society. I know you are very busy and the topic might be too general for you but in fact there is a lot of hard science in it. We are looking for a good speaker for the opening. Can I interest you in it?'

'I would be happy to help, but when is it?'

'It is mid-June. We deliberately chose June. It seems more feasible for most people. And of course there is the added attraction of the sea at that time of the year.'

'It will be my pleasure.' We talked a bit about the details and he said he would send me more information later. He thanked me and we had a warm hand-shake.

When we sat in the car, Fiona looked tired and pale.

I said, 'it was a good meeting.'

'Yes but a bit too long. If only Malcolm didn't give long lectures on safety issues! Sometimes I think he is in the wrong profession!'

'I agree with you but his knowledge is useful.'

'Yes, but it is too much!'

It wasn't a long drive to the station. And when we got there, there was half an hour's wait for the next train. Fiona stopped the car on a double yellow line.

'Don't let me keep you, you need to go back, I'm sure you've got a lot to do,' I said.

She ignored what I said and turned off the engine.

'I am thinking of quitting,' she said.

'What do you mean?...Don't be silly... Why?'

'I have had enough. It will be difficult but I see my life passing me by and I ask myself what am I doing with my life. Jane is growing up fast. Soon I will be left alone. I want to live too.'

'But you are doing very well keeping up with the work and your daughter. You are doing well for yourself.'

'What is good about it? I don't have a moment of rest. Do you know? This is my moment of relaxation, in a car by the station talking with you, threatened by the train's arrival! I have had enough.'

'All of us think that way from time to time. I was thinking the same the other day!'

'Were you?'

'Yes!'

'I thought, out of all people, you would be the last to

feel that way, or if you did, you would be the last to confess it. You're getting soft old boy,' she said.

'So am I losing my appeal to the young and the glamorous?'

'You'll never lose that. Not where I am concerned!!'

'That's reassuring.'

'Not for me! I want to get rid of you,' she laughed.

'Now you contradict yourself.'

'That's what makes me attractive, of course, apart from my irresistible presence!'

'Do you need to say these things now that I am leaving?'

'This is just a train trip David. I am not dead yet.'

'So when are you coming down.'

'That's something else. When I feel like it!'

She was laughing. She wasn't pale any more. I could see radiance in her eyes with wrinkles around them as she laughed. I looked at her thin lips with stale red lipstick. I thought that a minute later she would be going back home and would warm up a ready-made dinner to have with her daughter. She would go to bed with a book while her daughter stayed up watching television.

The train was empty. A young couple were busy at the end seats. I sat by the window and flicked through the newspaper. The train was warm. I closed my eyes. When I opened them, there were other passengers on the train and we had arrived.

25

I had plenty of time to prepare for my talk in June but I was intrigued by the topic and I had been thinking about it since I had come back from the proposal meeting. I had, of course, my usual reservations: it was too woolly, too general; anyone could talk about *Today, Science and Society*. Lying on the sofa I had started the dialogue in my head already: 'So what if anyone in the street can talk about this topic. Does that make it less attractive? Does it make it less topical? And, should a scientist feel that his point of view is superior to other people's just because he knows something other people don't know much about?'

'Clearly, the scientist has expert knowledge and this puts him in a special place.'

'But does this mean that his views are superior?'

'Well, in a way, yes! Throughout history scientists have had a special place in society. They have improved the quality of life; they have created a civilised society!'

'Sure, but does that mean that a non-scientist's opinion is less important?'

'I would say in many cases it is irrelevant. If someone doesn't have a clue about microbes and animals' physiology and responses, their interaction with each other and nature, the genes; if someone does not know about the structure of atoms and subatomic particles, about the stars and galaxies and the rules of nature, then he can talk about how a society must be run, what we should eat, how we should bring up our children, until the cows come home, but his views would be rudimentary, naïve and uninformed.'

'So one needs to be a scientist to be a good parent, a good citizen? What you say is absolute arrogant trash! The scientists used to believe that planet earth was the centre of universe, that the sun rotated around the earth, that the earth was flat, that human beings were the ultimate creatures, that the moon was a piece of glass, should I continue?'

'But then there were other scientists who found out that these weren't correct …they moved science forward while ordinary people were baking potatoes!'

'Yes, in your opinion scientists have moved things forward; you think they have created a civilised society! Hah, civilised! Is it civilised behaviour that we attack each other en masse and kill each other under the pretext of bringing civilisation to another country? Of course it is civilised to leave people to die from hunger, in spite of all the advances of science!'

'Scientists are not all that rounded in their personalities but remember that other people implement the ideas. And there is a difference between scientists and politicians.'

'Now you are hiding! Your argument leaves me cold.'

'You can use science in your home to warm up.'

'Yes, and what if I don't have the means?'

'You seem to me to be a miserable old martyr!'

'Yes, but thankfully I am not a scientist!'

I was getting into a serious quarrel with myself when there was a knock at the door. I wondered who it could be.

'I am sorry to bother you like this.'

It was Anita at the door.

'Not at all, do come in. What a nice surprise. What is the problem?'

It was Saturday midday and I expected the bistro to be busy.

'It is not an urgent problem but I had a sudden feeling to get out of the bistro, the kitchen, everything.'

'Who's dealing with the customers?'

'Oh, Hanna is there. I will go back soon. I just wanted to see a familiar face I could talk to. I know all the usual customers of course but I cannot talk to them, not like this.'

'Sure, but what is bothering you?'

'I don't know. Hanna came back from school yesterday, she looked tired. I was tired too. I think we had both a long day. And today, I really didn't want to get out of bed. I hadn't felt like that since I was a teenager. I dragged myself out of bed.'

'We all feel like that from time to time. You've had a hard time recently. Maybe you have a cold?'

'No, I can't remember having a cold ever! John used to make fun of me saying I am a robot! Working hard and not taking time off. But I am not sure what to do if I take time off. Anyway, I cannot take time off now. I felt so guilty today.'

'I am sure you are going to do excellently. In no time you will be expanding your business,' I said.

'You think so? Sometimes I think about selling it.'

'Really?'

'I don't know, I don't know... I'd better be going. It will be too busy for Hanna to handle things alone.'

She left in a hurry. Carol came out of the bedroom. She had a towel around her head. Her wet hair showed from under the towel.

'Who was that? Sounded like the bistro girl.' She went to the kitchen. 'We are getting too popular aren't we?'

'You have a one track mind. Can't people have other issues?'

'No! And believe me, I know.'

'And obviously I don't.'

'Yes, your highness should confess that he is naïve about certain things.'

'When it comes to women, all men are naïve. I can't dispute that. Anyway, cup of coffee? Perhaps with some toast?'

'Perhaps you prefer to have your lunch at the bistro? You'd better be hungry when going there.'

'Maybe you can teach an eager naïve old man a thing or two over the coffee?'

'I take your offer on-board.'

'Delighted madam, one coffee coming up and toast will be with you in a minute!'

We had a nice cup of coffee. We did not talk about women. Instead, we talked about the weather in Rio.

26

First thing on Monday I had some urgent work to do in the office. It was drizzling and I was in a hurry. As I arrived at the entrance to the building, there was a group of students and a few members of staff standing in front of the door facing anyone who wanted to go in. As I was going to pass them, a lecturer from another department approached me with a notebook and some pamphlets:

'You are not going in are you?'

'Yes, why?'

'Haven't you seen the flyers?'

'No!'

'They were everywhere, anyway, take one now.'

He pushed a hand-out into my hand.

'I don't look at flyers very often. I suppose you are on strike then,' I said.

He looked at me angrily but with a controlled voice said:

'Yes. And we hope you'll support our case.'

'Sorry, I am not into this sort of activity.'

'Why not? What are you protecting? Your future? Your promotion? Don't you know they have already made up their mind? We must not be passive. We must show them we have a voice. A united voice.'

'I am not sure if I understand you. Now I have to go in,' I said.

'So you want to taint your name with us!'

He became a bit aggressive I thought.

He continued: 'so if you have a problem, don't rush to us for help.'

'I'll remember that, thanks!' I said.

As I was going in he shouted:

'Responding like this, we will never have a change; people like you encourage the system.'

I was already in the lobby of the building. I went to my office, made a strong coffee and sat down to work but heard noises coming from the street. I had a look out of the window; the students were carrying colourful flags. There was a knock at my door. It was Richard.

'Yes, what can I do for you?'

'I came to thank you for your help.'

'That's fine. It is my job.'

'But nobody is in today. It is only you!'

'And you,' I said.

'Yes but I don't count!'

'Why is that?'

He ignored my comment.

'So, what can I do for you?'

'I wanted to ask your permission to put your name as a reference.'

'Why do you want to use me for a reference?'

'I hoped that you, as my tutor, would write a reference for me.'

'Of course I can write a reference for you but are you sure you want my opinion?'

'Yes! After all, it is just a reference.'

'What do you mean, it is just a reference?'

'I wouldn't have bothered you if you weren't my tutor.'

'It is not necessary to have a reference from your tutor. You can get a reference from any of your lecturers who know you; perhaps you can get one from Michael.'

'Oh, I have asked him. He is writing one for me.'

'And you still want one from me?'

'Yes please.'

'Fine.'

He didn't say anything but stayed there.

'Anything else?'

'No.'

'Good, now I have other things to do.'

He left. I started to pull a document out. There was a knock at the door.

'Yes, come in.'

It was Richard again. Sorry sir! When can I come to collect it?'

'Collect what?'

'The reference.'

'I don't give references out like that. Whoever wants it should write to me and I will respond to them directly.'

'Dr. Michael is giving it to me. I will collect it from him later on today; other students have got their references from their tutors.'

'I am not Dr. Michael or any other tutor.'

'OK then,' he said.

'Yes,' bye.'

He left. I wondered why he got on my nerves so much. I had no answer. I wasn't a 'totally by the book' person but he always wanted things that I couldn't or wouldn't do. Then I started to think about what I was like at his age. What I would do, how I would behave. I sat back and slowly it dawned on me that I was behaving like a grumpy old man. I thought I was quite a miserable man to have been affected by such a brat! Then I began to realise I was repeating things in my mind, repeating myself to myself, and that it was only the morning and if I kept on repeating myself to myself I'd better resort to an aquarium. Just a few minutes ago I had jumped the picket line to get to the office to clear some of the backlog. I had created a great image for myself passing through the picket line: one who was part of the system, one who jumped with the smallest whims of the system, a puppet, a selfish bastard! And after all that I had got to my office to be visited by the boy I didn't like, to have him looking at me as if I was a hard, inflexible person who couldn't understand people and their problems, one who could ruin someone's life!

Maybe I was over-interpreting a simple encounter, a non-event just because I liked to be noted, no matter in what capacity, but noted, counted. After all, why should I bother about people's views about me? People think all sorts of things. Anyway, since when had the view of the masses become so important for me? I wasn't like that before! We used to have long chats starting from the freedom of individual and slavery and finishing with the ads and subliminal suggestions in the media. Kate and I used to enjoy the debate. Could somebody's death have such an effect? Such a negative effect? Who was I then? I had lost not only a friend but also part of my character! The part that I was happy about! I started thinking about her face, tried to remember her face. It shouldn't have been so difficult! But I had a definition of her behaviour, her movements in me, not a picture. I am sure that had I been a painter, I would not have been able to draw her! There was an emptiness, a vague presence in me that I could not picture! I could guess and act all her words, sentences, I could remember her movements when she was lying next to me but her face was eluding me, evading me. And why was that? How important was she to me? Now, this was the first time I had started to think about a woman, assessing her importance in my life. No, I was not a bastard! One of those…! But I didn't like to build a structure where a woman, any woman and I were the essential part of it. They were more like a river, passing by, moving. Perhaps Kate was the same. Perhaps that was why I couldn't remember her face. But what about all those discussions? What about her diaries? Now, suddenly, I had arrived at something I had put away, ignored. Why did I keep her diary? What was my response to her words? Could I ignore them forever?

I stood up. It wasn't drizzling any more. I had managed not to do a single piece of work. I tried to console myself. I had filed so much rubbish while thinking. Now my office was tidy. I decided to go to the pub for a quick bite.

It had to be Ian sitting there. I asked myself, why did I go to this pub? He was always there. He was the last person I wanted to see, the old man with his silly problems, his album of stamps and his wife. 'What do I care?' I asked myself. I was going to turn back but then I thought, why should I change my plan just because of this miserable man? I went up to the bar:

'Half a pint of lager and a smoked ham on white,' I said.

'Mustard?'

'Yes please.'

I looked around and Ian was sitting nearby looking at me.

'So you've been a bad boy,' he said, 'not very clever passing through them.'

I sat next to him.

'If you like, news travels fast,' I said and remained silent, drinking slowly.

'You look preoccupied,' Ian said.

'Not really, a bit tired,' I said.

'I decided not to cross through the gang standing there, didn't have the energy to argue with them. If they wished to stay out, good for them. But they looked at you as if you were a criminal.'

'It does not bother me,' I said.

'But it bothers me! There are things to be done.' He adjusted his glasses, 'I don't want to be thought of as an outsider.'

'But if you are not with them, then you are an outsider, surely!'

'I suppose, but I don't even know what they are talking about. OK, they want better education, they want more money, they want ...what else?' he asked.

'Is there anything else? It is good for them to voice their views though, to vent it. We have a democracy.'

I wasn't sure if he could understand me. I didn't care either. But I felt as if I was talking to Kate now.

'I don't believe in these sorts of activities; I think of them as a waste of time. Do you know, for some people it is a form of entertainment. They are bored. I remember when I was a student and we went on strike and staged sit-ins, there were groups who played poker all night in the occupied building, there were others who ended up playing football all day in the garden; and why not? As long as it didn't get out of hand, it was good for everybody concerned. They would release their frustration and soon the strike was off. Now, things are a bit different but the main thing remains: boredom, excitement and, in extreme cases, martyrdom. As for me, I like my whisky,' I said.

'I wish I could be as indifferent as you are. I cannot tolerate it when they stand there with their self congratulating postures looking down at me.'

'Why shouldn't they? After all you are, to them, a sucker for the system. They like to believe that. They enjoy it. Why do you want to deprive them of their moment of satisfaction?'

'I am not in the business of satisfying people. There are special people and special places for that sort of thing.'

'Now you are being too melodramatic. Just relax,' I said.

We started somehow to talk about stamps and that they don't make stamps the way they did in the good old days. When I came out, I was craving for some coffee. I needed fresh air. I walked to my flat.

The street was shining after the rain. I walked, slowly, thinking about myself. I started to compare my situation with that of Ian. I thought this was the first time I was comparing myself with others and I had no control over it. It seemed as if I was rolling down a steep slippery road. I had no logic for my comparison. I always mocked this man in my head and now, now I was thinking that his life wasn't that bad, that miserable. He would go home to a wife who would nag at him because he wouldn't pay enough attention to her. He was wanted. What a reassuring state to be in. I had my hand in my jacket pocket. I pressed it to my body to keep the breeze away. I would go home and cook some food, read something, go to bed until tomorrow to go back to the office and face, whom? Richard Farmbaker, or for that matter Michael who would lecture me on how to treat useless students who shouldn't have been there to begin with. And then there would be another night. Yes, there was Carol with her temporary body, with her desire for a man and a life in Rio or anywhere else, there was Fiona with her daughter whom I hadn't met. I thought about Fiona taking me to the train station. There was something about her that attracted me but I could easily forget. And of course, there was Anita whom I was going to see in a minute asking for coffee. And yes, the memory of the old coffees, which had stayed with me and would stay... but there was no Kate.

I was close to the bistro. Suddenly I decided not to go in. I had no energy in me to listen to Anita and her problems; I couldn't sit there with my coffee listening to her and her potential plans to sell the bistro and go back. I tried to imagine the bistro. What would happen to it? I suppose it would change hands quickly. Knowing the area, it would become a sandwich place, then another sandwich place, then it would remain empty for a while, then I would see some building activity. It might become a hairdresser's or perhaps a health food shop. I would pass it by... remembering the bistro but gradually I would forget about it; forget that it even existed there. I would have another person deducted from the list of people I knew. Perhaps for a while I would get a postcard from her, saying how difficult she finds it adjusting back in her own town, then no card, no news. Then after a couple of years I would receive a card inviting me to her wedding, or perhaps a letter asking me to do something for her daughter who wants to come back and go to university to continue her studies.

I put the key in the door and went in. Carol was in. She was sitting on the bed varnishing her toenails. She looked at me.

'What has happened? You look like a dead man. Look at your face. Pale. You are like a 14-year-old fallen in love with her mother's glamorous friend. Ah... did she touch your face?'

'Good to see someone's happy, and her toes happy too!'

'Oh! My little toes are making themselves ready for a party. They can take you as well if you say no to your mother's friend and take a hot bath.'

'What is the party in aid of?'

'The desperate, the idle, the lovely!'

'I know which one I am, I don't know about you.'

'Count me as any of the above, but I know you know I am lovely!' she said.

I had to start to think seriously about my plenary talk. I still had plenty of time but it was in the back of my mind and was starting to become a permanent resident. Carol wanted me to go to the party with her; she wanted to be with someone. I didn't care one way or another and actually I thought that it might be good for me with the state of mind I was in.

27

The party was on the second floor of a large block of flats. There was a large sitting-room joined to a dining room. We were the last ones to arrive. There were about 60 people moving about in a confined space. It was a party of young students of arts, marketing, advertising, that sort of people. A young man came over to Carol.

'So how's the young lady of adventurous travels?' he said with a camp accent.

'Marvellous, couldn't be better, I'm off in a couple of weeks.'

'And when will we see you again?'

'Who knows, start praying!' Carol laughed.

'I shall remain sleepless darling! And who is this young man? He will be shattered without you!'

'This is Professor Hardag.'

'Oh, my! A professor! How did that happen?'

I said, 'things happen, some have the wrong genes!'

'Thank you darling, you are on my side! I keep on telling my mom but she still accuses me of depriving her of grandmotherhood! Do you want to see my mom? After all, this lady is vanishing! So why not be generous? Make a mother and son happy!'

'I am against charity.'

'And why?' He had a sip of a pink drink and continued:

'It is very fashionable these days. You might get a promotion too!'

'I am afraid it doesn't appal to me.'

'Then you must see my mom. She must appeal to you. I will order her!' He laughed and moved away.

'I can see we are going to enjoy it tonight,' I said.

'Would I take you somewhere boring? Now, I am going to mingle. Do you want me to introduce you to anyone?'

'No thank you, I am quite OK. If I feel left out, I will ask the charitable boy for help.'

'I am sure he would be more than happy to oblige. He is ever so nice.'

I stood by the table where the snacks were spread. I had no interest in talking to people but was in a happy mood. There was a couple standing next to me.

'We could have gone to a movie,' the guy said.

'Why? Don't you like it here?' the girl said.

'Not particularly.'

'But you can meet lots of people.'

'I would have preferred for us to be alone.'

'We'll have plenty of time for that; don't be like this, let's enjoy it.'

'I am enjoying it, just that I thought we would have enjoyed it more had we been alone.'

She was facing him but then turned towards me and smiled.

'Hello, I am Amanda.'

'Hi, David.'

'Oh, this is David too, my fiancé, we are getting married next month.'

'Congratulations. Have you been together long?'

'Yes,' the girl said, 'we have been together for a year now, nearly.'

'It is a nice party; do you know many people here?' I asked.

'Not really, just Robert. He is an old friend of mine, really, we were brought up together, we were neighbours. And you?'

'No, I came with a friend who knows people here.'

We stood there for a couple of minutes. The man did not say a word.

I was getting bored. I needed fresh air. Carol was laughing away with a couple of boys on the other side of the room. I slipped out; out on the street there was a sharp blast of cold air. As I started to walk down the long narrow street, I warmed up. Was I getting old and intolerant? Why did I keep condemning myself for what I was, for what I was becoming? Yes, I would have mingled with people a couple of years ago, perhaps even a couple of months ago. But so what? Am I to be blamed because I didn't want to stay and talk about the couple's wedding preparations? I thought I might have been intrigued by them on another occasion; it all depends on one's mood. Yes, I liked that logic but then it was obvious to me that I was in a peculiar mood these days.

'You didn't help that boy, you know, Richard; you didn't go to the hospital to see Kate, you didn't even phone her. You don't like talking with your colleagues much: take Ian. You didn't even want to talk with Anita! Don't you think that you are behaving like one who has decided his time is over?'

I didn't like my train of thought. I started to walk faster. As I was turning into another street, I bumped into a man. 'Watch it! Can't you see?' he said.

He was a very well dressed middle-aged man with a serious face.

'I am sorry.'

'You think that's enough?'

I didn't say anything and started to move on but he stopped me.

'Wait a minute, you think you can walk so carelessly and then expect nothing to happen? Not even to receive a notice?'

'But I said I was sorry! You seem OK,' I said.

'Hah, I am OK but am not sure about you. You look to me like a desperate man in search of anything in the air. Watch where you go!'

Then he walked away. I never thought I would be shaken by a silly accident like that, but I was. I just couldn't continue. I thought to take a taxi and go home but I felt that I couldn't face being alone in the flat; there was no taxi in sight in that street anyway. I turned back and hurried to the party. When I arrived back, the two couples were standing together arguing and Carol was still at the other side of the room. I found my way to her. She looked at me: 'Where have you been hiding? I wanted you to meet my gorgeous friends.' She introduced two men to me. I couldn't register their names. They were both in their early thirties with imposing shoulders and had one hand in their pockets, another hand holding a drink.

'What do you do?' one asked.

'I teach science,' I said.

'Interesting.'

I thought he was insulting. I was about to move on but Carol stopped me: 'David! This is the man who introduced me to Fernando.'

'So he is the culprit.'

'I am so thankful to him.'

I was getting angry.

'Do you do this sort of thing very often?' I asked him.

'What?'

He was looking somewhere else.

'Do you like to bring people together? Are you a matchmaker?'

'You might say that; actually I have my own Estate Agency.'

'I see! Once an agent, always an agent! And here you've been the agent of love, cupid!'

I hated my sentences. I don't know why I had engaged in that sort of dialogue. The other boy said to Carol, 'I see you have a colourful friend!'

'Oh! I love him to bits but he doesn't see me. His eyes are glued to Eastern European greenery!'

'What rubbish,' I said and I wouldn't let go. I turned to the estate agent:

'I wonder how come you haven't found Carol a nice flat. She has been looking for nearly six months.'

'She doesn't need a flat of her own; she needs a man

that goes with the flat, preferably a house. So I told her I had one but she had to travel to South America to claim occupancy.'

'I see! And what is your rate?'

He just ignored me and said:

'This is a lovely party, don't you think so?'

Carol said:

'Yes, nice friends, good atmosphere,' and she looked at me:

'I need a top-up. David, would you be an angel? My Bacchus?'

I couldn't wait to go. I made my way through the crowd. When I came back, she was talking with some other people. I gave her the drink but didn't stay with her. She seemed to have preferred it too. But then this man with a glass of wine in his hand came towards me. 'I noticed you are with Carol,' he said.

'Well, in a way.'

'I adore her, you are a lucky man.'

'Not that lucky, we live in the same flat, she is leaving.'

'Oh, you are separating? I am sorry.'

He didn't seem sorry at all.

'Don't be, and we are not separating, it is not like that. We are friends; she is going to Brazil for good,' I said.

'Oh, why?'

'There is always another man! But you should ask her not me; anyway how do you know her?'

'She wouldn't remember but we were at the same school.'

'An old flame then?'

He remained silent. Then he said: 'She was podgy then, she was a real heart throb.'

'And many of them were successful I suppose.'

'I wouldn't know, wouldn't like to think that way.' He paused, then he said:

'It is a strange feeling, after so many years.'

'Why don't you go talk to her?'

'Me? No, no!'

'But why not?'

'No!'

I was surprised to see a man of his age, mid-thirties, to be so shy. He even blushed for a second. I suppose he was still living in the days of his early youth. He was still trapped in those days of walking to school with his heavy bag, with his mother or father at his back all the time. His mind had gone back to the times when a smile, a kind gesture that he thought was meant for him would remain with him for a while until he would find out that it was just an expression without significance. He had hoped for discrimination, but it was a world of equal opportunities, and this was a game he wasn't prepared for or perhaps wasn't made for. So he had gone back to the days when he went to school with sleepy eyes and unkempt hair. He had become more silent; more reserved and had heard his parents talking about him: 'Do you think he is ill or something?'

'No, can't be.'

'Perhaps he is taking something.'

'Oh, God, I hope not.'

And he had kept his silence, this time as revenge

against them, against the girl with the generous smile, against the whole world around him. After all, how could his parents think like that about him? Him taking something! Perhaps he should! But he wasn't interested; at the time he would have reasoned that he didn't have the guts for any radical action. He had established in his mind that he was a wimp. So how could he do anything properly, effectively? He had become increasingly reserved, and this was a cosy state of affairs. He had created a picture of himself that others had accepted. He was shy, dreamy, absent minded and studious. He studied all the time to achieve just better than average marks. This way, everybody was happy. And he had kept Carol's image in a hidden corner for himself. He would refer to her image from time to time and particularly when he felt lonelier than usual.

'So what do you do for living?' I asked.

'Oh, I work in a bank. I am an accounts analyst.'

I thought about the life he could have had with Carol! Him and her! This was an absurd picture. Him, coming home with a bunch of flowers bought from the station and kept carefully not to be crushed in the rush hour train; and her… cooking food? No, no! He would go home and start cooking, hoping for a day that his wife permitted him to become a proud father. Then he would take the child to his parents on Sundays to tell them, 'look, this is your grandson, from a boy you thought was a junkie!'

I smiled at the thought, I felt jolly! Perhaps it was the depth of religion in me saying, 'look, it was for the best that they didn't get together; what a misery it would have been. Whatever comes is good. There is a divine logic in it!'

But then, immediately, I cringed. I started despising myself. I felt Kate standing next to me saying: 'I told you, you and all your pretence about your love for Nietzsche! Deep inside you are superstitious.'

I walked out of the party for the second time. This time I stopped outside the main door of the block of flats on the ground floor, waiting for a taxi to come. I knew it was too much wishful thinking to expect a free taxi to come this way, but I had no intention of walking to the underground station; I didn't want to take the same route that I had taken earlier either. I stood there outside the heavy door for about ten minutes I think, then the door opened and Amanda, the future bride, came out. The bridegroom-to-be was not with her. I said, 'coming out for fresh air?'

'No, I've had enough,' her face was red and her hands were trembling. She took a cigarette out of her handbag and lit it, 'I've had enough.'

'What happened?'

'Nothing new! Are you waiting for someone?'

'No, I'm just hoping to catch a taxi.'

'What? Here? Now?'

'I know it's unlikely but I didn't feel like walking to the station.'

'Come on, I'll take you, I have a car.'

'That's kind of you, what about the lucky groom?'

'He might be out of luck! Actually, I can do with talking to someone. What about a drink somewhere?'

'Fine, yes. I am not in a hurry.'

We ended up in this pub with a warm atmosphere. She looked nicer now sitting the other side of the table than standing next to her future husband in the party. Her face was relaxed and was even attractive.

'Tell me David, you said you were with a friend.'

'Yes, she is having a good time right now.'

'So you just left her there like that?'

'It isn't that catastrophic, she knows her way back! Anyway we are not getting married next month!'

'Ah that! We would have wanted to get married next month for a long time. It is becoming a very private joke for me!'

'A bride with a sense of humour! But the joke is on him I suppose?'

'I think he will know it too late. What was your plan for tonight?' she asked.

'To have drinks with you,' I smiled.

'Is that all? You seem to be more adventurous than that.'

'I wouldn't refuse exciting challenges.'

We didn't talk much. There was a short drive to her place.

Her skin smelt of oranges. It was good that the next day was Sunday.

28

'Is that Elizabeth?'

'Yes.' Her voice was distant on the phone.

'It's David. I was thinking about the memorial.'

She sounded pepped up. 'Yes? I thought you weren't interested.'

'Oh, no, I am actually ready when you are.'

'Oh, that's very nice of you David. This is very good news. I'll talk with people and come back to you by tomorrow.'

'That's fine.'

Actually, it didn't take until tomorrow. She phoned back in the afternoon. She had organised everything. All she wanted was a date from me, she had some dates ready. We agreed on a Thursday, 3 p.m.

29

I walked fast to the fourth floor where the library meeting room was. I was thinking that if Kate was there, this was the time we would go for a coffee. I had the talk in my pocket, just a few lines as aide-memoire; the rest I had left to be said spontaneously. I didn't want to make a formal, distant talk. As it happened, I didn't need the paper in my pocket. The room was more than a meeting room, I think they had it for some induction events for students, there were some chairs. When I arrived, around forty people were waiting already. Elizabeth was standing near the door. We exchanged greetings; she then went and sat on a chair; there was no need for introduction. I stood behind a table by a board. I felt animated:

'It is awkward. It is the norm to say it is a sad occasion, and it is a sad occasion but I'll skip those expected words. It is awkward like going to a foreign land, you don't know the language, you want to get into a train and you feel things are unfamiliar, strange… unsure. This is the way I have felt since Kate left us. I have done my daily routine…of course…as we all do… feeling someone was there, not for me per se, but someone who could be there for me too. The sheer existence of her made the moments familiar, friendly, acceptable. I do the same things now as I did before but they are different, I cannot put my hand on a single thing and say, Ah! This is it, this is how things are different, but they are! Perhaps I say this to avoid facing the loss of intimate moments, to make things easier for myself to be able to continue. And how do I continue? It is difficult. It is not that I do anything differently in any tangible way, but I live differently. We didn't live together, we didn't have a family together, but we had those moments that for me go beyond description. I know I am talking about myself not about her. But whatever I say is her. This is her. I know she would have liked this. She was always ready for a discussion about life but what happened to all that? If the cup of coffee was an ingredient of our moments of intimacy and intrigue, then those moments have gone although it is difficult to accept it. She would say: 'You are too vague. I am not sure if you know what you are talking about yourself.'

But I think I am quite clear on this.

She would say:

'But that's what you think and that is surely not enough, you will need to have an audience who understands and if this audience didn't, for whatever reason, then you are responsible for it!'

I feel responsible for having lost her. The dialogue for me is not only a mixture of words. The touch of skin, the breathing together, the glances you have as you pass by, what you have in your mind and never utter, to me all these are dialogues and I am responsible for losing the dialogues. I know, this makes me a partner in crime, the crime of creating a situation where her body does not exist any more. And if I didn't want to create it, if those moments of coffee and Nietzsche were so dear to me, how come I participated in a process of losing her? I know I seem confused, I know what I say might not make sense but perhaps she would have made sense of it…she could explain it all… But this doesn't make sense because she is not here any more. This is not acceptable. When I live with a project, a proposal, I crave to attain it, I crave to see it materialise. If I am unsuccessful, I apply again, and again, there is a hope. Here, since she has gone, everything is strange, foreign, awkward. This is a checkmate. Here, there is no hope.

Then I stopped and I left the room. I didn't look around, just left. I walked out of the building. I wasn't sure where I wanted to go. It was still early afternoon. I walked around the streets for half an hour. Then stopped at a coffee shop and had a cappuccino. I thought about my words earlier on. Why did I leave like that? There were perhaps 40 or more people in the room; some had come from other departments. I didn't know she was that popular.

30

'You are a rude man'! The ticket man in the train station announced in the loudspeaker for all to hear. And by that he meant me! I suppose he was right as far as the passengers on the platform were concerned. I suppose he was right even by my own standards but not for the occasion he was referring to. I had waited in a short queue to buy a ticket. He was making jokes with an old local woman who was looking into her wallet for the right change. At first I was in good humour. I wondered why old people have this problem with paying. First of all, they love to pay cash rather than use their card. Secondly, they always look for the exact change; always look for that small coin which is mysteriously hidden in a corner of their wallet. But the ticket man went on and on with his bland joke and I got bored.

'Can we have some attention here too? The train will be here any minute.'

He said: 'I am serving this lady. I will deal with you when it is your turn!'

I was furious. I thought that I had been tolerant enough and the ticket man must attend to the passengers properly. I said: 'with this service I will be lucky if I catch the last train of the day!' I dashed to the automatic machine which wasn't working either. I decided to get to the train anyway. The train came only five minutes late. It was three stations later that the ticket man appeared. 'Tickets please!'

I asked him for a ticket and while issuing the ticket he said, 'there will be a fine.'

'Why is that?'

'You need to posses a valid ticket to the destination when you get into the train, sir.'

'The ticket office was slow and I would have missed my train. The automatic machine wasn't working.'

'You can complain sir,' he handed me an A4 pink form, 'and I am sure they will return the fine back to you. You will need to fill in this form for that, but for the time being you will need to pay the fine, I am sorry.'

For a moment I felt that I had lost all my resolve to fight back. I paid the man and closed my eyes to go to sleep. Every now and then I would wake up with the screams of a little girl who ran playfully along the length of the corridor. I was in a drowsy state; there were the voices of teenage students getting in and out of the train at each stop. Then the train stopped. The guard came in to say that we were going to experience some delay because someone had jumped onto the track; the driver had stopped smoothly in time. I thought how selfish some people can be. They are the kind of martyrs that think everybody should know about them, their misery; should feel sorry for them and feel guilty for their life. I told myself, why don't they kill themselves in the privacy of their homes; in any case in a way not to interfere with other people's lives? The train was packed with people who had all sorts of things on their minds, all sorts of things to do; the last thing they wanted was a delay. But no! Those martyrs cannot let go! They have to cause problems because everybody else is guilty but them! People are guilty for their unhappiness!

After half an hour the train started to move. The delay was less than what I expected. The next station was very close. As the train slowly passed the platform, I saw a young girl with dishevelled blonde hair leaning against a policeman in a yellow overcoat, limping away. Three other policemen were accompanying them. The guard came in again. 'She survived,' he said, and then he mumbled some sort of apology for the delay. I looked out and the girl was fading away from my sight. Then there were trees under the hazy sun.

As the train arrived at the station, I suddenly remembered Kate. I am not sure what it was that reminded me of her but it was thinking about her earlier that took me to the Gallery, drove me to go through the trouble of taking the train. As I got closer, I noticed the ads for a temporary exhibition. From across the road, I looked at the wide glass window of the Gallery. Three vertical advertising flags were moving in the wind in front of the window. It was the last day of this painter's exhibition.

There was a long queue for the exhibition and no chance of getting in in time. I passed it by and went into the permanent collection. I walked through the rooms as if I was a lieutenant checking his orderlies. All those painters I knew, or I didn't care to know. Kate and I had planned to go to the Gallery together again and again, and it had never materialised. I would have told her:

'How come galleries are full of women? Just look! For every man, and they are all old, there are four or five women.'

She would have replied:

'Obviously because we are more educated, more interested in culture… in all things refined.'

'Do I sense discrimination here?'

'So?'

'And yet, these are women who always complain about being ignored, discriminated against.'

'I am sure no man is going to oppose my statement.'

'I do!'

'Well, perhaps you are pretending!'

'Look at the arrogance!'

'Me? It is just enough to look at me to see how wrong you are to say that.'

'Oh! So you are resorting to your looks! Yet another feminine device!'

'Ah, who is discriminating now?'

I stopped by a painting, a woman on a chair next to a bed where a young girl was lying sick. How many painters have done mother and sick child? I wondered if the sadness in the eye of the mother was from feeling sorry for herself, having had to devote herself to the child.

'I would have left your father years ago, if it wasn't for you. All those years! I spent all my youth on you! What a fool I was! And look at you now! It is a miracle if I hear from you once in a blue moon.'

'Do NOT touch the railing. Can't you understand it is dirty? How many people have touched it with their dirty hands infested with microbes?'

How many children, grown up children, men, women, have heard this? And why do we have such a loving feeling towards mothers? You say something against them and you are damned forever! You are branded persona non-grata! Great, get abused and then when you just voice your true feelings, be condemned. And if this is the holiest part of the human institution, what do you have to say about the rest of it? Humanity based on self-gratification, ever self-righteous individuals forming the 'benevolent' society based on sacrifice, martyrdom and phoney feelings, justifying its own existence while at war with itself, its neighbours, and peoples of the lands far away!

I sat on a wooden bench in a small room in the gallery. A huge painting was in front of me showing an outdoor scene with a horse, some trees, grass, water, a couple of young girls holding their hats in the wind, a young boy looking at them from a ramp a little distance away. I thought, what a waste of paint!

Then I thought, what is wrong with me? Why should I condemn the painting? Perhaps the painter was full of passion painting that scene. Perhaps he was commissioned to do it! So what? I am tired; I have nothing else to do so I start criticising the painting! But what makes the difference between two paintings of the same object, the same scene? The shades of light, the depth of colours, the strength of the brush? All these are of course important. But I am talking beyond the techniques. Is there a difference between paintings because of the suffering of one painter and happy life style of another? And is that enough? Can you see the blood poured deep inside the canvas?

I needed fresh air. I went out, fast.

31

Carol says, 'we are so similar, I don't know why I am going, I don't know why I should go thousands of miles away, distance myself from you; I don't know why you don't insist that I should stay, that I should not leave you.'

In fact, I had thought about it myself but I think she is living in a dreamland. We might appear similar in our daily routines but deep inside we are miles away. I look at her as we sit under the rays of the afternoon sun with the newspaper on my lap. I have flicked through all those fat pages from gardening to cooking to the movies of the week, I have tried to ignore the headlines, forget about yet another set of changes to education, yet another proposal for the running of hospitals and directives for the conduct of government at war. Carol is touching her naked feet, massaging her toes and I hate this. I don't know what is so attractive in this for some people.

'I might come and visit you,' I said.

I thought the way I said it was as if she was going to be admitted to a mental hospital or condemned to internment.

'Would you?' she said. There was a sense of disbelief in that.

'Yes, if there is a conference, I would like to see Brazil.'

'So it's not to see me.'

'You too.'

'You didn't go to see that librarian dying in the hospital in the same town so close to you and you say you'll come to see me in another continent? ...And she meant something to you, didn't she? I don't understand you.'

I remained silent. I was reading the achievements of someone climbing a dangerous mountain somewhere. What do people get out of these sorts of activities? I fail to understand. The media is full of these things. The woman who went around the world on a bicycle in record time, a man who designed the largest balloon to go around the world but the wind was such and such. I would say what boring, desperate people. Isn't there something less boring? I was so happy I didn't have children to need to teach them on Sundays how to ride a bicycle or how to do homework! Let alone making myself busy with problems of getting a special-design balloon! I was happy to sit there reading rubbish but not being on that mountain range, not to try to repair the lamp shade! I was happy about all the things that I didn't have and didn't want to have! And Carol was thinking that we were so similar because those were the things she was craving for!

32

I worked late Sunday night in the flat. I knew that the next day I would be hassled by a gang of students wanting to discuss their marks. Carol had long gone to bed. I could hear her breathing and now that I had finished the work, I wasn't sleepy. I had in my mind the picture of the girl being carried away on the platform after her suicide attempt. She was looking at a point beyond the people gathered on the platform, at an empty space. I had thought she was selfish, using such a method to kill herself, affecting so many people. But now I was thinking differently. I had her picture in my mind and I was sad as if I knew her, as if I had lived with her. Why did she try to kill herself? Maybe she didn't have someone to talk to, even the sort of talk I have with Carol, mundane but perhaps vital to her. I have seen, repeatedly, two women having dinner together with a bottle of wine between them, talking and talking and getting into moments of laughter, stupor. What would they do when they go home? Is there someone waiting? They make sure they drink so much they would go to sleep, fast. It wouldn't matter if anyone was there when they entered their flat. It wouldn't matter what "he" would do, what they would do. And the next day? Hopefully there is a job to go to, lose yourself in the daily gossip and usual annoyances and... one day you might not be lonely, until the next event. But why did the girl on the platform affect me so much, to think about her while Carol with her warm skin and intimate breathing was sleeping in my bed? I had no answer for it; but it was disturbing to see myself with two different, in a way opposing, views in a short period of time. What about my integrity? How could I believe in my own arguments? How could I convince anyone if I am vacillating so readily, so dramatically? Oh, I needed Kate to argue with to feel better. Had I grown dependent on her? Perhaps Carol's comments about me and Kate were not that far away from the truth. I always belittle Carol's views; after all, she is the one who doesn't know what she wants. I don't believe at all that she has understood or thought through her desire to go to Rio. So, do I think she is a fake? Yes! And what about myself and my views? I change them so quickly. So she was right in saying we were similar, but we are similar in our phoniness!

33

I saw Elizabeth the next day as I was passing through the lazy corridors with most offices empty, answer phones ringing in measured intervals. We didn't stop, just exchanged greetings in passing. I hadn't seen her for some time now. She was paler and had lost some weight. Not that she was chubby at all but she was even skinnier now. What surprised me was that I felt she had aged over this period. I wondered what she would think about me. Had I aged too? What a silly question! As if I was different! But OK, people age differently. Some age much later. What about that singer? He looks like plastic vegetation. He doesn't seem to perish but what do you do about the dust sitting on the plastic leaves? I suppose you can always dust it, use shining creams! I am among those who prefer perishing flowers. They give you a sense of living, companionship. They smell differently, not only at different times of the day, but also on different occasions, they behave like a dog. They seem to feel your feelings. I know I am entering into the realm of the esoteric but this is what I think. Yes, people age differently and I hope to age late, but at the same time,

I am not interested in growing old like plastic vegetation! So, do I expect a lot from my physiology?

This is only on growing old; but what about death? Of course people believe in death, in its inevitability, but only for others. They even find it difficult sometimes to accept it when it happens to a friend or to someone they know. But what about its inevitability when it comes to themselves? Never! Have you ever seen someone with an incurable fatal illness? How do they continue? What makes them tolerate the pain, what makes them accept all sorts of humiliation, indignity? It could only be possible if they believed an amazing cure existed somewhere, and that they would come across it sometime. Why do we insist so much on keeping a terminal patient on a series of machines just to help them breathe? This is the sanctity of life for you! As for me, of course I'd say I believe I'll die one day but that day is too hypothetical, far away. And what is all this? I see an older colleague passing by and I start thinking about ageing and death! How do I concentrate on my work? What percentage of our daily work do we devote to our work really? I am now not talking about times when we have coffee with others, or gossiping away in the labs and offices. I am talking about the times that our minds fly away somewhere while sitting by the desk. We don't even remember where our minds had gone, a little later as we are sitting in a bus going home. Had we thought about our death?

34

'I am not convinced by myself. I am not convinced about anything when it comes to myself.' This is, I think, what I said to Kate at our last meeting. I remember her now. She looked frail. Yes, I know, I didn't mention it to her; I didn't even mention it to myself. So how is it that I remember it now? I should have registered it somehow; I should have found it of some importance, at least to keep it deep somewhere in my mind. Keep it to remember one day! And now it is the time. Was it because I was so interested in expressing myself to her, to talk about myself, that I could ignore her look? What would I have done if I knew then that she was dying? Would I have continued to talk about the mundane, myself? Perhaps I had guessed it and didn't acknowledge it because I couldn't face her not being there any more, I couldn't face the coffee shop without her. I can hypothesise until tomorrow! I can talk! That is my escape from it all.

35

She said, 'I think I'll go on that trip anyway.'

'What trip?' I had totally forgotten about it.

She didn't say anything. She laughed.

'Really, what trip?'

'You know I am a dreamy person. Sometimes I exaggerate.'

I ignored her statement. I said, 'I am not convinced, for example, that I am wholeheartedly devoted to research.'

'You must be joking. You breathe research; you sleep with a proposal in your arm!'

'That's kinky!' I said.

'Don't evade my comment. You are devoted to your research, but I think you are confused and that is your problem; there is no question of not being convinced. Yes, you might be unhappy about some aspects of your life but knowing you, even as little as I do, one would say you are pretty well in line with your passions.'

'That's a great statement! I'm not sure…I'm not sure at all,' I said.

Even now, sitting in my office, I am not convinced, but Kate is not around to argue with me. If anything, I am less convinced. I didn't notice Kate and her frailty walking to death and all I was concerned about was me, talking about me while she had this statement in her mind, *'Sorry, I am afraid this doesn't look good, you have only so long to live.'* Surely I would have been concerned about her. But was I? Clearly I wasn't, as my behaviour showed. Now I can be concerned… now that it's over. I can be sanctimonious about it. So which one of these people am I? I know one thing, that I finish work, go home, pour a glass of whisky, read a bit, perhaps listen to some music, and go to bed; something on those lines. Perhaps have dinner with Carol. Even the lure of skin, the intrigue of touch is becoming a question mark and here, I am afraid: you question something and that is the beginning of the end for it; things should be left alone, why destroy things by questioning them? …But is this true? You start a project with a question, you design experiments, it might take years to find an answer, a partial answer that leads you to another one and yet another. If you are interested in something though, in Kate's words if you have a passion for it, then you don't question it, you go for it! You act!

Oh! I don't know. These thoughts make me exhausted. Have no answer. You might say age is creeping on you. Yes, you are right but I suppose I still have time, I still have the interest! I know, I know, I am contradicting myself. I cannot accept that I have totally lost the appetite for certain manoeuvres, strategies, actions. But I have to say, I am bored with people's minds. I don't see much excitement there; always mundane things. But again, what about myself? No, I resist, I am not mundane. Never!

36

I sit at the table in the bistro. Hanna comes over. 'Hello Hanna, how is the new school?'

She smiles. She has braces on her teeth. 'Yes I like it.' She looks happier than before. 'And where is your mother?'

'She is at the back, will be here soon. Can I get you something?'

She talks like her mother. I suppose they have an intertwined life, one in which physical attributes and boundaries become hazy, difficult to identify until there is a revolt, a heartbreak, a mother feeling martyred, a daughter's guilt – and that goes with a subsequent freedom – rediscovered. What a beautiful contradiction! I shall remember that!

'Yes Hanna, could I have a whisky please? I'll have dinner after.'

'Of course!'

I sat there by the window with my whisky and watched people passing by. I felt exhausted, I needed a holiday but for no good reason. There was no extra pressure; the work was going fine apart from the usual hitches. But I was tired. What would people do on these occasions? They would go to the pub with their pals talking sports, women and work. Some would go home to their family, play with their son, relax looking at their little daughter talking baby talk, complain to their wife about anything that comes to their mind, try to taste the old naughtiness with her for a brief moment and go to bed. This image made me happy. I was happy that I didn't fit in that picture. I stretched my feet under the table until it hit the foot of the chair on the other side. I was surprised that just a single whisky had relaxed me so much.

Anita came over. She looked preoccupied. She made a friendly gesture. 'Can I talk with you for a few minutes?'

'Yes, of course.' Only one other table was occupied and Hanna was dealing with it.

'I wanted to ask you something,' she sat on the chair next to me, 'there is this man who comes here very often, you might have seen him. He is a calm and quiet sort, doesn't talk. He comes here when there are only few people around, eats his usual, always the same, no change; sits there for a few minutes afterwards and goes. The other day he asked me if I could join him at his table. I did of course, he is a longstanding customer. Then he asked me, suddenly, if I believed in God. I was afraid, you know. He was looking at my face as if I had done something wrong, as if I should repent.'

'What did you say?'

'Well I tried to avoid answering, not because I had no answer, but because I was afraid of him. I began to think that he was ill with some sort of imbalance, a mental disorder or something. People don't start a conversation with someone for the first time asking about their beliefs, do they? He was looking into my eyes. I looked away, trying to avoid his glance. Then I thought, if I answer him, it might calm him down. I said, 'yes, I do.'

'Do you really?'

'Yes of course, don't you?'

She asked me with such innocence.

'Not really.'

'Oh!'

'But are you disappointed?'

'I had guessed, you being a scientist. It is normal isn't it?'

I thought she had a trace of Kate in her. Now she was making assumptions about me without knowing me much!

'So what did the man do when he heard your answer?'

'Nothing! He just said, hum, and left.'

'So that's alright, you shouldn't worry really.'

'No, I am afraid. John is not around any more and I think this man is dangerous.'

'But how do you know he is dangerous?'

'Just a feeling; anyway people don't go around asking people if they believe in God,' she repeated.

'But perhaps some people are sick; they are sick because they don't know how to communicate with each other. I sort of like what the man did!'

'Maybe you are right, but so what if I believed or didn't? What did it have to do with him? It is none of his business.'

'Perhaps he adores you and wants to have a mental picture of you. Perhaps he wants to know your beliefs before trying to get closer to you. Some people have strong beliefs.'

'I suppose you might be right. But what am I to do if he comes back with a knife?'

I laughed, 'bring him a chicken, but make sure it was cooked well!'

She stood up and looked at me with a smile as she was walking away.

On my short walk home I thought about Anita and her fear. Does fear alleviate loneliness? I suppose if you think you are watched, that someone might even hurt you, then in your mind you create scenarios with yourself at the centre of someone's attention. In a funny way, you might be pleased because you are wanted. Why should she want to tell me about her fear? The fear makes her bold enough to talk about herself and bring another person onto the scene. But it was also interesting for me to see that she was alarmed by a person approaching her, out of the blue, questioning her belief in God. Would she be as alarmed if the man had asked her about her views on a question of fashion, or a film? I am sure she wouldn't be so alarmed. So it is obvious what it was that made her edgy. The question of God! But after all, is God that relevant to our lives? I go to the office, I see colleagues, I get into a routine day after day and one day I drop dead. I suppose that is where God becomes important; God and his paradise. I know that most people I know do not subscribe to the idea of paradise or hell but then it seems that there is an internal defence mechanism to the potential danger: what if there was something after life? So when people are asked about God they would move a bit in their seat and say 'I am not sure about God but there must be something.' But why? Why should there be something? A scientist tries to justify it by the laws of physics; lack of vacuum and the like, but all is a premise with a vague guarantee based on rules and regulations and codes of behaviour. In essence, there is no answer. But as a safe measure man has decided that he needs God. Seems quite harmless; although the harm is so obvious.

They say: So what if I believe in Him? Don't ask any more fundamental questions. People tend to get impatient when it comes to this sort of stuff! And if they don't, they start an essay on the benefits of believing in 'God'. They do want something to pray to. So if that's the case, why shouldn't it be a piece of wood or a statue? It would be cheaper, economically much more viable and certainly more tangible. Yet, people are afraid, in degrees, and ask for a secure way out. Security in ambiguity!

37

Carol was getting ready for her move. I still couldn't understand how one could decide like that; leaving a life behind, going to another country she had never been to, in the hope that a man like Fernando would accept her into his life. But then, in reality, she didn't have any life here. She was living with me, sleeping in my bed; she had no job and wasn't trying to find one. So perhaps she knew that she wouldn't lose much. Clearly, I wasn't interested. Perhaps it would make a difference for her had I been more forthcoming. But then she knew how I was and how I lived. Still, the thought of the possibility that she might go all that way just to find out that she had made a mistake, made me nervous. I don't know why. I didn't have any sympathy for her. After all, if someone wishes to ruin her life, it is her business. But why did I even think about it if I didn't have the sympathy? Perhaps I admired her for her courage. Perhaps this was something I lacked; the ability to make serious decisions. It is funny that I thought she was making a serious decision while she couldn't think what life was all about! Now I was attacking her in my mind. The woman had decided for her life, her future; something that I have never done.

But why should I make decisions when I am not in a decision making situation?

Carol was putting her stuff into the red suitcase she'd bought.

It reminded me of my mother. I wondered why. My mother was a totally different character and as for the suitcases, there was no similarity between hers and those of my mother. My mother rarely travelled. The suitcases were there mainly to keep her personal stuff. Nobody would go near them. When I say nobody, there was only me and my father. I am not sure if my father was even aware of such things and if he was, he didn't consider it his business. As for me, I was afraid of getting anywhere near my mother's territory. I would have been happy just to be left alone; and most of the time I was. I was curious to know what was in them. And of course, as is usually the case, you get to know about the contents when the person is dead. This somehow takes away the intrigue but gives it that melancholic feeling from then on for years later. I opened one of the suitcases with a demonstrable reluctance. Perhaps by that time I knew what to expect. There was little emotion involved. I did it as part of my responsibility, to go through the motions. My father had died five years before, and apart from monthly visits, there was little between my mother and me. 'Cup of tea my dear?' she was always elegant in her later years. She made sure her hair, now very thin, was tidy with some sort of thing in it, a small decorative flower or the like.

'No, thanks. I'm OK.'

'I am going to have one myself, are you sure?'

'Yes, thanks.'

She would bring the tea in her best china; old china with small flowers. I remember it from my childhood. I wondered how she managed to keep it intact. She would bring the tea on a silver tray with the biscuits she liked. I brought them for her every time I visited her. I see the same brand in the supermarkets. I wonder how the biscuits would taste now. Would I immediately think of her if I tasted them? This will mean a rush of all sorts of memories, events of a lifetime. Imagine me sitting in a meeting with colleagues, and those biscuits on the table; what would I feel?

'Are these the biscuits your mother loved? Did you buy them from Alberto's? He has the best.'

'I find them a bit on the sweet side.'

'Going out of fashion though, aren't they?'

Then she would sit quietly having her tea, looking at me from time to time with a polite smile as if she was entertaining a guest. How she had changed!

'Everything alright at work dear?'

'Yes thanks, I am fine.'

I suppose things changed between us after I left home. She did try to control my choosing partners, buying the flat, even what I ate, but she soon gave up. I was surprised about that as I expected to have her reign for longer; but it was welcome. We got more detached after my father died. I always wonder how some relationships are linked together. A child dies and the parents separate as if they were waiting for an event, an excuse. I suppose I am very harsh here, but this could be one interpretation. As for the children, they have great hopes for their family, their relatives; but then there is a divorce, a separation. People then start feeling sorry for the kids. Perhaps the kids wished it! Perhaps they were much better off after the parents separated. Do we assume things to follow a linear logic?

Carol, putting stuff in her suitcase, asks me: 'Do you miss me? Will you miss me?'

'What a question, of course!' I say.

'Not enough to come over to visit me though.'

'Not at the moment, no!' and I laugh.

'So, maybe sometime in the future?'

This reminds me of a carpet seller in a bazaar who never despairs, who never accepts that you are not interested in his carpets. *'You want to think about it? Maybe later?'* He brings you tea or sherbet, talks about all sorts of things, shows you, one by one, layer over layer of carpet and when you don't buy, he doesn't bat an eyelid, smiles and says 'maybe later'. I think this is amazing. It is as if selling is a side issue; for them, showing their stuff and having a chat is the main thing. I would like to think that they have a good amount of capital hidden securely somewhere, otherwise how could they continue? I get so self- conscious going to a shop and coming out without buying anything. How do these people live? Have you ever thought about that? Day in day out they go to the shop, sit there waiting until some intrigued tourist enters, then the ritual starts, a cup of tea, perhaps some rose water or a Cola if you prefer. It is hot outside and the fans are in full swing inside. *'Why not have a look sir? You don't have to buy.'* How do they respond when they go home to their family day after day sitting there to eat dinner and the wife asks: 'How was your day? Have you sold anything today?' Maybe they don't even talk about it. Have something to eat and go to bed, get ready for tomorrow to be fresh and active. But worse than that is the case of those who frequent coffee shops and restaurants with a bunch of red roses in their hands. The carpet seller has a big bank account, but what about those people? Have you ever seen couples sitting in a restaurant buy flowers from them? Even if they do, one or two stems...how much is that? How do they survive? I cannot even think about that. I try to look busy or to go to the toilet as they come near. I feel so embarrassed. It is as if I am responsible for their misfortune. I am the guilty party.

Carol asks me if I would go to Rio to see her and I feel embarrassed to say no, it is finished, it had finished when you tried to leave the first time. Why do I feel responsible towards her and not only her, towards Anita too? I even feel vaguely responsible towards Fiona. But why is that? I suppose it goes back to my loneliness. I am essentially a lonely man. The funny thing is that I don't mind it, I even enjoy it. I enjoy it differently at different times. Most of the time it gives me a sense of independence. It is great to go home and not have another creature move around the house. I can't understand people who don't have a family but keep cats and dogs. Just thinking of it...! The smell, the cleaning, the need for taking the miserable dog for a walk, the shopping. Shopping! Shopping for the pet! Have you seen the rows and rows of stuff for pets in the supermarkets? It is bizarre as far as I am concerned. I love this sense of independence that comes with being alone, and being alone has to bring with it loneliness no matter how much people say they are two different things. Of course, when I get tired of loneliness, there is always the good old 'feeling sorry for myself' option. I can accommodate both feelings in my home and be a happy lonely man.

Carol is looking sentimental with her stuff. The last thing I want her to say is, 'would you please take care of this for me?' An ugly stuffed woolly thing. What is it with women, particularly for her type, that they should always have something to cling on to? A large bear in bed, a syndrome carried over from their early teenage years. You might disagree; *'it is the stereotyping from childhood.'* I suppose they want to say, 'although my boyfriend was lousy, I can always have my teddy bear.' What a miserable state of affairs! It is also an invitation. They want to show how sensitive they are. This is an open, morally acceptable invitation to their private lives, a statement about themselves! But Carol doesn't say anything, though she looks sentimental all the same.

'How long do you think you're going to be?' I ask her.

'Why? Do you have a plan for me?'

I don't feel like joking. 'Thought we could go grab something to eat.'

'Yes, sure. This will take me hours. We can go when you are ready,' she says.

'I am now.'

'Let's go then.'

It was a good suggestion considering she was getting flustered. We got out of the flat and there was a nice breeze.

Coming out of the flat, Carol suggested a new restaurant we hadn't been to before. When we arrived it was packed. We waited for 20 minutes in a congested part of the restaurant where the waiters with their plates passed by and the new customers with reservations accumulated. The table wasn't ready when we sat. A hasty waiter came with a small automatic brush to clean the table. Carol's mood had changed. She was now talkative and jolly. 'There is good food there, good meat, the sea,' she said.

'I am sure you will enjoy Brazil.'

'And the group is energetic; they get together after rehearsals in small restaurants with a good atmosphere.'

I wondered if she was telling me this or was trying to reassure herself.

'They organise dinners too, it is a ritual! And each time one volunteers to bring the food. They have lots of fun.'

'I am sure they will have more fun when you go there.'

I don't think she got my remark. The waiter came and I ordered some wine.

'I have already been invited to their party in June.'

'They must be well organised. I thought artists lived chaotically.'

'Oh you must see them.'

'But you haven't seen them yet, how can you encourage me?'

'I am sure you will like them. One in the group is a professor of history.'

'Surely he doesn't dance?'

'No silly, he is the boyfriend of one of the dancers. She is gorgeous; I've seen her pictures in performance. She is on the way up. You will see her on magazine covers. You will, mark my word!'

'And what about Fernando?'

'What about him? He is there. He is trying to continue with his group. It is not easy. It is not like going to a classroom, teach and come out.'

'Well, teaching is not exactly like that,' I said.

The dinner was good. We talked about her future in Brazil, what she would do, how she would spend her time, what galleries she would visit. She had read about all those. She could even give me the names of local birds!

Going back home, we asked for a taxi but there was none available for another 40 minutes so we decided to go out and try our luck. Walking slowly, Carol was leaning on me with her hand wrapped around my arm.

'You must answer my calls, you must return my messages David,' she said.

'What do you think?' I said.

'I don't know about you, sometimes I think I know nothing about you. Sometimes I am afraid of you,' she said.

'Afraid of me? That is a novelty.'

'I am, I am. You can be cruel.'

A taxi came and stopped for us. He was going home and we were on his route. It was lucky.

In the bed, Carol curled next to me and pulled me close to her.

'You must promise,' she said. And the next moment, she was in a deep sleep.

Next morning I woke up early with palpitations. I didn't have breakfast, left the flat quietly not to wake her up. I was in no hurry. I was not thinking of the day-to-day events. No noise in my mind from the office. I just wanted to walk to end my thoughts and my thoughts gave no indication of abating. It was as if I had been ambushed. It happened before I knew it and it affected me where I was vulnerable. Funny feeling, walking in the streets early in the morning, remembering years ago walking slowly in a street with plane trees on either side one early morning. It has been difficult for me to talk about my early youth. It is as if my life started when I was 18 and everything before that is blanked out. But then, from time to time, this image comes back....when I was 14 walking with someone who seemed to have been wiped off my memory. I remember walking in that street next to her with tall plane trees losing their leaves.

'Can I have a picture of you?' I asked her.

She had her hair loose, barely reaching her shoulders; a nice day with a cool breeze. Now I could feel her walking slightly ahead of me. I try, I cannot remember her face but I can remember the smell; the perfume in the breeze. The street is calm and there is no one in sight.

What would I do if I had her picture?

She would be eating with her family now, probably three kids and a high flier husband who goes to church on Sundays and plays golf with colleagues but has time to spend half an hour a week with each of the kids aged 8 to15. Perhaps she has finished eating and is now watching a series on the television. I can imagine that she has become a bit chubby. How would I fit into this picture? Not even as a neighbour who brings you the letters delivered to him by mistake.

I am the first one to admit. Yes, I could not fit into that sort of a picture. Yet memories have come back and forced me to walk by the river bank. Tomorrow I shall feel better.

38

It was early morning when we came out. It was still dark and it was drizzling. Carol had two big suitcases and two small bags plus her handbag. The taxi was waiting. I put her suitcases in the boot. We didn't talk much on the way. It was a combination of early morning feeling, drinks the night before and going to the airport as if you were getting ready to go to war. Did you take everything? What a stupid question! What is everything? You mean passport, purse and ticket? Is that all? You mean toiletries? Would you please remember to say goodbye to such and such for me?

The airport was quite busy for the time of the day and for the middle of the week. I suppose it is always like that. I think, for some reason, our minds shift to useless dialogues, mundane things, ridiculous statistics; our eyes see little, just brush over things, and we hear repetitious announcements without taking them in.

We stood in the queue for a long time, in front of us people with big suitcases, children climbing the trolleys, couples arguing, children screaming. We went to the restaurant. We had plenty of time to have a big breakfast.

'So, here we are,' I said.

'It is all your fault. You know that!'

'Don't start again! We've done this before. You can hardly blame me for your actions.'

'It takes two to tango you know.'

'Do you want to tell me you have cold feet again? This time somebody is waiting for you and you can warm up your feet together with him in a land where tango is appreciated.'

'Last time my mother was so sad that I didn't go to her. She will be disappointed again to find out I didn't go to her to say goodbye again,' she said.

'But what difference does it make for her if you are here or in Rio? She is miles away anyway. In any case, this time she would be more understanding; after all, you are going to join someone a bit more masculine than your mother I suppose!'

'Do you have to make jokes about everything? Is anything serious for you at all? Perhaps you are afraid of real things in your life. Do you know what is wrong with you? You don't have the guts to take responsibility for anything. You are so full of yourself; there is no place for anybody else. I suppose I should be glad you accommodated me for those few days,' she said.

'Yes, you should. I think you should announce an annual thanksgiving from now!'

'You see, you cannot be serious, Oh why do I bother?'

'Exactly, you will be on that plane in an hour and you can wipe away any traces of that irresponsible man from your life. Think about Rio, think about good weather, good energetic friends, dance and parties.'

She stood up, came towards me and hugged me and stayed for a short while. 'Let's go. I want to go now.'

I did not stay to wave as she went through the security. I wouldn't have stayed in any case, even if I were able to see her after that point.

As I was going to catch the metro, the sun had come out. It was a good feeling. I wanted to be in my office. I wanted to have the journey cut to a few minutes. I had the feeling of someone who is hurrying to go to a pleasant meeting with an old friend. The metro was full of tourists and their suitcases, intrigued about new places to visit, looking through their maps, looking at the main tourist attractions on the map, talking in languages I couldn't translate; and I liked it that way. I wanted noise around me but didn't want to participate in anything. I closed my eyes and imagined my flat.

It was quite sunny by the time I entered my office. The campus was unusually quiet. It was the examination period and most students were busy preparing for or sitting exams. I made some coffee, sat at my desk and did some paperwork but I couldn't concentrate on anything. I was quite hyper and couldn't think why. I dialled Fiona's number without having anything to talk about, but there was no answer and I didn't leave any messages. I thought that any minute Richard would come in with some request, but no, nobody came in. I tried to start with one of the many small niggling chores. The phone rang. It was Carol. 'Hello, hello!' A voice in a hurry. I said, 'hello, where are you?'

Where do you think I am?' her voice was angry.

'What happened? I thought you were on the plane by now.'

'Yes, that's what you wish isn't it?'

'What do you mean? I thought you were enjoying your drink in the air.'

'No such luck, the bloody flight got delayed. Aren't you happy to hear my voice again?'

I didn't know what to say. I did not expect her call. I thought briefly of the breeze outside in the airport.

'You see, you cannot even bring yourself to lie. Come out with it. You are delighted that I am going, that I have gone. You wanted to get rid of me and you have done it now, haven't you? Anyway you are lucky, they are calling now.' She put the phone down. I didn't feel like staying in my office any longer. I went to the library and looked through the latest issues of journals. Wrote down details of some papers for my team but didn't want to go to the lab. I read in the library for three hours and was quite happy about it. Coming out of the library, I remembered the first time that I met Kate. I had taken some journals to her to take out. I thought I hadn't seen her before. 'Are you new here?'

'Not really. I've been here for more than six months now.'

'Oh! This shows how often I come to the library,' I said.

She didn't say anything, stamped the journals and gave them to me.

'See you,' I said.

She smiled. I remember her smile but I don't think

it had a particular imprint on me. I think there is something special though, about a smile. I can identify, in my mind, people I have met through their smile. It is like fingerprints. Different in different people but it lingers in your mind and as you think about them, you smile years later, perhaps sitting in a train looking at the countryside as the trees pass you by.

The flat was silent. The bed was unmade as we had left it earlier in the morning dashing out to the airport. I tidied it up and went to the kitchen. I wasn't sure why, I didn't even feel like having a drink. I stood in the kitchen asking myself why I was there. Then I went to the sitting-room, sat on the sofa for ten minutes. I wasn't sure what I was going to do next. The door to the wardrobe was open with some empty hangers. No letter was left on the desk for me. I scratched my face, could hear my nail on my skin. I thought that Carol should be asleep on the plane by now. I felt sleepy too.

I had lived like that before; always alone but with friends, seeing them in their places, in restaurants, in parties and in my place too; but I always kept my flat, its tranquillity to myself. I never craved having someone live with me, like those single men who arrive at the point of no return: 'I have done my singles years, now it's time to have a family, I cannot tolerate Chinese take-away any more ...' For me, it will always remain bliss to be alone. In a sense, I have chosen my partner: it is my flat, it is the place I live in. So I have a dialogue with my place as I enter it. But this time, it was the flat that was lonely, it wasn't me. But I was sure it wasn't because Carol had left. I had a feeling of freedom, one of those feelings that one has after a long period of studying, having finished the exam. The feeling of coming out of the last exam not knowing what to do... a sense of suspension without any obligation.

I sat on the sofa looking at objects in my flat. The table, the salt and pepper in the middle of the table, the coasters, the shelves, the books, and the books on Nietzsche that Kate had given me. I started to think about her, tried to remember her when she gave me the books. What was she wearing? Was it a sunny day? She wasn't there any more to oppose my ideas or agree with them for that matter. The books were sitting on the shelf. I thought of having a look at them. I stood up but then I decided against it. I went to the kitchen, had a glass of water and came back.

It was an hour later when I woke up. I had dozed off on the sofa. I opened my eyes having Kate's diary in my mind. I had forgotten all about it. I took it out from the corner of the drawer. Had I really forgotten it? If so, how come I remembered it so forcefully now that I was alone in my flat? Did I want to protect it by not referring to it while Carol was there? The wet pages were now creased and gave it an older look. Perhaps this was more to Kate's liking. How could I ignore her diary now that I had read some pages? It was as if I was invading my own privacy, and by doing so I was taking away the sanctity of it all. Was I getting religious again? Very appropriate topic for discussion with her! I opened a page arbitrarily:

'Today on my birthday, I received a bonsai tree from a colleague. A very thoughtful present, he is always very meticulous. What you expect from a good librarian. He knows I like plants, he knows that I live in a small flat, so what better than a bonsai? I was so touched by his attention to details. But I am now faced with a difficult question. This bonsai is equivalent to a 50-year-old tree. But it is the size of a short stem. What about the potential of the tree? I keep it inside, water it regularly, have to feed it with a particular chemical and have to learn how to cut the roots and branches. The tree needs open air, rain, cold, sunshine, breeze, wind and I will be depriving it of all these. This is a serious problem for me. What should I do? Keep it? By doing so I will create a dependency on both sides. I am not keen on watering it, taking care of it, learning how to prune, limiting myself to certain activities which I am not interested in. Throw it away maybe in a waste bin? The plant is in flower! Small white flowers, each time I look at it I feel uncomfortable. But can I throw it away? After all, even if I don't think about the plant, this is a gift from someone who has thought about me. Should this act be considered as a binding factor? Definitely not! So I am left with a dilemma. I must discuss this with David. Yet another exciting topic! Now, I am looking at this as a topic for discussion, what about the life of this plant? I am becoming unscrupulous. Can I simply ignore it? I am entangled, in my small flat, with this plant. Each time I come in I feel the heavy air; the atmosphere is full of the dialogue, the presence of the plant. But, after all, am I taking things too seriously? We have all these varieties of dogs with different shapes and sizes, all of them cross bred to become strange creatures, and their owners love them. What about the dogs? I read somewhere that they suffer from all sorts of diseases from weak joints to different kinds of infection. Yet their owners take them to barbers' shops and special clinics! And what about those women with their feet deformed in tight shoes from childhood? All this in the name of beauty! But aren't things beautiful when they express themselves with their full potential? Oh, I don't know. What I know is that I am becoming too choosy about everything. Everything poses a question; everything poses a different meaning as soon as I try to look at it. It is good that I got this off my chest but I will get up tomorrow and my eyes will catch that bonsai and I shall feel heavy in my heart. Then, the question will repeat itself... until?'

I closed the diary and put it on my desk. I wondered how come she had not discussed the bonsai with me. I thought of what I would have told her:

'Oh, come on! This is not a big deal. You just give it to someone who likes bonsai. I am sure there are loads of people out there who would be delighted to receive it. They will take good care of it too.'

She would say: '*Deal*! *Deal*! This is an unfortunate word you use here. This is an emotional thing for me and you say *big deal* as if it is a business transaction.'

'It is a figure of speech.'

'Yes, an unfortunate one.'

'OK, but you do see my point.'

'I do see your point but you don't see mine! You can't see that I have received this as a present from someone and it is really awful to pass it on to someone else.'

'And what's wrong with that?'

'Everything! I am surprised you ask. Can't you see? By giving it away you reject someone's feelings.'

'Is it that hard? We do it all the time. A student comes to me and pleads for a better mark! I always reject their feelings!'

'This is totally different and you know it.'

'In any case, what about your feelings towards the poor plant? You cannot see a plant deprived of its full potential! But the damage is done! Perhaps you can put it back into the soil? Is it possible? The poor plant will probably die like those wild animals people keep confined, and are then released into the wild, probably because the owners got fed-up with them or they can't afford to keep them. Then what happens? The poor animals die as they cannot survive. They have forgotten their origins. In a way it would be better if they killed the poor creatures. But no, they can't face their guilt. They console themselves by releasing them, condemning them to a death they don't witness!'

'Thank you for your added confusion.'

'But what do you say about all those people who are deprived of their potential every day, every minute of every year?'

Kate would remain silent to see what I would refer to. I would have seen in her eyes a glint, a smile on her lips.

'Do you know how many of these thousands of students we get into our universities are doing what they really want to do? It is our duty to bring out the best in them, to help realise their maximum potential, both for their own good and for the survival and betterment of society. Then what do we see? Groups of demoralised, indifferent young people sitting in the lecture rooms with their mobiles on their desk, day-dreaming! No! I am too optimistic here. They do not have a dream left in them. By the time they arrive in the classroom, they are not even a shadow of themselves. They are 'creatures' in search of money to survive to enjoy the banal, to enjoy imitating bloodless heroes where pictures are displayed everywhere for them.'

'You are too animated now. I do agree with you but this doesn't mean that I should not be concerned about my bonsai. You deal with your students, I will do something about my bonsai!'

Am I thinking too much about people around me and what they think?

Kate has gone now. It seems several years have passed. Yet, the dialogues with her continue in my mind. Would it matter if she still existed in the flesh? It would. We would get closer. There would be more emphasis on the physical side of our relationship, and then? Maybe the dialogues would die! We would wait for each other, go home together, talk about our colleagues, think about reducing costs by her moving in with me and then getting a bigger flat. We would continue going to the cinema, some alternative theatre, a poetry reading once in a while and all the time the dialogue would become thinner and thinner. And then the quarrels would start, criticisms, accusations, bitter nitpickings, and of course the making up, apologising over glasses of wine, making love as a sign of reconciliation while with each movement a wound would move in us, waiting to bleed again on a different occasion. Then it would be the case of buying a dog, taking it for long walks, the blissful moments when you walk the dog, alone with the poor creature that would seek other dogs but would be bound by the leash. But you would be relaxing, sitting on a bench looking at the tulips in bloom. Maybe a child would be a good idea? Yes, that would be the time to transfer the faded hopes, to create other ones. After all, why should you be the only one to suffer?

But there is no Kate. Now, there is none of it. She has gone, the dialogue has stayed. Carol? She seems irrelevant. I do remember the scent of her skin though. Why should I assign some values to people, to appreciate them? My life is made up of these moments, slipping away while I try to weigh them. And all the time the moments creep out, taking away with them all their being, just like Kate and Carol. So I didn't form that bond with any of them, I always wanted to go to my flat alone, with only brief lapses when other people breathed in my space. Am I unique in this? I see couples with their children walking, going to cheap restaurants that their kids love and they can afford. Is this what they have craved for? 'Come here, don't go far. Stay with your mum! Be careful! Good boy!' And what happens to those intimate moments? The moments of youthful desire, plans for the future! What plans? These are so predictable!

Who said, for the first time, that man is a social animal? I dispute that. Man needs other members of his species for his basic needs. That's all. Anything more than that is subject to a big question mark. When I look, things that cause dependency are those that are not essential for our being but, over the years, we are led to believe are necessary. Perhaps man would be much more creative than what he is now, if only he could get away from his fears.

I went to bed. Carol's smell was still in the flat. From the shelf I took a book that I had wanted to read for a long time. I read some 20 pages before I fell asleep. As I was going to sleep, I thought of the bonsai.

39

In the office, I started to do some clearing up of the papers collected over the last semester. I had some time to spend on it. I left the door to my office open and had done a couple of paper stacks when Ana came in.

'Could I see you?' she said.

'Yes, of course. How is your research going?'

'Fine.' She paused.

'Do you want to discuss it?'

'Just wanted to say that I have thought about leaving.'

'Oh, yes, and?'

'I have decided to go.'

Suddenly, I had no time for her. Maybe it was because I didn't expect her to arrive at that decision and that was why I was angry. I tried not to show it much.

'Well, that's your decision. I am sure you have thought about it carefully.'

In a matter of seconds I had lost all my interest in her. Now I wanted her out of my office, the lab and my sight but she wouldn't go. It was as if she expected me to insist on her staying. But that would never happen now.

'I wish you all the best,' I said.

'Do you think I have made the right choice?'

'I don't know Ana, I gave you my opinion last time.'
I knew I was cold but I didn't feel like parenting her.
She said, 'thank you,' and left quietly.

I kept on clearing the stuff. I thought I couldn't understand modern women. They insist so much on going to work, being equal to men. They make sure to imitate men's behaviour in pubs and discothèques; they consider that their appetite for sex and sexual behaviour is identical to men's. But then they are so subservient on other occasions. They are prepared to change direction with just a whisper of a promise.

I was getting tired of filing and dealing with documents I had no particular files for. The phone rang.

'Is that the idle man?' It was Fiona on the phone. The call changed my mood. She had a special way of... how should I say... a way of always expressing herself with double meaning.

'You could have been in trouble my friend! How did you know it was me? You could have dialled a wrong number,' I said

'I didn't! But after all, all men are idle!'

'Now you are placing us in an elevated position.'

'Only trying to please you,' she said.

'I am pleased! You don't need to try! Where are you? You are, I suppose, in that cold and dreary town.'

'Could any place be dreary if I am in it?'

'It depends on what mood you are in. You can be quite off-putting you know.'

'Oh, thanks very much! I suppose this is in retaliation for what I said? I don't budge. You men are all idle!'

'If you say so! I am what you say as long as you

phone, it's OK! Anyway, what's the occasion? You don't phone me just to say I am idle! I would prefer it if you looked into my eyes and said it!'

'I will! Just wondered if you are going to that lousy meeting Juan suggested?'

'Yes I am. I told you.'

'But you haven't confirmed it with them!'

'I thought everything was taken care of by your beloved colleague.'

'Don't be stupid! Are you new in this?'

'Clearly someone is! It would have helped if he had sent me the necessary information. I have been waiting for the stuff.'

'I will remind him of that. So we can have dinner together somewhere warm for a change.'

'Great! I have to start writing the talk.'

'I am sure you will do that at the last minute.'

'Wouldn't you?'

'No! I wouldn't have accepted the talk. It is too general for my liking.'

She would evade or argue whenever she felt like it.

'But you would write at the last minute an article very specific to your work anyway.' I said.

'Well, perhaps.'

'Don't argue with me on this. I know how you work. Do you have to argue about everything? I suppose you practise it with your daughter all the time, poor Jane,' I said.

'Now you feel sorry for Jane! She is a young devil. She was a mischievous child and now, she does her best to get on my nerves. Don't remind me of her.'

'This is a mother-daughter syndrome! I thought you, as an educated mother, were much wiser.'

'Now don't be patronising!'

'Would I see you before the meeting?'

'Only if you bother to travel to the dreary place.'

'Have things to do at present.'

'So do I.'

'Then we shall be in touch anyway! Don't get serious! It will be nice to meet and forget about all the things around us.'

'The things around us? Certainly,' she laughed.

40

On my return home, I stopped at the bistro for an early supper. Hanna came over, happy to see me.

'Where is your mother then?'

'In bed! She has a cold.'

'It must be difficult for you running this place alone.'

'Yes but Mark is helping us now.'

'Who is Mark?'

'He is a new one. My mother employed him just three days ago.' She went red.

'Does he know how to deal with the customers?'

'Yes. He was working in another restaurant until last week. He is a part-timer. He is a student of arts.'

'How did she find him?'

'I don't know. I think my mum put an ad in the local paper.'

'How old is he?'

'I am not sure, may be twenty.'

'Is he handsome?'

She blushed again. 'I don't know.'

I had a Whisky and a borsch. I didn't feel like having a big meal. Then I asked for a coffee. As Hanna brought the coffee, I noticed she was wearing small earrings.

'Nice earrings.'

'Thanks. I had my ears pierced last week. My mum finally agreed.'

'Do you like to have some tattoos as well?'

'My mum would kill me,' she smiled, 'I am not sure... I sort of like it but then I don't know how it would look on me, most girls in the school have done it though.'

'Are they happy with their tattoos?'

'Oh, yes.'

I sat there with the coffee cup in my hand. I just wanted to sit there and do nothing, just look at the customers coming in, ordering their food, talking, arguing, complimenting each other, leaving, eagerly looking forward to their future hours, leaving sleepy, bored, hoping to get to bed, wishing they could sleep there and then. Was I in the right profession? I was asking myself this question again. I did enjoy my work, the research, the teaching, the travel, meeting people, so what was the problem? I suppose I am very intense. I must relax a bit more. Why should I always check my actions, the best line of action? Who is there to question me? Even if I had a family to go to, did I have to be so regimented? Can't I be all these things? Hanna came over. 'Do you need anything else?'

'Thanks Hanna, you take good care of me. Could I have a large brandy please?'

'So not another whisky?'

'Not this time.'

'Of course.'

I held the brandy glass between the palms of my

hands, the cold glass was warming up. The bistro was now full. Mark was serving at the far corner. A couple were sitting at a table close to me. The man was complimenting the woman and she was laughing. What is so important in a compliment? Does it matter if it is a lie? You want to create a good atmosphere. The people around you enjoy your comments, so is there something wrong with it if it is a lie? I was, again, thinking about right and wrong. Perhaps I was becoming a lonely old nagging man. Perhaps none of these questions would matter if I had someone to go to, a family to take care of rather than a single body ending up in a flat with just enough time to go to bed. I was finishing the brandy. I wondered why I asked for the brandy. I don't even like it. But it was nice that night. Hanna came over with the bill.

'Tell your mother I was asking about her.'

'She knows it already. I told her. She is still in bed.'

'I am sure she will be OK soon.'

I came out and went for a walk. When I arrived at the flat, it was after midnight.

41

The large hall was completely packed. I wondered how it would feel after three hours with so many students breathing with anxiety in a hall with closed windows, late May. The sun was out; inside Michael was announcing the exam regulations. I was watching as students fidgeted in their seats waiting for the start. I wondered why the students subjected themselves to this. It was so nice outside. They could sit on the lawn, have a pleasant chat, read a book they liked, enjoy each other's company. Instead they were in this hall answering questions that most of them couldn't find any use for or any relevance to their lives. Michael mentioned plagiarism in his announcement. They must, by all means avoid doing it otherwise they could be expelled from the course. But what made them plagiarise, go through the trouble of preparing the material to use in the exam? Maybe they have a secret desire to beat the system and this was a way to enjoy a double success. This shows how uninterested they are in what they do. Maybe they lack the self confidence for it but, for whatever reason, they lack interest. Cheating has a clear message saying they want out, out of the situation. So perhaps we do them a favour by throwing them out. In an hour's time they would have to put down their pens. 'All remain seated until all manuscripts are accounted for!' Now what did they think about? Now that they had passed a hurdle? Going out to the park? The sun was still out. But somehow I doubt if they were interested in the park.

We walked back to the campus central office, large envelopes of exam papers in our hands. Michael was in a happy mood. I thought he liked this sort of thing: instructing the students, talking about rules and regulations, having a pint or two with 'mates', talking about old colleagues who died some years ago, with anecdotes about them.

As we were walking he said, 'all went well,' as if something unpleasant should have happened.

'Yes, but what could have gone wrong?'

He laughed. He was more than happy to explain:

'Many things. Somebody could have fainted. It happened two days ago. We had to call paramedics. There could be a fire drill! That is a real pain. What do you do? You know nothing is wrong but then you have to evacuate. Then it is case of whether they should go back to continue with the exam or not; what if there is plagiarism? You must write a report for the Subject Board. Do I need to say more? I prefer it the way it happened today. Nothing happened.'

'Will you be going anywhere this summer?' I asked him.

'No. I have lots of work to do at home. I am doing

up the old kitchen. Keeping the wife happy. What about you?'

'I have an invitation to talk and haven't thought about what I would do after that. Don't mind getting away for a couple of weeks.'

I looked at his shoes. They were brown, old but polished. I thought, each morning he spends some minutes shining his shoes. He had gained weight over the years I had known him. I suppose I had too. It is always easier to observe others. We walked without talking, passed through the park, green and colourful. I went to my lab when we returned to the campus.

42

'Does your mother feel better?'

Hanna was talking with Mark outside the bistro.

'Yes, thank you.'

'Is she in?'

'Yes.' As she was going to show me where she was, Anita came out of the kitchen. She had lost some weight, and that in only a few days. I remembered a schoolgirl when I was at the school. Sometimes I saw her getting on the bus in the mornings. Each time I saw her, she looked different; sometimes podgy and other times she looked emaciated. The bus was always full. I used to lean against the window in a corner. She would come in with her books and notes wrapped in this leather belt. It was fashionable, but I could never have them. My mother thought they weren't clean and tidy enough. I suppose I have inherited this obsession with tidiness, and only this I hope! But why did I remember her? Just a change in weight?

Anita came out too. 'Such a lovely day,' she said.

'It is always a good feeling when you recover from an illness,' I said.

'Yes, but we haven't had such good weather for some

time. Days like this, I wonder why I ever thought of leaving this country.'

'I suppose you want more of things like this.'

'Yes, but so what? It is impossible.'

'It must have been difficult for you to be ill now, with all the customers, and John gone.'

'Not really. We can manage well, Hanna and I, and I have got this boy, you have met him, Mark.'

'Yes.'

'Why don't you come in? Come in, have a coffee. This is on the house!'

'Oh, thanks very much. I would like that.'

We sat at a table by the window. Hanna came over, 'what can I get you?' looking at us playfully.

'Coffee and cake,' said Anita.

'I am still not sure if I want to continue with this place.'

'But what has happened? What has changed? OK, John has gone but you liked it here not because of John, didn't you?'

'I am not sure. Yes, I like the place but is that enough for me to stay? I think of Hanna. What would she do if we go back? It would be a big change, particularly for her. And now, there is Mark.'

'Oh, yes. How did that happen?'

'Well I needed someone to help here and he found me from my advert at the grocer's. He is a nice boy.'

'Nice enough to make Hanna unhappy if you decided to go back?'

'Anything can make her unhappy!'

We had the coffee together and the cake was fresh. I

looked at Anita. The wrinkles under her eyes were deeper than before. Her skin looked tired and pale. She had put on some make-up that made her face oily. I patted her hands as they were sitting idle on the table. They were cold. 'All will be OK. This is a period of adjusting.'

'To what?'

I thought perhaps I had put too much emphasis on John in my mind. It seemed as if Anita had moved on already. I stood up. 'Better be going, too many things to do! Come over to my place sometime, whenever you like. Bring Hanna and Mark too; that is if you prefer. In any case, see you around.'

'Yes, I'll do that,' she smiled.

'Thanks for the coffee; the cake was delicious.'

There was a cold breeze. I turned into my street. I wasn't sure what to do next.

I walked past my flat and continued on. I hadn't gone through that street before. The street got narrow towards the end and through a curve continued on. It was darker there, there were fewer street lights and I could see the lights coming out of the windows of terraced houses with the same shape and design. But it seemed that the developers were only interested in the houses at the start of the street where it joined the wider road. I continued on. It was a long street. I could hear the odd words through the low windows as I passed by, the TVs, the music from time to time, mainly from the first floor rooms. I could picture the interiors in my mind: sitting-rooms downstairs with a TV in them. The husband watching TV, the wife coming and going between the kitchen and the sitting-room where a table was placed at one end, wallpaper with large flowers, perhaps small flowers if the occupants were younger couples, narrow staircase leading to the first floor where a teenager was listening to music. Walls full of motor-bike pictures, young celebrity pinups and odd things hanging from the ceiling. Smell of feet and other smells mixing with the smell of cooking. I suddenly felt I couldn't continue. I stopped and turned back. I started going back fast, nearly running to get to my flat. Once inside, I poured myself a large whisky and dropped onto the sofa. Was I becoming increasingly detached? I took the newspaper and flicked through the headlines. There was nothing that could attract me. The so-called political titles, editorials, banal arguments. Now the broadsheets covered crime reports on their cover page. They talk about disillusionment of people with politics; yet loads, millions go out to the funerals of celebrities. The whole structure is robust, working successfully. What are they afraid of? I put the newspaper aside. Why did I get it everyday? A habit! It is like buying milk. They go together; one is incomplete without the other. Did you add milk to your morning coffee? Did you glance through the newspaper while drinking your coffee?

I had a sip of the whisky and stretched my legs. I thought of Anita. She was considering leaving her restaurant, something she has acquired by luck. Now she was not sure because of her daughter. Is it because of her daughter though? Hanna is growing fast, exciting times ahead with Mark around. I could imagine Anita having a dialogue with herself.

'It was your fault, you employed him. Did you really need someone else?'

'Of course I did. How could I run the damn place on my own with Hanna going to school?'

'Was he the only one?

'He was the right one.'

'So, what's your problem?'

'I don't know.'

Perhaps her problem was not Hanna, was not going or staying. She was lonely, that's all. But was she craving for one of those terraced homes I was passing by? She was a good cook! And what about the other aspects of married life? The emotions, the arguments about the curtains, the garden over-growing, the rubbish man not taking the cut branches. And what about the touch of skin after you had that argument? Now you were in bed. You paused. You waited for the other. Perhaps you took the initiative. You approached it logically. So what if he was a real pig, irresponsible. This was the bed and it was supposed to witness your bodies coming together, in harmony, for a few minutes, OK?' She would turn around facing him. 'How was your day darling?' as if nothing had happened, as if there was no shouting half an hour ago. And fifteen minutes later, her eyes closed, she would think of her skirt when she was 18, the one that Piotr touched. It was an early evening and the whole group of them had gone out to this restaurant. Lying on the bed she would feel her body warming up. She would feel her skin and eventually she would go to sleep. Outside there would be the sound of the siren of a passing ambulance and then silence.

I woke up and didn't know what time it was. It was dark and raindrops were hitting hard at the window. I looked at my watch, it was after 2 in the morning. I listened to the rain. I remembered that I liked the rain in my childhood. I liked to walk under it, splash in the puddles, run on the edge of pavements parallel to the cars passing so that I would be splashed. I made sure they splashed me!

I listened to the rain for a while. I opened my eyes. I could see the drops under the street light that shone on the window. I remembered my earlier thoughts. Anita would be asleep now in the room above the bistro. My mind wouldn't go further. I turned in the bed. I couldn't go to sleep. I always slept well. You go to bed, you sleep! It was a matter of seconds not minutes for me to go to sleep. And if, for some reason, I couldn't sleep, it would be a catastrophe. 'I couldn't sleep last night!'

'Why?'

'I don't know.'

'What were you thinking about?'

'Nothing, nothing serious. It was raining; I woke up and couldn't go back to sleep.'

'But surely you had something on your mind. Otherwise why not go to sleep?'

'No. I just woke up and couldn't sleep after that.'

Then the thoughts came. How many friends did I have? None! And what about family?

'What? Family? Yes there are odd relatives here and there. I don't see them really.'

'Don't you want to have a family?'

'Don't be silly. Me? I am OK the way I am thank you very much.'

'So what do you do when you get old and frail?'

'I die!'

'Yes, but before that?'

'So you are telling me that I should have a family, change my desirable life-style now because sometime in the future I might need someone to take care of me? Is this a reason for having a family? And anyway, since when should one lose the happiness of the moment for the ambiguous security of the future?'

'But we all do that.'

'Not me!'

'So perhaps that's why you can't go to sleep!'

'And what about all those with their families snoring away? Are they all in a deep sleep now?'

Then I thought about couples sleeping next to each other. One curled away, one clinging to the other; some facing away, some breathing into each other's face. I thought of all those tiny microbes getting exchanged, pushed from one into the other. One sleeping under the background snoring noise of the other. Waking up as the partner is going to relieve himself. One getting up earlier than the other in the morning going to work.

'Bye.'

'Bye.'

Why don't they have their own bed? Have the space, the fresh air, the freedom?

'You can't understand love!'

'And what is that?'

'Just all those things to share!'

'Yes! I am in love with all the commuters in the

morning then! I share the same bus with them. Sometimes I breathe their breath directly as we are pushing against each other, standing tight so as not to fall on the other with the sharp brakes.'

I listened again. The rain was subsiding. I had a feeling of weakness. Then I went to sleep.

43

The sun is shining through the window into my office. The exams are finished, the Boards are held, the results are announced. The corridor is silent. I am sitting in the middle of piles of useless paper trying to get rid of them. Each year I decide to organise my room. Each year I throw away less than a quarter of what I should throw away. Each year I am left with more rubbish. Piles of filed marked exam scripts are sitting in the corner waiting for me to return them to the central office; exam paper documents have filled my top drawer. Double copies of projects are waiting for their owners to come and collect them but no student has ever come. I think about writing my talk but I cannot work in this chaos. I look at the boxes of papers sitting next to each other on the shelves for years. I need the courage to throw them out. Did I say courage? Why courage? I haven't referred to most of them for years. I don't even know what is inside most of them. Yet, I cannot throw them away. I have to look at them one by one to decide. And looking into a box, it takes time.

'Oh, I need that paper. I am going to read the other one, this is really important and I have to keep it, what about this one? I *had forgotten about it but it is so useful. I should remember to keep it somewhere not to forget!'*

So the box goes back to where it was. And it is funny that I am famous for having the tidiest office. Yes, I have all the good intentions to get rid of stuff but I end up keeping them. Is the same true about friends? I mean people I know? Why is it that I cannot say no to some of these people around me?

There was a knock at the door.

'Come in.'

Richard came in. He looked happy.

'So, you are now prepared for society!' I said.

'I have been ready for this for a long time.'

'So what is your plan?'

'I have a job waiting for me already.'

'Oh, that's great. So you've been writing lots of job applications.'

'Not really. It was a good interview for my first application.'

'Congratulations. You are a lucky man.'

'I don't know. I wanted more money but they said it will come in six months.'

'That is not bad at all; given the situation in the job market at the moment.'

'Well perhaps. I just came to say thank you and goodbye!'

'I didn't do anything. I wish you well.'

'And as for the calculator.'

'Oh, forget about it. I have forgotten already.'

'Thank you.'

He left with a grin on his face. I wasn't sure why he came. I wasn't interested in him and he knew it. Perhaps he came to show me what a successful person he was. It was a sign of *I won, you lost!* I thought of many better students who don't have a job but he had got it with his first attempt. I wondered if his family had pulled some strings for him. Perhaps, but he came across so confident that anyone could easily get fooled by his disposition. I suppose once they find how useless he is, they will get rid of him. But by that time it might be too late to admit their bad judgement. And how does this help society? We create these cases. Each student is a case. I suppose he will be a bully, an arrogant businessman with a pin-striped suit and a house in the country. A commuter who reads his newspaper on the way to work every day to look more informed when he arrives at his office. I suppose he will be one of those young employees who are greeted by the smiling, inviting faces of their female colleagues. He would sleep with most of the hopefuls and go up the ladder and then, nobody would be able to approach him; he would be an isolated man with great influence! Yes, he is the student who went from one office to another to improve his marks through complaints and appeals. He did everything but studying for a better mark. Now, he is ready to start in a job in this posh block in a green square. He would promise things to everyone and part deliver those which he thought would be useful for his future. He would look into your eyes and confidently say, 'trust me, it will go through, it will be OK.' But can you trust a man who is prepared to do anything to get what he wants? Perhaps yes. He shows how committed he is to his own success.

44

'I've had enough.' Ian was sitting at his usual table in
the pub. He was rolling his large beer glass between his
hands.

'What happened?'

'Nothing in particular; I think it is about time to
leave this dump.'

'Something has happened, surely.'

'You'll be surprised to know that nothing new has
happened. Do you expect anything new to happen in
this place? There are lots of forms for you to fill in.
That's all. Even now that I am leaving.'

'What? You are leaving?'

'I told you I've had enough.'

'Why the sudden decision?'

'They've offered me one of those offers you can't
refuse! This is the honourable way to bow out. Everyone
thinks you have been so valued, even you yourself get
convinced. In reality, a couple of hundred here and there
to motivate your moving out. Basically, this is a scheme
for those who want to leave but need a positive jolt. I
just drank to the jolt! Handed in my letter and had my
drink!'

'Oh, well. There is only so much that one can do now.'

'Sure.'

'What can I get you?'

'The same would do, the usual, thanks.'

I got the drinks. As I came back, he was searching his pocket.

'Had an address, I think I've lost it... It was for this stamp shop, one of those traditional shops with old style service.'

'There you are, you have already started your next assignment.'

'Yes. The wife would love to hear this!'

'You haven't told her you're about to leave the job?'

'Not really. She should have guessed. She will know tonight alright. She doesn't need to know. Anyway, we will have more time together. That's what she wanted, so no reason to be dissatisfied.'

I finished my drink. As I was coming out, he was still sitting at his table with another full glass. I thought, it will be a long night for him. I wasn't sure if there would be a goodbye 'do' for him. It was summer and most people had gone away.

The flat was warm. The sun had shone all day while I was away at work. I opened the kitchen window, there was a nice breeze. I poured a whisky, sat on the sofa and opened the book I had taken from Kate's flat, *The life and times of an Andes flower*. It was as good as new but I knew she had read it, meticulously, and perhaps had taken notes too. I just turned the pages without knowing why. I didn't have the slightest interest in that topic. I actually wasn't sure what it was all about; and yet, I was flicking through without reading it. Then, there was a thin piece of paper towards the last pages. It was her handwriting. I had a sip and took out the paper. The thin paper sat in my hand. I could see the lines of my hand through it. It was somehow difficult for me to start reading it but I did:

'I am in the library. I have just come back from the coffee shop. I had the most exciting moment with David. He speaks with such passion about everything. It doesn't matter what, it is bliss. I am fortunate to have these moments. It is so good to have the library silent at this moment. It is as if everything has gone silent for me, to let me feel my moments with him. I know I am going, I know that all the tests and appointments and repeat tests will end up in disappointment. This is something I do not want to share with him. I want to see him as energetic as he is. I want to keep this memory for myself. It is not that I am afraid of his response. I think that is irrelevant. I think my illness is irrelevant to our relationship. So, I will have no contact with him after a certain point. I just hope to linger the moments, the dialogues. I don't care what happens later, the bed, the smell of the hospital, the bored nurses, the enthusiastic ones, the humanitarian ones. The flower by the window, the plastic white curtain between the beds, the tube-light, the subdued noises. Those will take their own time and I shall deal with them when they come. Those are specifically made for me and no-one else, not even for David. The days are even more unpredictable now but the moments are dearer. And for now, the silence is going, I see students coming in so I'd better go with the flow. There are books to be stamped. I shall ask David if he thinks we are stamped?'

I put the paper carefully back in the book and returned the book to the bedside table. I walked around the flat, went to the kitchen, to the sitting-room and back to the kitchen. Then took my jacket and went out. I rushed into the bistro. It was busy and both Anita and Hanna were serving customers. Mark came over.

'How are you?' he said. He had a grin on his face.

'Fine. Could I have a whisky please and a soup a bit later?'

'Sure.'

I wanted him to go. I don't know why I couldn't stand him at that moment. He hadn't done anything wrong. I expected Anita to serve me, to have a chat, to get involved with her daily mental chores. But now I had to do with Mark. He came with the whisky.

'So are you happy working here?' I said.

'Yes, it gives me the money for my studies.'

I suddenly felt that I could not create a dialogue with him.

'Good,' and I started with my drink. He left.

I looked around. Anita was talking and laughing with a customer. Hanna was taking the used plates back to the kitchen. I thought how well she had learnt to serve. Mark came out of the kitchen and passed her by. I thought that there was no reason why I should dislike this boy. But I did. I think it is true that our feelings are shaped by faces. I couldn't put it into words but there was something in his face and posture that I didn't like. But then, so what? It was no business of mine. Perhaps it was because after John, I now considered myself as the man in their life! Strange! I wasn't involved with them but it was an interesting feeling. Perhaps in a strange way I felt responsible for Hanna's future and I didn't like Mark playing a central role in it. He came with the soup. He was very friendly. He put the soup and the bread on the table. He had even heated the bread. But I immediately thought it was Anita who told him to do it. I did feel guilty for my thoughts about him though. A warm piece of bread, a newly acquired guilt!

45

It was an early flight but I looked forward to it. I arrived much earlier too. Somehow everything happened smoothly; there was no queue for the check-in, there was no waiting for the security check and there was no customer at the exchange desk. So I found myself sitting at the tall table in the coffee shop with a coffee in my hand and a pastry on the table. I was still sleepy but I liked the feeling, coming out of sleep gradually just to go to sleep again on the plane. I finished my coffee and started to walk idly in the hall. Most of the shops were closed. I stood outside the pen shop. A young girl with unkempt hair was opening the shop. First the metal security door was opened, then the door after that. I wondered, who needs so much security for a shop in the airport? Who would rob the shop in the airport? She went in and I started looking at the pens in the window. She put her bag by the counter. Took a mirror and started with the lipstick, then combed her hair as if she was in the bathroom. I went in. She looked at me and said 'Could I help you sir?'

'No, just looking at the moment, thank you.'

'Just let me know if you are interested in anything.'

I thought, if Fiona had said that, we would have a great time conversing around it. That made me feel good. I was going to see her at the conference. Five days of talks and dinners and being idly busy! I needed a break. The girl's mobile rang.

'Hiya.'

I hated that word. I do not know why but I still do. I shiver whenever someone says it. There are certain words that I feel so much hatred for. It is strange. You can hate someone, hate being in a particular situation, you can hate the weather. But a word? I suppose it's the way people use the words, particularly the young. One of words is 'like.' You can hear them saying it all the time, 'I told him like...' The girl was talking loudly. 'Why not? It will be fun, it's just a lunch... OK, whatever...' Yet another one of those words. The call was surprisingly short I thought. She came over. 'Do you want to see our latest designs? They are kept here.'

'Yes actually, I don't mind.'

There were four famous brands. Then, suddenly I remembered that I wanted to buy Kate a pen and I never did. I had seen the pen I wanted, I had thought she would like it but I never got down to buying it. I felt the colour of the airport lights, and the noise of the people was increasing. A group of Japanese tourists came in. I left the shop. I walked toward the gate. It was still early but I walked to the gate which was unusually announced early. In the waiting lounge, there was only one other man sitting and working on his computer. I sat in a corner and took a pocket book out. I was a tourist!

46

I went to the conference registration desk in the afternoon. It was the Sunday before the opening of the conference and some of the participants were already registering. I got the big blue plastic conference bag with the logo and name of the conference in white. Two thick volumes of proceedings, bits and pieces of loose advertising material and my name tag were put in the bag which was already losing its shape under the weight. There was the smell of new plastic in the hall. I sat at a long bench looking at the list of participants when I saw Fiona approaching. She had a pink shirt on with a large light brown handbag. 'Looking tanned already! Do you come here every year?' she said jokingly.

'Only if I have people complimenting me like this! How was your flight?'

'OK. Just arrived, left the bag in the hotel and came over; hoped to see you here.'

'Keep on talking, I like what you say.'

'That's enough for today's dosage! Now I must register.'

'Get your act together. Drinks are warming up!'

We walked by the sea. The promenade was calm in

the mid-afternoon. Across the road, the coffee shops and cafés were open but it was too early for the evening customers and the lunch customers had already gone.

'It is good to be here, eventually,' she said, 'I was getting a bit rotten in my good old town.'

'Have you considered changing to another university, another city altogether?'

'How? I must think of Jane. She is still studying there.'

'Nothing is impossible. You say it as if it is a big deal.'

'It is easy for you to say. You don't have any kids.'

So, it was the old argument, I have heard it hundred times: 'You cannot understand,' 'you don't understand the situation, you are a lucky man.' And while they say this, they look at me as an unfulfilled man while they are jealous of my situation. The only one who could understand me was Kate. Of course with Fiona's state of mind, there was no point in telling her not to feel a martyr. The discussion was fit for me and Kate only.

The conference bags were a nuisance. Fiona had her own bag too.

'I can see you aren't enjoying your parcel! Perhaps we'd better go back to the hotel.' I said.

'I thought you would never ask! By the way, are you ready for your talk or do you need to spend some time with your slides? It is tomorrow morning, isn't it?'

'Yes, it is tomorrow morning but I don't need to practise.'

'Good. I was beginning to feel sorry for the old man with his slides! So you don't need help.'

'Who said that? Even the most competent man is in need of help from a friend!'

'Don't worry; I am a charitable woman when necessary. I am in search of the ultimate charitable act though.'

I looked at her thin pink shirt with open buttons. 'I can see the potential for charity to begin at home!'

We went straight to the bar of the hotel. Coming from outside, the bar was dark and there was no one there. I rang for the barman. We had a couple of liqueurs and went up.

Fiona's room was somehow larger than mine, though marginally. She hadn't unpacked. Her small suitcase was sitting in the corner. She put the bags down. I went to the large windows overlooking the crowded street eight floors down. I looked at the serpentine of jammed cars. As I turned around she was standing in the middle of the room smiling. Her lips were sweet with remains of the liqueur and her body still had the warmth of the sun outside.

47

I had my talk just before coffee time and now I was in the long queue for coffee. Fiona was talking with a group ahead of me. This young boy came towards me. 'Your talk was interesting,' he said.

I laughed: 'Oh, that was the idea. I tried!'

'I was wondering though. You don't have much respect for scientists do you?'

'You think so?'

'You are a scientist but you don't have much respect for us. I am still baffled how you could compare us to the pastors of the church.'

'I thought I explained why. In any case, being compared to a priest is not that much of a sign of disrespect.'

'For me it is!'

'Sorry to have offended you. I suppose there are priests out there who will be offended if they hear they have been compared to scientists.'

'That's their problem. But it all depends on how you look at it.'

'Exactly! I thought it was quite simple. We, as scientists, have assigned ourselves goals, rights and wrongs, and routes to achieve the goals. As far as I am concerned, this is a religious approach to science,' I said.

'But this is for scientific enquiry.'

'Not at all, this kills the spirit of investigation. A real scientist goes for an unending search. He doesn't know what he might achieve. He guesses some things and hopes for others but cannot prejudge the results. And results are part of the search. But nowadays whenever you want to submit a proposal, you have to take into account the goal, the deliverables of the project, the milestones of the investigation, its so-called timeliness, together with a long list of dos and don'ts. Our churches are our campuses.'

'But science has created so much for humanity and religion has taken so much away. Don't you agree?'

'Sure. But religion has given a lot too. Look at the great architecture of churches and cathedrals; look at the paintings, sculptures, the list is very long indeed.'

'All wars are because of religion.'

'And science is innocent? I can't believe that you don't see the damage, destruction and death all around us being inflicted on us under the good offices of science!'

I saw Fiona coming over smiling:

'That was a good one. You like to be controversial don't you?'

'Apparently I've been successful in that. This gentleman thinks I've been unfair to the scientists.'

'You mean the boring lot? It is a favour to humanity to be unfair to them.'

'I suppose you are a scientist yourself,' the boy said.

'They say I am. They have even given me classes to teach, but I deny it all. This is a terrible accusation taking me for a scientist. But I have lived with it. I think there has been a serious mistake somewhere in the registry,' Fiona said laughing.

The boy was now in a hurry to get his coffee and go.

Fiona said, 'what was that? Do you have to collect boring people around you?'

'Not always. Sometimes impostors infiltrate as scientists!'

We took our coffees and went towards a long narrow shelf near a tall glass window.

Malcolm came over. He had a couple of fingers in his colourful light waistcoat which had curved over his belly.

'Interesting one! I am sure you have found yourself at least a couple of pen pals. You will receive some hate mail.'

'Fame at last! But if they disagree, then they should have some respect for their own ideas and not send hate mail just because they are threatened by the opinions of the others.'

'Scientists are opinionated.'

'That's exactly what I was trying to convey. They don't consider seriously other opinions on a common matter. The moment they see something remotely different from their ideas, they start opposing it, they start finding faults in it with the ultimate aim of rubbishing it.'

'And that is fun!' Fiona said.

The bell rang and people started going back to the

lecture hall. Malcolm started talking to someone.

'I don't think I will go to this one. Do you?' I asked Fiona.

'Do you want someone to bother you as you walk in the park enjoying the sun?' said Fiona.

'Oh, that is the only wish I have now.'

We walked slowly to the park along a narrow road with lawn on both sides.

I said: 'I saw a bird once in a cage. The door to the cage was open. I waited for a long time. The bird flew away in short flights, but eventually it went back into the cage. Our scientists are like that I thought.'

'Don't be too severe. You have finished your talk. Now, it is the time for fun.'

She took my hand. Her hand was cold.

'Do you always have cold hands?'

'Most of the time when I try to avoid serious talks! I have been serious enough in my life. Now, at forty-five, I want to avoid being serious. It is not worth my while. It makes more sense not to spend time on serious matters as much as one can.'

The flowers in the garden were already wilting under the midday sun.

'Some chilled beer is a necessity.' I said.

'Necessity?' she said, 'I would say vital!'

We didn't need to go far. We went into a small café on our way. Three local men were standing at the counter drinking tea.

Fiona sat across the small table. Thin lips, sharp eyes with corners up, small bony face, dark hair short of reaching her shoulders. I was waiting for her to say something. But we were both silent and remained silent until the waiter brought the beer.

'Do you drink much?' she asked.

'It depends on what you consider to be much.'

'Oh, come on, you make an issue of everything. This is a simple, innocent question.'

'Yes.'

'What do you mean yes?'

I started laughing. 'Well I answered your simple question. I drink a lot.'

'You don't look it.'

'I will drink even more if this conversation continues the way it does.'

'Boy, we are touchy today.'

'No I am not. Just trying to answer your question honestly and you don't want to hear it.'

'This is not a court. I promise you I won't hold it against you now.'

I wasn't sure if she was getting into that joking mood.

'I love it if you do, here and now!'

She ignored me. I thought it was a cheap try. I was glad that the beer was starting to have some effect.

'I thought you talked very well but it was irrelevant to the audience,' she said.

'So it was a failure.'

'Yes, but for them. You really expect a lot from your audience. These people are there to be praised, to hear what an important role they play in the well-being of society as scientists. They don't want to be compared to rigid priests. And you told them exactly that.'

'So I should have said something I didn't believe in?'

'No.'

'So I shouldn't have come?'

'Then you would have lost the pleasure of my company,' she laughed.

I asked for more drinks.

'Listen, you can give a talk without trying to be controversial.'

'But I didn't try.'

'Yes, I should know. It is in your blood.'

I took her hand. 'We should enjoy this moment.'

'We are, well, I am.'

We finished the second large beer and walked to the hotel. I liked the sharp contrast of the room with the outside. It was cool inside. Fiona drew the double curtains. There was a sense of losing yourself in the darkness. There was a sharp but small ray of light through the middle of the curtains. I could see her skin, the small body, the pause.

'Are you philosophising?' She was jolly now.

I did not answer. I was thinking of how it would have been if Kate was there. What she would have thought about my talk, what would we have discussed over the beer, and how would it be now.

I stretched my hand to reach her skin. She came over. We were silent throughout.

48

The gala dinner was crowded. It was as if all participants had registered for it. Round tables, white table-cloths, bottles of wine, one white and one red already on the tables; we all arrived in coaches. The dinner was held in this old palace, now in the hands of the ministry of Science and Higher Education for special occasions. Before the dinner, we had drinks and aperitifs in the gardens. We queued in two long rows. Fiona was talking to a couple of people behind us.

'It's lovely here isn't it?'

'Yes, marvellous. We couldn't ask for better. We've come a long way and this is really like a holiday for us.'

They started introducing themselves. I wasn't really interested. I made myself busy with the person in front, a serious man in his 30s, with a small dark blue tie and a navy suit.

'So what is your interest in this conference?'

'I am an archaeologist but am interested in human behaviour now and its effects on society in comparison to old societies, more specifically those of 1000 to 1500 years ago.'

'Any particular society?'

'Not really. I look at them in general terms actually, it is interesting to look at the geographical issues as well but that is an exhausted topic.'

'And how have you found this conference so far?'

'It's OK. Hoped to hear something new, something more challenging.' He didn't ask me about my interest and I left it at that. I was interested in his research area but not in him. One of those things, you get a very exciting collaborative project and you end up with people you find difficult to work with, just because you don't like their tie, or their way of moving their hands, or something like that, let alone their attitude, their views.

'Glass of champagne please.' I was at the long table. I took my glass and moved towards the gravelled area, away from the crowd. Fiona came over.

'It's OK isn't it?'

'Yes. Good choice of venue.'

'It is 18th century. I am sure they used to enjoy themselves in this garden, more than once...a routine matter!' she said.

'You think so?'

'Yes, I can feel it!'

'I am glad you are here. It would've been pretty dull.'

'Pleasure is all mine! It is a holiday for me, being away from that structure. Just for a short break. Talking about that, I'd better see what Jane is doing, sorry.'

She walked a little further towards the trees and dialled her mobile. There was a nice breeze with the smell of a flower I couldn't place. It was dark now. A girl came over with a tray of bits and pieces. I took one.

'Do you like it working here?' I asked her.

'I do not work.' She spoke with an attractive accent.

'So, what do you do? Are you a lady of leisure?'

'Pardon?'

'What do you do then?'

'I study.'

'Oh, what do you study?'

'Tourism.'

'That should be fun.'

'It's OK.'

'You don't seem to like it.'

'I like, my boyfriend not,' She smiled.

'Why not?'

'Want me work only.'

'Ah, what does he do then?'

'He study too.'

'Tourism?'

'No. Computers.'

Someone came over to take savouries. I smiled and moved back. Fiona was having a heated conversation on the phone. She put the phone in her bag and came over.

'Oh, I don't know why I bother.'

'What happened?'

'She tells me she wants to go and stay with her boyfriend for a couple of days.'

'So?'

'What do you mean? She is too young for that.'

'Is it OK if her boyfriend goes to her?'

'Surely not.'

'But it is irrelevant whatever you say. They are seeing each other, both at your place and at his place, you can be sure of that.'

'Thank you for the support.'

'You don't need to let it get to you. They are young and this is part of their activity, part of their life.'

'Some life! Easy for you to say. She is my daughter you know! I am responsible for her.'

'Yes, but you are not her prison warder!'

'What a thing to say.'

'She just asked you because she wants to have your support. You can help her that way rather than behaving like an opponent.'

'You mean thoughtless.'

I laughed, 'would I say that?'

'You have already said it.'

'So what? I want you to be happy at this moment and happy with your daughter. She does what she wants to do. It's just that you make her feel guilty, she does it anyway, she feels more guilty, eventually she can't cope with the secrecy so she does something for you to find out by yourself, there will be an almighty fight, after which she convinces herself that you cannot be part of her life and you convince yourself that she is no good and why bother. There will be a hurt-ridden truce.'

Another girl came with a tray of drinks. Fiona took one. My glass was still full. The guests started to move to the dining hall. I took her hand. It was cold and bony. The hall was bright with the chandelier lights.

We sat at a table with a chubby bald man, perhaps in his 60s, on the other side of Fiona. A young tiny man with a pale face was at my other side. He was talking with the girl next to him.

I introduced myself and Fiona to the chubby man.

His face was red and he spoke in short sentences. 'Absolutely gorgeous weather,' he said.

'Yes, and a good conference too,' I said.

He laughed. 'I wouldn't go that far my boy.'

I wasn't sure if I was happy to be called his boy.

'I take it as a compliment. Although I am young at heart, you are right there!'

'Anyone in this conference is young compared with me but their ideas are older than me. Nothing new.'

'Did you go to my talk?'

'I don't think so. What was it about?'

Fiona said, 'David thinks scientists today are not much different from priests... only their books...their terminologies are different and their place of work.'

'Good one. They have different outfits too,' he laughed, 'so he thinks highly of them!'

'It depends on your views on religion,' I said.

'Not really, the fact that you think scientists are anything, you have placed them highly. What does this bunch of good-for-nothings do?' He laughed again and had a sip of the wine. He had no grudge, he was just merry.

'You don't consider us as scientists of course,' Fiona said, intrigued.

'Well, I am testing! If you take offence at what I said, then you are a scientist, you have proved to be a scientist, and so I was right and I don't care if you were upset! If you see my point and find it amusing, then we have a rapport and we will enjoy the dinner together!'

I said, 'how about having the dinner and seeing what we are by the end of it?'

'Challenge eh? Fine by me. What about the young lady?'

'Anything for a good laugh!' Fiona said.

'We are on then,' he said, and poured us some white wine.

'So how long have you two been married?'

Fiona laughed. 'I don't marry people who don't have faith in the church!'

'And I don't marry those who don't believe in science,' I said.

'So I am safe either way here, I knew I had positioned myself in the right place! But what do you do if you are not busy being married?' he said.

'Are you married?' Fiona asked.

'Do I look it?'

Fiona was getting fidgety, 'I don't know, you could be.'

'I am the proud father of two girls and grandfather of one.'

'So what have you taught your daughters?'

'Not to take anything seriously!'

'Can anything proper happen in this demoralised world of ours if one was not serious?' I asked.

'Well of course.'

'I doubt it. One needs to have ambitions, aims, plans, and be serious about them to have a firm grip on things, otherwise things slip out of your hands.' I liked to be controversial.

'All that happens is that one gets over-occupied, obsessed and exhausted. And as for an achievement, the enjoyment of it is short-lived.'

'So you belong in the wily-nily land,' Fiona said.

'I don't belong anywhere, even this argument, for me, is not something to stick to! But I think that if one does things that one enjoys, then the aim is secondary, only part of the process. If you achieve your goals, fine, if not, at least you have enjoyed the process.'

'So you are a calculating man. This is a business deal: 'how to behave to be happy.' You do have rules and regulations for this and you are defeated by your own principle.'

'You think so? So be it. He drank a last gulp of the white wine and started on the red. 'May I?'

'Yes please,' said Fiona.'

'Just a little for me,' I said.

'You are very cautious my friend! Are you a tightrope walker? You can't walk there if you are cautious.'

'I haven't fallen so far.'

'Perhaps you fall without feeling it, without being aware of it. This is sad: missing the opportunity to walk tall and missing the opportunity to see things, a double calamity!'

His face seemed to be in flames and the way he talked I wasn't sure if he was serious or was acting. He spoke as if he was in a Shakespearean drama.

Fiona said, 'I think we are taking ourselves too seriously! I drink to the jokers of this world.'

'You will be drowned,' he said.

We drank too much that night. In the coach back to the hotel most guests were asleep. Fiona had her head on my chest and I thought how the night would be if Kate was there at the dinner table.

The driver drove slowly. He had put on calm music, with low volume mixing with the sound of the engine and occasional snores. I was sitting by the window looking out. It was a country road passing through the woods. I remembered the only time that we went to the countryside, a day out, with Kate. We stopped at a pub for lunch. It was crowded but only with the locals. They wanted to know where we were from, how we liked their village, what we did. I said I was a salesman working for a computer company. It was an impulse of the moment. I felt playful. Kate went along with it. She said she was my second wife and we had married six months ago but because I was so busy, we hadn't gone for our honeymoon yet. They insisted on buying drinks for us and invited us to their village for our honeymoon. In their jolly mood, I had some words of advice from them. An old man in a country sport jacket said, 'you should know better! One lives only once. You must enjoy your life, every minute of it.'

The other said, 'life is tough these days … we had it easy.'

We came out of the pub laughing. 'I feel bad,' I said 'pretending those things.'

'Well I don't,' said Kate.

'But those were lies.'

'Fantasies, we are permitted to have our fantasies. What are we without them?'

'But that wasn't a fantasy. I have no interest in being a salesman, let alone a computer salesman.'

'OK, stories then. We like to tell stories, like a child. I don't believe that children lie. They just live a life which is much fuller than ours; a life parallel to their daily activities: *'Have you brushed your teeth? Did you take all your notebooks? No, not that shirt! I told you not to!'* And we crush them for living their life. We crush them because we have lost a big chunk of our life growing old, shedding stories, avoiding complexity. Do you know, through this we become boring. And if we aren't, we get into this sea of guilt as you have dived into it: *'Have I lied? Did I really do a bad thing?'* You went back to your childhood for few minutes, that's all.'

Fiona moved her head closer to my face. There was a smell of perfume and wine. The coach was getting into the town.

'Did you have a good nap?' I asked.

She mumbled something and slept again. I tried to imagine her at her place coming back home, her daughter still out. Lonely nights, no family, no friends. Similar to me? I thought not. She liked her head next to something comforting. I liked my head single on the pillow. But where did that assumption of mine come from? How did I reach the conclusion that she had no family or friends? Was it the way she had her head on my chest?

The coach stopped. Sleepy passengers walked out slowly.

My room had been cleaned and I went straight to bed. Throughout the night I dreamt of the driver of the coach losing control and the car going off the road and down into a deep ditch. I got up to drink water and go to the toilet. When my alarm went, I was already awake, very sleepy but awake. It was the last day of the conference and I wanted to hear the closing session; I also wanted to look at the posters. At the breakfast table I saw Fiona with swollen eyes. 'Did you sleep well?' she asked.

'Not really, and you?'

'Must be joking. I want to go to bed right now!' And she did, after breakfast.

49

There were around 200 posters. Some so lousy I wondered why they bothered. I suppose they had to show some effort in making a presentation in order to be funded by their departments. I saw a puny East European girl standing by her poster. I went closer. Her face was small and very pale.

'Is this your work?'

'Yes. She gave me a one page A4, a very small reproduction of the poster. There were pictures of cows in a farm and smoke coming out from a city flat. The background showed people walking from the farm into the town. I thought she had chosen a clever picture.

'What do you study?'

'Social behaviour of Man.'

'It sounds a bit generic but do you know? This is my personal hobby.'

'I hope you like the poster then, I mean the text.'

I spent some time reading the poster. Somehow I always find it difficult to read a poster thoroughly but I read her poster. There was nothing exciting about it but it was a good, solid piece of work.

'How much is left for you to finish your studies?'

'Another year.'

'Do you have any plans?'

'Yes, I'd like to travel, perhaps for six months.'

'Good idea, should be fun. I suppose it can be in line with your work too.'

'Thank you.'

I looked at some other posters and went to the garden. I sat on a bench. An old man with the conference bag in his hand was walking slowly to the conference room. I remembered Ian after he had handed in his early retirement letter. He started using a rucksack and somehow his behaviour changed during the last days. He behaved like a young researcher; he wore sports shoes and didn't mind stretching his legs onto a low table; a sense of freedom I suppose. I thought, I still have time. But time to do what? Should I always do something? Can't I just enjoy the sunshine sitting on a bench? I suddenly felt that if Fiona didn't come soon, I would have nothing to do. I don't know any of the conference participants apart from Malcolm and Juan. But Juan was an organiser and I hadn't had a chance to see him properly. And as for the man we met at our table the night before... I didn't feel like seeing him again. I thought I was becoming bitter, but I wasn't sure why. It was bliss to find myself outside a bar near the venue. I went in. There was a middle-aged man at the bar drinking beer. The barman was drying a glass. 'Could I have a beer?' I said.

'Of course.' The barman was a young local boy.

I started with a big gulp.

The man by the bar said, 'come a long way?'

'Now everywhere is near, don't you agree?'

He sounded as if he was thinking about a serious problem in life.

'I suppose so!'

'And you?'

'You can say that, a different continent!'

'It must be exciting.'

'I wouldn't put it that way. Calming! Calming it is. I am on my honey moon if you want to know.'

'Oh, congratulations. So, you must be excited. Where is the lucky bride?'

'There is none.' He inhaled deeply. The cigarette in his hand was hand wrapped.

'I thought you said you were on your honeymoon.'

'Yes, and I have enjoyed it thoroughly so far.'

He was clearly enjoying having me confused. I wasn't particularly interested but it was a good pastime.

'Do you like mysteries?' I asked.

'Not really. I suppose that's why I am not successful in my marriages.'

'Marriages?'

'Yes. All three of them so far and some more to come I suppose.'

'But you are on your honeymoon. Which number is this one?'

'This is after the third.'

'I don't need to be a mathematician to say this; it is your fourth marriage then?'

'No, it is not.'

'Well, you have managed to confuse me.'

'You see, we live in the century of definitions, expectations, stereotyping.'

I agreed but remained silent.

'I am on my honeymoon. I love every moment of it; after that horrible divorce I needed a honeymoon to be alone by myself regaining my sanity, tranquillity, independence. Honeymoon means a month of sweetness. This is what I have now!'

'So, if it is so good, why do you predict another marriage?'

'Because I can't help it. I grant you, that is my weakness. Give me another month and my resolve dilutes in a sea of women passing by. It's the way they move, the way they just manage their body, and I am gone!'

'But why should you marry?'

'Permanence! I love security, permanence.'

'But you just told me you like your freedom, independence.'

'Yes, I know. It is a dichotomy. I vacillate! But there you are. This is mythological! You know the myth of Sisyphus? There you are.'

'But he suffered all the time, he was condemned.'

'This is what Homer wanted us to believe! Nothing in life is exclusive, pure! You cannot have only joy or only pain. There is always some impurity. That's what makes it so fascinating.'

'But we try to achieve pure joy! You just said you desire permanence! But by what you say now, there can't be permanence.'

'Well of course. I did say I am searching for permanence but it doesn't mean it can be achieved!'

I had a couple of sips from my beer. We drank in

silence. Then he said, 'I know I am full of contradictions. I am alive! But enough of me, what brings you here?'

'I am at this conference here.'

'I noticed there is a bit of movement around!'

'It's about science and society.'

'Well you should be happy; I solved all the problems for you. We are not social animals… or maybe we are!'

A group of young university students came in with their poster holders. They were laughing loudly. I thought it was getting too crowded.

'Have a good rest on your honeymoon!'

'Yes I know! I will need my strength for the next stage!'

We laughed. He was gazing at his beer glass when I left.

50

We flew back on the same flight. I knew that Fiona's mind was now totally occupied by her daughter and the backlog of work.

'So, when will I see you again my religious scientist?' she asked.

'Not for a while I suppose.' I wasn't sure when. My mind was focused on nothing special. I was thinking of how to get back to my flat. I was happy that I had no plants waiting for me by the kitchen window dying of not having had water for several days.

'You are silent. Is it my effect on you or has the conference has left you spell- bound?' Her eyes were shining.

'Do you have any doubts?' I said.

'Always… a small but persistent doubt is good for you. Didn't you know that?' she said.

I thought she would have made a good journalist. She could make up anything she wished.

'And you like it?'

'Every minute of it.'

'But you don't have doubts when it comes to me.'

'I don't discriminate!'

51

My flat was dusty. I had been away for only five days and it looked like a person ignored, left alone. I opened the window in the kitchen, opened my suitcase, put stuff out to be taken to the cleaners, hung the rest; put the items back where they belonged. I started dusting. I didn't want to think. I wanted to avoid thinking as if it was a dangerous thing to do. I was both angry and sad but couldn't find out why. I had had a good trip, a good time, my talk was received well, and so I had no obvious reason to be dissatisfied. Yet I was angry. I cleaned the flat, took a shower and went out. I couldn't face myself alone in the flat on a summer's evening, having nothing to do. I didn't know what to do but it was obvious that I would end up at the bistro. Anita came over smiling but looked tired. 'Hello David, you are already back?'

'Just an hour ago, practically.'

'How was it? Did you have a good conference?'

'Yes, everything was good. How's everything here?'

'Well, Mark left.'

'Oh, why? What happened?'

'I really don't know. Just phoned one day saying he

cannot come any more. You know, I was very disappointed.'

'Well of course, and what about Hanna? Did she know he was leaving?'

'Of course not, not at all. And he didn't say goodbye to her at all. She is very hurt.'

'I can't blame her. Of course one gets hurt. How is she now?'

'She is in the kitchen, you will see her.'

'Well, that's too bad. Maybe I will talk to her.'

'Yes, please do. It will help.'

'Anyway, enough of us. What would you like?'

'Just a whisky please.'

She left and did not return for a long time. Other customers were busy eating or chatting away. Nobody seemed to bother. Then she came with the glass of whisky on a plate.

'She does not want to come out. She says she is not in the mood to talk.'

'I understand that. It's quite natural.'

'Yes but for how long?'

'That we wouldn't know. But you must give her a breather.'

'I don't know, let's see. I don't have any choice anyway.'

I had the whisky quickly. I thought about Ian when I saw him last in the bar. What was he doing now? Perhaps sitting at a round table at home with a couple of stamp albums looking at them methodically, row by row. And what about his wife with her interest in dance clubs? Perhaps he has enrolled her in dance classes. What does he do with the rest of his time?

Anita came over. 'Another one?'

'No thanks. Better be going. Keep in touch, let me know about Hanna.'

'I will.' Her face was pale.

I came out. Now it was dark. I went to the other side of the road and started walking. I had no plans.

I walked for a good couple of kilometres without thinking. There was just a sentence in my mind repeating itself. 'I am a fake.' It just started repeating itself when Anita told me that Hanna did not want to come out to talk. Now, after some fresh air, I started at myself again. Why did I stick to that sentence? I was a man, alone, without any commitments. I kept myself to myself. So where did this 'being fake' come from? OK, I did not make an effort to see Hanna. I did not insist that I must see her. So what? Does it mean that I was not honest in showing my sympathy? Perhaps it was better for her to come to terms with the facts of life. Why should I have protected her, consoling her for a very day-to-day event? How many other people had gone through a similar thing on the same day? These sorts of events were not exclusive to her! But this reasoning did not convince me. I had the sentence ringing in my head. I sympathised with Anita and yet I didn't do anything. And what about Carol? All I did was to take her to the airport a couple of times! I was actually happy that she was leaving, going out of my life. Letting her stay in my flat before her leaving was no big deal. But was there a meaning for me in all that? I could have done much more for her and I didn't. But why should I have done anything anyway?

I was walking faster and it had started drizzling. I thought that I was even a fake with students. I wasn't bothered about Ana's future. I wasn't bothered about her leaving her PhD programme. I showed concern but in reality my concern was for my research, my group's progress. But what is wrong with that? I was entitled to have my research group and be concerned about its integrity. What about Richard? He was just an undergraduate student. Did I expect initiative from him? a miracle? By not giving him the exam timetable, did I want to teach him a lesson? Give a lesson to a miserably dependent student! Great. I was convinced that I was right too. I am sure I was, but how relevant was my act? I was just doing it to prove my authority. I was a fake.

I was getting wet under the drizzle but I just couldn't let go. I had just come back from the conference. How much attention did I give to Fiona? I say I like her but all the time I was dismissive. I had a good relationship with one aspect of her only. So what? She was happy with that. Yes, she was, but was I? I stopped. I turned around. The drizzle had turned to rain now. But I wasn't finished with my thoughts yet. What were my feelings about Kate? Had I ever faced them? Yes of course we had good conversations, enjoyed each other's presence. But this doesn't say much. Why didn't I go to the hospital all those days when she was dying? Had I ever thought about her after her death? OK, I didn't promise her anything. I didn't promise anyone anything but does it make me an honest man? Shouldn't I be happy with myself rather than seeking to find approval from others? She was always content anyway. So was Fiona. But what about me?

Maybe I am too harsh on myself. I criticise myself all the time. I am under constant criticism. Does it matter how I am? How I behave? I am alone, I do my job, I have some friends, perhaps better call them acquaintances; I do my bit for them from time to time. So who cares whether I do this because I like my image, because I want to leave a good name! Hah! If I died in my room, who would know? The first one to know is a top floor neighbour going down one day, smelling something unusual. So, do I care for my name? What happened to Kate? At least there was a memorial for her! Then, the ambulance will come and if Anita is standing outside the bistro, she might think, what is the ambulance doing in front of my flat. She might put two and two together and ask about me. But then, she might also think that I have gone on a trip for my work.

I slowed down. The thoughts had stopped as if I had accepted that I, or whatever was left of me, was now lying down in that ambulance. There was no sentence in me any longer, there was no repetition. And the rain had stopped. I walked down slowly to my flat. On the way someone said hello, I didn't stop. He called me by my name. I looked back. It was a young boy. I suppose, one of my students. I arrived at the flat, put the key in the lock but did not have the drive to turn it. I stood there for a couple of minutes. Then I turned the key. I went straight to the sofa and dropped my body on it. Sitting there, I looked around. I saw Kate's book, I remembered the thin paper inside it. I tried to remember it. I had a good feeling thinking about it but I couldn't remember the contents. Then I closed my eyes.

52

I woke up with a knock at the door. At first I wasn't sure where I was. Then I thought I was in the hotel at the conference. It was a good feeling but then I realised I had slept on the sofa. I was at home. I was very slow. There was another knock at the door. I couldn't understand what was going on, what time of the night or the day it was. I turned the light on. It was 3 a.m. I went to the door. It was Anita with a pale face. 'Please help me.'

'What's the matter?'

She was incomprehensible; uttering some words I couldn't make out. 'Listen, just calm down. Tell me what the matter is.'

'It's Hanna. I have called the ambulance.'

We rushed to her flat above the bistro. The street was completely quiet, only the sound of our footsteps. As we arrived at the door next to the bistro, the ambulance arrived too. The paramedics went in carrying gadgets and I followed them up the steps. Then we went into Hanna's room on the right of a small landing. Hanna's face was pale, her eyes closed and one hand had fallen out of the bed; no movement. Anita was standing next to her motionless, looking at the bed. I wasn't sure what to do. I tried to get close to her but at the same time the paramedics moved and transferred Hanna to the stretcher; they acted fast but calmly.

The hospital was empty. I was surprised. I always had the idea that the emergency wards were crowded with people rushing around. It was nothing like that. Paramedics talked to a nurse and the stretcher disappeared into a corridor at the back of a long waiting room. Anita followed them but came out soon. 'They didn't let me stay.'

'It will be OK,' I said.

'No. How can it be OK? It is already bad.'

'But things have changed since our time. They can do a lot nowadays.' I noticed I had used the plural, which I shouldn't have.

'Nothing has changed; people still die even of simple diseases, don't they?'

I couldn't say anything. I felt incompetent.

'But tell me what happened?'

She did not answer. She walked to the door and back. The rows of metal chairs in the waiting-room were empty. There was a vending machine at one end.

'Look, we have to wait. So, it's better if we sit and talk. At least our minds will be busy talking,' I said.

She sat on a chair in the front row. I bought two coffees from the machine.

'Perhaps it is better to go out?'

She didn't say anything, just stood up. We went out of the waiting room. The door opened onto a car park. It was starting to lighten up. There was a cool breeze.

'Listen, she will be fine. You will see. In a couple of hours you will be laughing. Once things have gone back to normal, perhaps we can take her to a play, keep her busy with things to do.'

'She has lots of things to do. I just wonder why she did this. Was he that important to her? It was my fault. I should have known better. But I was just hoping... Just hoping.'

She did not have the coffee. She left it on the concrete edge and said:

'Let's go in.'

We went in but there was no sign of the nurse. Then a car drove close with a fast braking noise. Two men came in, a third one with blood coming out of his face somewhere near his eyes. A nurse appeared as if from nowhere. At the same time another car stopped and a man and a woman with a child came in. A boy of six or seven was in his father's arms. He was pale and I could see he was suffering. Anita was walking in short steps in the waiting-room. I took her hand and we sat on the metal chairs.

'Is Poland like this? I mean how do they deal with emergency cases in hospitals?' I tried to divert her attention.

She looked at me as if I was stupid.

'I have heard the medical service there is excellent,' I said.

'If we were there, this wouldn't have happened to us to need to go to the hospital,' she said.

'But listen, you can't make hypothetical cases. You are here and this thing has happened.'

Then I noticed that I had been harsh. My last night's thoughts came back to me. I stopped talking. I thought a long time had passed. The sun was out now, just.

Then she said, 'thank you for coming with me. Please go now.'

'Not at all. I will stay to organise taking her back. I suppose by lunch time everything will be OK.'

She started walking about again. Now I was getting worried. I knew that they had to do their job, but we were left in the dark for three hours. I went to the nurse who was moving fast. 'Sorry, could you tell me what's the situation with the young girl, Hanna, we brought her in some while ago?'

I couldn't be sure if she knew anything about this. I thought she must know; only three patients had come in during the night and she had been here all the time. But she looked very distant.

'I will check and let you know,' she said, and disappeared behind the door.

'It is impossible, what a shame,' said Anita.

We waited for another two hours. It was nearly the mid-day when a thin young doctor came out. He had faint blue eyes with thin golden-framed spectacles. He asked for Anita.

'We have done all we could and hope that the danger is past,' he said

Anita interrupted him. 'What do you mean you hope? How is she?'

The doctor could not be interrupted. He had a monotonous but considerate voice.

'Your daughter was in a very critical state. All I can

say at the moment is that we have removed the poison from her body. She is detoxified. It has had some effects obviously. We will observe her closely. She is in a coma and we hope that she will come out soon. We have transferred her to the ward.'

Anita was silent. She was suddenly calm. 'Can I see her?'

'Yes of course, but you won't be able to communicate with her. You will need to be patient. We hope she will come round soon.'

'What are the chances?' I asked.

'It is difficult to say. We will do all we can; such a nice young girl. We will do further tests.'

We had to wait some more and Anita filled in some forms. Then we took the lift to the fourth floor. We passed through a silent corridor with the smell of antiseptic and overnight human smells. A nurse took us to her. Hanna was lying on a bed with tubes hanging from her and a curtain on the other side of the bed, a small cubicle. You could hear noises from other curtained spaces around it. Hanna's eyes were closed and her face was like a mask. Anita stood there but did not go close, did not touch her, just stood there. I took her hands. They were very cold.

'It is good that the danger has passed,' I said.

She ignored me. As we were going down she said again:

'What a shame.'

Then we came out. It was noon. I kept my eye open for a restaurant. Walking for ten minutes in silence, we arrived at a small local Italian.

'You must eat something,' I said, 'you have been under pressure. You must take care of yourself to face this.'

'I am not hungry.'

'But you must eat.'

I practically pushed her in. It was a silent lunch. I did try to talk about the conference but it was very irrelevant. Even at the right time it would have been irrelevant. Then she started talking. She talked about her husband.

'He was a handsome man. We had a couple of good years together, but he couldn't be a husband, a father. So I took Hanna and came here. I wanted to be as far away from him as I could. I wanted both of us to be as far away as possible. Now I don't know where he is to tell him about her.'

'Do you have to?'

'He is her father. He might want to know.'

'Has he been in touch?'

'No, but it doesn't mean...'

'It means something. You have spent all your time with Hanna and he hasn't contacted you even once, this should mean something.'

'I don't know. What a shame. I don't think...she will come back.'

She said this with a melancholic voice. Still there were no tears.

'You mustn't let despair get to you. Give it a bit of time, it is only few hours. There is a very good chance...'

'Of what? She is damaged. Even if she comes back, she is damaged for life; and for what? For someone we didn't even know properly. I should have managed the shop myself.'

'You must think positively. OK, she is ill now, but you have a shop to run. You must be positive.'

Then, for the first time, I thought that she saw the gravity of the situation. She turned her face away. Hanna wasn't there to help and she didn't have anyone else.

'I don't think I can do it.'

'Yes you can. I will help you find someone. Just be positive. Don't let it get to you.'

We came out after a short lunch but I didn't want to leave her alone. I suggested to her she might come to my place to rest and have some tea.

'No thanks. I need to be alone. I need to take a shower.'

'Then I will come and see you later.'

'Yes.'

We said goodbye and I waited for her to get into her flat above the bistro, then I went home. The sun was shining in. There was little noise from the outside. I fell on the sofa and slept.

53

It was the start of the term and the corridors were full of new and continuing students moving about to see their tutors, organise their studies, enrol, register and get inducted into the system. It was cloudy outside as I went into my office. On my way to the university I stopped at Anita's place. There were a couple of customers eating their breakfast. She was cleaning the tables and the chairs, and moving the things around. She had her hair tied back and was working fast and seriously.

'Hello. I can see that you are getting ready for the rush,' I said.

'Yes. I am going to the hospital later. Burt is coming soon.'

Together we had found Burt, a middle-aged, out-of-work man to help her. He was calm and had a good composure. The sort of person you trust.

'Any news on Hanna?'

'No. As time goes by they say it becomes less likely she will come back.'

'Yes but there are exceptions.'

'Yes I know.' She was dismissive and abrupt.

'I am off now, shall see you later.'

'Yes.' She had a distant smile.

On my way to the office, I thought to call Elizabeth. I hadn't seen her since Kate's remembrance day. When I called her, she seemed very busy but was accommodating.

'Oh, hi David, how was your holiday?'

'OK I suppose. How was yours?'

'Fine, needed it. We went to the Canary Islands, loved it. What can I do for you? It is mayhem here,' she said.

'I know, I am sorry to bother you at this time. It is just that I wondered if you could give me Kate's address, you know some details to find her, I mean the cemetery?'

There was a pause. 'Yes, actually I have it. I'll get all the details and let you know as soon as I can get a respite from the invasion.'

'Thanks Elizabeth.'

'Not at all.'

Since I had come back from the conference I had wanted to do this but hadn't done it. Kate had gone away. Why would I need to go there? I didn't see her in her last days in skin and flesh, now I wanted to go to the cemetery for what? To console myself? To portray a considerate, compassionate picture of myself? And to whom? To her? It would have been a great case for discussion with her I am sure, this topic of compassion. Now, how would I relate with a decomposed body? *'Listen, I am here to discuss with you my dilemma. Yes, my dilemma and it is about you. I don't think that anyone has occupied my mind so much. Why? I don't know! You tell me. I just want to share with you my thoughts that's all but this time, no coffee. Just dry thoughts.'*

54

I worked well that day. It was early in the term but it felt like end of the term. I felt the weight of a semester's work. I hadn't managed to organise the paperwork that needed to be filed in yet. When I came out of the office, it was getting dark and it had started to drizzle. I went to the bar near the office and had a large whisky, then I walked for some distance before I got on the bus. The bistro was crowded. I went in and sat at a table in the corner. It seemed that this table with one chair was my usual place now. It was part of my flat! Burt came over. 'Nice to see you David! A drink first?'

'Yes, why not. Just a whisky please Burt.'

'Of course.' And he went to the kitchen.

Then I saw Anita. She had the same dress she had worn in the morning. Her face was pale. She came over, took a chair from the table near me and sat across the table.

'How was she?'

'The same.'

There was silence. 'They say you never know. I never knew anything anyway! I shouldn't have brought that boy in. I thought I was doing the right thing. But who knows? When I left Piotr and Poland, I thought I was doing the right thing. What was right about any of the things I have done? And now, I don't know what to do. I wanted to sell this place and go back, then that boy appeared and I thought maybe I should stay. Now there is no reason to stay but I can't leave with Hanna in this state can I?'

'You shouldn't think like that. If you do then everything is wrong, then whatever we do is wrong, one can find mistakes in every action.'

'But look at me. What is my choice?'

'Do you really want to leave? To sell this place? You are doing so well and people love you here.'

'I don't know. I don't know anything any more. I didn't know anything anyway.'

'It is a difficult time for you but you shouldn't whip yourself like this,' I said.

'What if this situation continues like it is? What if she doesn't come back?'

'This we don't know and precisely for that we shouldn't speculate. The only effect of your thinking would be to pull us down. You must look at things positively.'

'I don't know David. I don't know. I have to go.'

She stood up and produced a dry smile. Then she went to the kitchen.

55

It was a Saturday. I woke up around 8, shaved, took a shower, had a coffee and a well-browned slice of toast and went out. I was in no hurry but I wasn't concentrating on anything special either. My mind was in a state of its own, somewhere unknown but nowhere special. I was walking in a haze. I took the bus that came in ten minutes; I got off one stop before the last to take another one. I had to wait for the second bus for half an hour. Then there was a long drive; first the tall buildings went, then the provincial shops, the dress shops with long thin flower-patterned dresses and shoe shops with long lasting shoes and the odd hardware shop. Then the bus passed by rows of lanes in parallel with identical terraced houses with green and blue coloured doors. Then it went towards the suburbs. I got off at a stop isolated from any buildings. There was a large lawn like a football ground but through the lawn I could see the foot path made by footsteps passing over and over the same route. There was a partially eroded sign written in black over a corroded white background saying 'Cemetery.' It was sunny and as I got closer, I saw a large metal gate by which the footpath ended. It was just past eleven in the morning. The cemetery was quiet. I could see an old couple kneeling next to a fenced grave. There was a picture of a young man in uniform inside the fence. Further away, there was a young woman standing under a large chestnut tree. There were several old trees spread in a pattern in the grounds. Then I saw an old man with curved back and a large nylon bag, walking through the narrow space between the gravestones slowly but firmly. I walked far behind him. He stopped by a grave, paused for a minute and ran his fingers through his thin but tidy hair. Then he opened the bag, took out a small broom and began slowly cleaning the small area around the grave, starting with the stone, very meticulously pushing the broom threads through the stone carving then the ground surrounding the stone. He paused every now and then and continued for some time. Then he took out three bottles of water and some flowers. He replaced the flowers in the vase which was firmly placed at the bottom of the stone. He emptied the bottles over the stone, pouring the water slowly. The black stone was shining under the sun now. Then he put all the rubbish, the drooped flowers, the broom and the water bottles systematically in the nylon bag. He placed the bag in a corner and stood there solidly with no movements. He stayed motionless as if he would never leave. But then slowly as he had come, he took the bag and walked away.

I took a piece of paper out of my pocket. I had written on it, plot 63x238 east. I thought it was like a long-term parking ticket. Do not lose it! I passed through older graves and came to an area where the stones were new and the flower pots were not chipped and had fresh flowers in them. And then, there it was, a small white stone with some words on it, only stating the name, the date of birth and the date of death. There was no clever sentence and no poetry, there were no words of endearment and there was no flowerpot. I walked around the small plot in a circle. I wondered what she would have liked to be written for her. A sentence from Nietzsche? I thought that perhaps she didn't want to be buried at all; that she would have preferred to be cremated. Then perhaps I could have some ashes in my library next to her notebook. My mind was again somewhere else, somewhere unfamiliar for me and I couldn't place it. I made a move to go back. It had clouded over and there was a cool breeze.

But I couldn't gather the energy to move. I was fixated on the white gravel around the grave stone. Then I saw the bench at the boundary between the rows of plots. I dragged myself to the bench. It was metallic and cold. There was a paper bag next to it with a used can of coke. I looked at the big chestnut trees spread randomly in the wide space with plots between them. I thought I would never be able to stand up and walk out of that place. I thought of a cup of coffee, but those were the good days of talking and having coffee and discussing ideas and now I had been denied all that. I was just moving around doing the routine; that was me these days. What happened to all those passionate debates about science, responsibility, eternal martyrdom, feeling guilty? Kate's stone was looking at me a few metres away. So I was a martyr in this entire affair. She had gone but presumably I was to stay, and not only for a couple of months; It was a matter of years I suppose. Would I come here again? 'Don't be silly,' Kate would have said, 'I am gone. I don't exist any more. Do you understand? Don't even think about it.'

'But if I think about you and some feeling stirs in me, then it means that you do exist.'

'Do you really think so? Then let's go for a coffee. Do touch me. I feel cold today! What absolute rubbish you say.'

'You know what I mean. We talked so much about Nietzsche and others, they were alive to us.'

'We were just enjoying ourselves with stories. Once someone dies, he is gone. We create stories and love our stories. This is also to console ourselves. This is the choice of the weak, the resigned, the benevolent! They create stories to show how considerate they are. Where were you when I was lying in bed counting the minutes? Have you smelt the hospital ward in an evening when it rains outside? You were strong then. You didn't want to see me and you didn't; now you are weak. I am glad I am not there to see you like that!'

'I was weak then. I didn't have the strength to see you then and I am weak now because I cannot face this. But the only thing left for me is our dialogue. I can talk to you and you are answering me back!'

'You are convincing yourself. How can you be sure that it is me and it is not you talking to your image?'

'I know. I can feel your hand, your warmth, your skin, no matter what you say.'

There was no debate any more. There was a cold breeze going through the open space, over the lawn, whirling through the branches of the chestnut trees. It had started to drizzle again. I stayed on the bench for some time.